D E A D F A L L

Books by Sue Henry

Murder on the Iditarod Trail
Termination Dust
Sleeping Lady
Death Takes Passage
Deadfall

DEADFALL

AN ALASKA MYSTERY

Sue Henry

AVON BOOKS NEW YORK

This is a work of fiction. Names, characters, places, and incidents either are the product of the author's imagination or are used fictitiously. Any resemblance to actual events, locales, organizations, or persons, living or dead, is entirely coincidental and beyond the intent of either the author or the publisher.

AVON BOOKS, INC.
1350 Avenue of the Americas
New York, New York 10019

Copyright © 1998 by Sue Henry
Interior design by Kellan Peck
Visit our website at **http://www.AvonBooks.com**
ISBN: 0-380-97661-7

Library of Congress Cataloging in Publication Data:
Henry, Sue, 1940–
    Deadfall : an Alaska mystery / Sue Henry.—1st ed.
      p.   cm.
    1. Jensen, Alex (Fictitious character)—Fiction. 2. Police—Alaska—Fiction. 3. Alaska—Fiction. I. Title.
PS3558.E534D4   1998   98-10956
813'.54—dc21   CIP

First Avon Books Printing: August 1998

AVON TRADEMARK REG. U.S. PAT. OFF. AND IN OTHER COUNTRIES, MARCA REGISTRADA, HECHO EN U.S.A.

Printed in the U.S.A.

FIRST EDITION

QPM   10   9   8   7   6   5   4   3   2   1

For Alice Abbott

with love and thanks
for patience,
generosity,
friendship,
and,
especially,
a sense of humor.

*D*uring the early hours of the morning, the storm had renewed itself. Now, just before noon, tide at its height, the gale was howling like a banshee and had become a wrathful avenger sweeping across Kachemak Bay, pounding wind-driven salt water against the shores of mainland and islands in an enormous, resounding surf that cruelly battered everything in its path.

In the midst of huge waves crashing far up the beach of one small island on the south side of that arm of ocean, near the outer edge of a cluster of islands that protected the waters of Tutka Bay, an old man valiantly struggled to launch a small boat into the maelstrom. The stones that formed the shingle of the crescent-shaped cove shuddered and rolled restlessly with the force of the incoming breakers, shifting beneath the water in a deep, uneasy growl, giving him no stable footing.

He was soaked to the skin, though he wore a rain slicker with a hood covering gray hair that was pulled back and tied at the nape of his neck, and his rubber boots, heavily full of water, did not help him maintain his balance. Rain, pouring from the dark sky, combined with the ferocity of the sea's flying spray to continually drench the wrinkles and creases of his face, filling his eyes till half the time he could see only what was directly in front of him, often not even that.

He knew that launching the boat was a foolhardy thing to do under the circumstances. But he stubbornly persisted, would have been ashamed of himself if he had not at least tried to take out the small wooden craft, start the ancient motor, and make an attempt to reach a second cove that lay half a mile to the east, beyond a long wall of surf-washed cliffs. The woman was in trouble, pursued by a madman, and he was guessing she would head for this other cove, where she might be able to locate some shelter and obtain what she could to defend and sustain herself. If he could make it there and find her, he might be able to help her, and himself.

A large wave struck the boat, almost spinning it out of his hands, but as its crest crashed over him, he put all his strength into a desperate shove that drove the craft farther from the shore and dragged him to his waist in the frigid water. As he held to the side and the next surge lifted his feet from the bottom, he threw himself forward, trying to kick and hoist himself into the boat. As it tossed in the violence of the sea, the edge of the gunnel dug into his ribs, bouncing and bruising his body. Recklessly, he grabbed at the wooden seat, pulled hard, and felt a sharp pain as something gave in his side: a rib—cracked. Dammit, he thought, rolling into the boat, gasping and holding his arm tight against the hurt, but there was nothing to be done about it.

When he could sit up, he was almost flung out again as a wave hit broadside, all but overturning the boat. Quickly he yanked out an oar that had been stowed beneath the seat and, except for a groan or two, ignored the agony under his arm in order to paddle the boat around so it was headed into the oncoming surf.

Then, he leaned, with a grunt, to start the engine before the capricious sea could swing the boat again. Pulling the starter cord was a painful torment. On his first try, it coughed damply. On the second, well-maintained, it sprang to life with a roar that, in the thunderous bellow of the storm, was only a whisper and a puff of oily smoke that the wind greedily snatched.

Aimed east to run before the waves, the boat slowly began to move on a course that would eventually bring him parallel with the line of cliffs that he could barely make out across the rough waters of the cove. Each swell lifted the propeller out of the water, screaming in protest. The waves were even larger than he had anticipated—eight, even ten feet high—and he knew again that he had undertaken a fool's errand. Never, for himself alone, would he have risked such an endeavor. But the woman might have need of him, if only for company and support in her dangerous plight, and it was part of his old-fashioned, chivalrous nature to offer his assistance to women.

He thought of the cold eyes of the face in the mask, the person who had maliciously tricked and caught him off guard. Remembering his terror and tractable compliance at the threat, he was mortified and humiliated, though he could not imagine what he could have done differently.

In the deeper waters of the cove, the ocean swells eased slightly, grew more regular, and he instinctively fell into a small complacence with the rhythm of the rocking boat. Looking toward the cliffs that gradually grew larger, he had no warning—did not see the massive wave that rolled into the back of his boat, crashing aboard over the engine, drowning it instantly with only a sputter. Powerless, with nothing to hold the boat on course, it slid sideways down the back of the wave, half swamped, until the next crest plucked and flipped it like a balsa-wood toy, hurling its single passenger into the sea with a cry of shock and protest.

He fought his way back to the surface, choking and spitting, to find that the boat had been driven ten yards beyond him and floated upside down, the engine gone—ripped off in the disaster. In an attempt to reach it, he took three strokes and realized that it was drifting away faster than he could swim.

It was cold—so cold. He tried to recall what he had been told should be done to avoid hypothermia in the lethal temperature of Alaskan waters, and thought he should curl into a fetal position, *because he would lose the most body heat from his head, armpits, and groin, but he also knew, sadly, with dread, that any effort would be futile. There was too much water between himself and the beach, and there would be no rescue—no one knew he was there.*

Cyclic storm swells raised and lowered his floating form and waves came tumbling mercilessly in from the west to wash over and leave him gasping. Numb with cold and weakening quickly, he forced himself to put forth the effort to stroke toward shore, a singularly unproductive activity, but one that gave him an excuse not to give up.

As his body core rapidly cooled, he began to hallucinate and to talk gibberish to himself.

"Old fool. Millie? Where is . . . ? Thank you . . . yes, I know that . . . I'm so cold . . . Just remember . . . A martini would be nice . . . she should . . . till you're . . . don't like this . . . at all . . . home again . . . can't . . . Damned old fool . . . you were meant . . . for me."

He imagined the boat, upright, on calm water, and reached out for it . . . heard the tinkling of a piano . . . smelled sausage frying.

In a brief moment of clarity, before his limbs stilled and he slowly disappeared beneath the surface of the cove, he hoped the woman would be all right without his help. She was a nice person—had been kind to him, though he had frightened her at first.

Jessie . . . her name was Jessie.

1

As the sun went down behind a western stand of trees, staining the clear sky the brilliant fuchsias and golds that are often a part of fall evenings in south-central Alaska, the breeze, sharp with a hint of frost, stirred itself into a gust of wind that whistled around the eves and tugged a flight of fluttering dark yellow leaves from a tall stand of birch, sending them swirling through the air like a flock of small voiceless birds.

Climbing the front steps of her snug log cabin, with an armful of harness that needed repair before the new season of sled dog racing, Jessie Arnold paused to appreciate nature's generous pallet and the circuitous, soaring reminder of fall. The wind ruffled her already tousled honey-blond hair and flapped the tail of the jacket she had worn all day working in the dog lot. Though a little sad that all the brightness would soon be stripped from the trees to the ground in a patchwork of gold, leaving their limbs to stand in stark skeletal silhouette against the sky, she knew she would welcome the arrival of winter's clean silence that would blanket her world in drifts, smoothing all shapes to curves and roundness.

She had never been successful in deciding which part of the year she favored in Alaska's constantly shifting panorama of extremes, and vacillated between spring and fall, the two seasons when change was swift, seemed to occur almost over-night and with little warning. A turn of the head in April, and in what seemed a moment, when she looked again, everything was green and bursting into blossom. Then, one day in Sep-tember, she would notice that, along the full length of the tall stalks of fireweed, its magenta flowers had gone to fluff that drifted in the slightest current of air. Or the distant honking of a ragged arrow of geese would draw her eyes heavenward to watch their restless passing. She would realize that the pelts of the forty-odd dogs in her lot were richly thick with new hair, come out early one morning to find them sleeping in nose-to-tail curls, hoarding their body heat.

For Jessie, there was always a languid, peaceful thought-fulness that came with fall, a sort of drowsy contemplation of life's rhythms. Unlike the burgeoning energy of spring that quickened the blood like sap rising, it was a slowing of the mind and senses that harmonized with the environment, a summons to quietude.

The season suited her well, for she was born to it. The next day was her birthday and she knew that Alex had some kind of dinner celebration planned, for it had kept him grinning for days with anticipation, as he dropped tantalizing, cryptic hints that led nowhere. It was a deep pleasure and satisfaction to her that he liked recognizing significant days. It was a trait many men lacked, shrugging off its importance to the women in their lives. But Alex had been raised in a family that made much of holidays, savored every candle on the cake, light on the tree, or grinning jack-o'-lantern. Greeting cards and small, often humorous gifts for him came almost as regularly as letters from his mother in Idaho. It was clear that keeping the continu-ity of her family circle going was important to Keara Lacey

Jensen, and that it gratified her to please her firstborn son, for mail addressed in her handwriting often arrived for Jessie, too, though they had never met.

She looked down and smiled as Tank, her favorite lead dog, pressed his cold nose against her hand, reminding her that he was eager to go inside—a treat infrequently allowed—that there were still things that needed doing before the end of the day.

"Okay . . . okay. Come on."

With a last appreciative glance at the fading hues of the sky, and a deep breath of the pungent, earthy odor of fall in the air, she stepped briskly forward to open the door into the warmth of the cabin. Flipping a switch that illuminated two table lamps and an old-fashioned fixture over the dinner table, she dropped the harness in a heap by the door. She kicked off her knee-high rubber boots and went to add wood to the fire in the potbellied iron stove and water to the cast-iron dragon atop it that puffed humidifying steam into the room from its nostrils, then stood for a minute looking at the space which pleased her as much as the scene she had appreciated outside.

The room she had entered was as wide as the cabin and full of cheerful colors. A huge sofa, covered in quilts and afghans, littered with bright pillows, sat close to the stove. Near it, two overstuffed easy chairs squatted like blowzy housewives in print dresses, ready for a good gossip. A large desk, much in need of refinishing, took up space against one wall, cluttered with the correspondence and paperwork necessary for managing a kennel.

The back half of the cabin was divided. On the left was a kitchen area, open to the larger room. Though a cookstove, refrigerator, sink, and countertops crowded this space, the impression was that they had been arranged wherever they fit best, shelves added to the walls one or two at a time as they were required, then stacked with dishes and pots and pans. Under the countertops, blue checked curtains hid shelves designated for food storage. A much-used oak dining table sat close, surrounded by a rowdy crowd of mismatched kitchen chairs hand-painted in lively primary colors.

To the right, walls enclosed a small bath off a bedroom largely occupied by an inviting king-sized brass bed with a pile of fluffy pillows above a wonderful quilt Jessie had found on a trip to Ketchikan. It glowed with a variety of blues that were scattered with tiny silver stars, but the special delight of it was the subtle colors sweeping across it in swirls and curves that portrayed the northern lights. One wall of the bedroom was filled with shelves of books and keepsakes—including Alex's collection of mustache cups; another held hooks and more shelves, for the hanging and holding of both their wardrobes.

As she hung her jacket on a hook by the front door, the phone rang. Crossing to the desk, she picked up the receiver.

"Arnold Kennels."

There was the soft sound of an open line, but no one answered.

"Hello. This is Arnold Kennels. Hello?" She waited, frowning, then started to hang up, but as she began to take the receiver from her ear there was a sudden, short, perhaps two-second burst of sound followed by the click of a receiver being returned to the cradle.

Wrong number. Exasperated, she hung up. People could at least acknowledge her hello, couldn't they—apologize for their mistake? Shrugging, she turned away, dismissing the incident.

To fill the silence, she put some Celtic harp music on the CD player and went to the kitchen. Scrubbing her hands free of the dirt accumulated in feeding and caring for forty dogs, she stirred, then tasted the kettle of stew that simmered fragrantly on the back of the stove, added a little pepper, and was soon cheerfully involved in mixing a batch of biscuits to accompany it.

The better part of an hour later, Tank, who had stretched out luxuriously on a braided rug in front of the fire, suddenly raised his head in alert attention, and Jessie, at the desk with a book and a pile of papers, heard the sound of Alex's truck coming up the long drive to the cabin. The husky did not bark—such behavior would have been beneath his dignity—but made a small affectionate sound in his throat and sat up eagerly to face the door.

Boots thumped on the steps and Alaska State Trooper Sergeant Alex Jensen energetically blew in with a gust of wind that swept across the room to breathe down Jessie's neck, eliciting a shiver that hunched her shoulders.

"Hi, trooper. O-o-oh, it's getting cold out there."

"Yup. Going to freeze tonight for sure. *'O, it sets my heart a-clickin' like the tickin' of a clock, when the frost is on the punkin and the* . . . ah . . . something's . . . *in the shock.'* " He fanny-bumped the hand-hewn door shut, sealing out the invasive wind, and quickly set about divesting himself of boots and coat.

Jessie smiled, familiar with his periodic inclination to quote scraps of poetry, often in imprecise fragments.

"What's that? Kipling?"

"Nope. James Whitcomb Riley . . . I think."

Crossing the room in long strides, he leaned to kiss her welcoming mouth and cast a curious glance over her shoulder at the paperwork. "Whatcha working on?"

"Rest of the stuff for the last junior mushers training this week."

"Glad to be almost done with it?"

"Yes, but all four of the kids I've been working with are doing really well. Two of the older ones want to come out to work in the lot this fall, and I can use the help with the young dogs. You hungry?"

"*Starved* . . . and something smells good in here."

"Moose stew seemed like a good idea in this weather. Toss that pan of biscuits at the oven and we'll eat as soon as they're done. I'll be through here in a minute."

"Hey, making the biscuits is my job."

"Yeah, well . . . I had an extra couple of minutes after I

fed the guys, and I figured you'd be ravenous when you hit the porch."

"Just buttering me up 'cause your birthday's tomorrow," he accused her, clattering the pan of biscuits into the oven. "Won't work, you know. I'm wilier than that. Smell a bribe a mile away."

Content in his presence, she watched him moving purposely in the compact kitchen, a grin on his face like that of a mischievous small boy with a secret, as he closed the oven, lifted the lid to peer at the stew, and fished a long-neck of Killian's Irish Red Lager from the bottom shelf of the refrigerator. He held up a second bottle. "Want one?"

"No, thanks. When I finish this, I'm planning to dip into my sacred stash of Jameson."

"I'll get it. Ice water?"

"Yes, please. Now who's buttering who up?"

"A little spoiling, maybe. Not buttering. I save buttering till I have a real reason for it. Then you're in trouble, because no one butters better than I do."

He stuck his head out of the kitchen space and twisted his face into a comic leer, waggling the wide handlebar mustache on his upper lip suggestively. "I could, however, be persuaded to do some kind of buttering later tonight, if you're absolutely set on it."

Jessie laughed and, realizing there was no chance of gathering her scattered concentration long enough to finish her work, abandoned it and began to collect and organize the papers she had spread out.

"Hey. Whatever. Dirty old men need love, too."

Along with the clink of ice and glass, she could hear him at the sink, muttering a tongue-twister she had never been able to master—butter, obviously, still on his mind.

"Betty bought a bit of bitter butter, put it in her batter, made her batter bitter. Betty bought a bit of better butter, put it in her bitter batter, made her bitter batter better."

Where had all this silliness come from? What could have put him into such an exuberant mood?

He brought her shot of Irish whiskey in a small snifter and set it, with a separate glass of ice water, in the space she had just cleared on the desk.

"What, no butter?"

"No butter," he told her. "This is just a well-deserved 'Happy Birthday.' "

Beside the drink, he laid a small package wrapped in gold paper and tied with a matching ribbon.

"Alex!" She swung around to look up at him over the back of her chair. "It's not till tomorrow."

"So? Tomorrow's tomorrow. This is tonight's birthday present. And, if you are *really* a good girl . . ."

She reached up, took hold of his shirtfront, and pulled his face down to give him a kiss.

"You . . . are too much."

"Open it," Alex directed, and laid a gently encouraging hand on the nape of her neck.

Jessie picked up the present and held it for a moment in the palm of her hand, considering. She hoped he couldn't feel her heart beating wildly, for at first sight of the gift it had all but leaped from her chest. The package was tantalizingly close to the size and shape of a ring box. Was it? Did she want it to be? Slowly, she untied the ribbon and carefully loosened the tape, holding the paper to avoid tearing it.

Time. If this *was* what she suspected, she needed time to decide how to respond. Whenever the question of marriage had entered her mind, she had, with purpose and determination, resolutely shoved it aside. Now she found herself confused, both wanting and resisting the idea. Glad he was behind her, could not see her face, she held her breath and cautiously lifted the hinged lid of the jeweler's box she had freed of its wrappings.

"Oh, Alex! O-o-oh!"

Against black velvet a pair of diamond studs for her ears caught fire in the light of the desk lamp.

Exhaling a sigh that could have meant anything, Jessie brushed them with the tip of one slightly trembling finger, then glanced up to see the delight in his eyes.

"They're beautiful," she started to say, but, halfway through the words, her throat closed without warning and his face swam in unshed tears that blurred her vision. How could one be both relieved and disappointed all at once? she wondered fleetingly.

Astonished, Alex dropped his arm to encircle her shoulders.

"Jess. Don't you like them? What's wrong?"

Then, without waiting for a response, he swept her up and carried her to the sofa, where he sat down, cradling her on his lap like a child, and tipped up her chin, so he could see her face.

"No . . . no." She smiled, as the tears disappeared. "Nothing's wrong. Really. I love them. They're gorgeous. You just caught me off guard, that's all. Surprised me. What a present!"

He reached to the arm of the sofa for a kitchen towel she had forgotten there and handed it to her.

"Oh. Well, of course I never gave anyone diamond earrings before, so how could I have known this was the traditional response? Here, love . . . wipe your face and put them on. I want to see."

She hugged him hard for a moment and complied.

Much later, when they had eaten, washed the dishes, returned a reluctant Tank to the dog lot, and were half asleep in the big brass bed, under the quilt that glowed with northern lights as bright as those that pulsed across the autumn sky high over the cabin, Alex heard her whisper.

"Some kind of buttering, trooper. But we'd *better* be going somewhere tomorrow night where I can wear these!"

2

In the very early hours of morning, Jessie found herself suddenly wide awake and staring into the dark, filled with a strange tension.

A breath of wind whispered through the slightly open bedroom window, inspiring a small susurrus in the folds of the curtain. Then there was the soft, dry rustle of flying birch leaves against the glass, like spirit fingers scrabbling ineffectively to come in.

She lay without moving, listening hard. Instinctively knowing that no usual sound had raised her consciousness, she searched past those she could identify for something else. The sound was not repeated, though she held her breath till her chest ached with the strain of alert concentration, her body rigid. She could half-remember a sharp noise of some kind, then another—different. All her intuition insisted something was not right.

The wind eased as if drawing its breath, and deep beneath

the lowering of it came a distant resonance, a moan . . . no,
the pitch was too high . . . a whimper . . . of hurt, or distress?
Tank barked, suddenly, twice, and was answered by a yelp or
two from other locations in the yard. One of the huskies produced a single howl that faded into yips of disturbance.

Tossing back the covers, Jessie was quickly on her feet,
switching on a small bedside lamp, throwing on the clothes
she had shed when going to bed.

"Wha-at?" Alex asked, sleepily raising his face from the
pillow to see her yanking a turtleneck sweater over her head.
"What is it?"

Hurriedly, she yanked on socks and jeans.

"I don't know. Something's wrong in the lot. Maybe a
moose has them going, but they don't bark without a reason."

He sat up and swung his feet over the side of the bed.

"Doesn't sound like a moose. They get crazy for that."

"I know. I'll go see." She slipped beyond the light into the
front room, wending surefooted past dark furniture to her coat
and boots by the door.

"Hold on. Let me get some clothes on and grab the
shotgun."

By the time he had snatched the gun from its hooks on the
wall and, shirttail hanging, arrived at the front door, she was
anxiously peering out the window, unable to see anything in
the dark but the square shapes of the closest dog boxes, which
were a little paler than their surroundings. He shrugged on his
coat, crammed his bare feet into boots, plucked one large
flashlight from a hook beside the door, and handed her
another.

"Opening this door will automatically turn on the new
lights," he reminded her, tucking the rifle in the crook of his
arm. "We could slide out through the kitchen."

"No, it's okay. We'll need the light. Can't see much otherwise, and I want to see, fast."

As they stepped onto the porch, the motion-activated halo-
gen floodlights on their tall pole blinked into instant brightness,

casting a wide, white circle of light that illuminated both their trucks in the drive and extended far out into the lot. At a glance, there was nothing unfamiliar within the area it revealed.

Tank, closer to the cabin than the other dogs, strained toward Jessie as they came down the steps, pacing back and forth at the end of the tether that connected him to the iron stake near his box. He did not bark again, but whined and, when they reached him, turned and trotted ahead, as far as the tether would allow, toward the rest of the lot. There he stopped, and stared intently into the dark beyond the lights.

Several more dogs, inspiring each other, were now barking, making it impossible to hear anything else, though Jessie tried to ignore them, to identify once again the foreign sound that had brought her uneasily searching for its source.

"Let him go," Alex suggested. "He knows what it is, and where."

She unfastened her leader, but kept a tight grasp on his collar, knowing that the temptation of a moose would strain his usual disciplined behavior. Free of the line, he did not, however, hurl himself forward against her restriction, as she had half expected, but calmly, steadily drew her past the other dogs, into the dark half of the lot.

Okay, no moose. What, then? Jessie frowned.

"Show me, Tank. Good boy."

As they moved between individual straw-lined shelters for the dogs, weaving a crooked path through the lot, and left the circumference of the light, her night vision improved, but not enough. She switched on the flashlight she carried and swung its beam ahead of them. Nothing. She could hear Alex walking quietly, close and slightly to one side. In the narrow beam of his light, she caught the glint of an aluminum food pan, the gold of straw spilling out the door of a box.

The husky pulled her forward until they reached the outer edge of the wide lot, the last row of boxes, close to a hundred yards from the cabin. A few feet from one box in particular, he halted, stared at it, and growled deep in his throat. Hackles rose along his neck and back, bristling under her hand. Her light showed nothing but the wooden side of it.

"Alex?"

He stepped up beside her, the shotgun ready for instant use, should he need it.

Then Jessie could hear it again, a muffled whining that came repeatedly, and the familiar wet sound of a dog licking something, but the sharp crack that had broken her sleep did not come a second time. She shone the light over the outside of the dog box. Alex's light moved over the dirt that surrounded it, stopped, and returned to the ground close to the door.

Jessie caught her breath.

It was soaked with red—blotches of blood that continued into the box.

"God. What the hell?"

They stepped forward and leaned to peer cautiously in through the door. Her light found the dog that had struggled to crawl inside and lay on the straw facing them. The straw under it was also liberally stained with scarlet. The dog raised its head to look blindly into the flashlight beam, quivered, then resumed licking, but it had been enough for them to see the ugly metal trap that was clamped cruelly to the flesh of one foreleg.

"Oh, God! She's caught, Alex."

Jessie sprang up to heave the box over, off its base, frantic to get to her dog. The resulting crash startled the next husky into leaping, with a yelp, to the top of its own box.

"It's Nicky. Oh . . . dammit. Where did that thing come from?"

She dropped to her knees beside the young female, which whined again and shivered in shock.

"Oh, Nicky. You poor baby."

Alex held his light, while she raised the dog's head so they could see the trap on the injured leg.

It was the sort of steel trap that was still sometimes used

to capture wolves and other animals of somewhat large size, one that could be spread open, leaving its sharp, wicked metal teeth turned up, silently ready for the unwary to step into it and spring the release. It would then close its steel jaws with a vicious crack, imprisoning the victim, slashing hide and flesh, as it had this dog, probably breaking bone. It was not new, but still strong, though brown here and there with rust and layered with dirt, which made it seem even more loathsome.

"Help me, Alex. We have to get it off her." Her voice was quiet, but terrible with anxiety and anger. "Can you open it if I hold her?"

"Yes, if you can keep her still."

She slid forward and gathered the trembling canine body into her arms so that the dog's front legs remained on the straw, holding Nicky's head under one arm, the flashlight in the opposite hand so Alex could see what he needed to do.

Gripping the trap, pressing it solidly against the ground, he threw his weight onto it, forcing it open wide enough for her to lift away the injured leg, then quickly letting it go, allowing it to snap shut again with that awful sound—the sound Jessie had heard in her sleep. She flinched. Nicky yelped in sharp pain, and blood once again flowed from the crushed, severed flesh, but she did not snarl or bare her teeth, and the bleeding quickly slowed.

Tank whined, then growled again, staring off into the dark beyond the lot.

"Let's get her to the porch and the lights," Alex said, picking up the trap, "so we can see how bad it is. She's going to need a vet."

Jessie spoke not a word, but handed him her flashlight and rose, gently supporting the dog in both arms.

Slowly, carefully, they made their way back across the dog lot to the cabin. The floodlights, which had shut themselves off, once again blinked on as Jessie and Alex came within reach of the sensor.

*   *   *

Two hours later, back in the brightness before the cabin, Alex shut off the truck engine and turned to pull Jessie into the circle of his arms. All the way down the long road home from the veterinarian's she had sat beside him, staring out the window into the passing dark, stiff and silent for the most part, the lines of tears streaking her face, lost in thought and distress. Twice he had attempted to encourage her to talk, failed, and, noting the rigid line of her jaw, let it go, knowing it was better to let her work through her anguish and anger gradually. Now she almost fell, unresisting, to lean against his shoulder.

They had left Nicky with the vet, whom they had roused from sleep with a phone call, and who had been waiting in his small hospital when they arrived in Wasilla. The dog's trapped leg was broken, but the damage that concerned the vet most was that done to the muscles and tendons, and the possibility of infection.

"That trap may be old and rusty—God knows where it's been—but it did a very effective job," he said. "She'll never be able to run with a team, Jessie. I think I can repair some of this, but only so much, and I won't know how much till I try. The leg may not be salvageable. I'm sorry. Shall I put her down?"

"No!" Jessie had been adamant. "Oh, dammit anyway. No. She loves to run, but . . ."

She had been ambitious for this dog and was in the process of grooming her as a possible leader, but she had also grown more than usually fond of Nicky's sweet nature and patience. Thoughtful for a minute or two, she watched as the vet made a more thorough examination, then frowned.

"She'll be able to get around, right? In the yard, I mean."

"Sure. She'd be fine with three legs, if it comes to that. Let me do what I can and we'll just see how it goes as she heals.

She's strong and healthy, like all your dogs, and she's young. Give it a try?"

Jessie had agreed, all her focus on the dog and what was best for her. But on the road home Alex had seen her attention shift back to the idea of the trap and her anger renew itself.

Now, in the truck, he held her, saying nothing, waiting.

In a minute or two, she sighed and sat up.

"Let's go in."

"Yes. It's getting cold in here. Make us a cup of tea, will you? I'll be there in a minute."

When she had gone inside and closed the door, he took the flashlight and walked back through the dog lot to Nicky's box for another, longer look around it and those closest to it. It had crossed his mind that there might be other traps, but he found none.

The tea was welcome, as was the warm fire she had started in the stove. Alex sat cupping his palms around the heat of the mug, but Jessie couldn't sit still in her chair at the table and was soon pacing between it and the kitchen.

"Where the hell did that . . . *thing* come from?" She gestured at the bloody trap he had laid on the table on a double thickness of newspaper. "I've never had traps, for this very reason. Too dangerous. With dogs around it's a disaster."

"Makes sense. Could Nicky have dug it up from some old trap line, maybe?"

"Was there any sign of digging?"

He had to admit there wasn't. And he had gone over all the nearby ground he could examine with a flashlight in the dark.

Now, looking at the bloody trap in the light, he saw something he had not noticed before. A cardboard tag hung from one hinge of it on a short piece of string. He pulled it toward him to examine what appeared to be words written in block letters beneath a smear of blood. Aside from the reddish brown smear, the tag appeared to be new and deliberately attached, as if the trap had been labeled. The letters had been written in pencil. Bending closer, he was able to make it out: "Happy Birthday Jessie."

"What is it?" Jessie asked.

"Something's written on this tag," he told her, and hesitated, knowing it would disturb her. "I think someone put this trap out there on purpose, Jess."

She came swiftly back to the table, horrified.

"Why would anyone set a trap that near a dog? Knowing what it would do—what it could mean? I hate them—always have. Nasty, evil things. Besides, no animal a trapper might want would come anywhere near a kennel."

Alex frowned, looking across the table with concern.

"It's not the trap that's evil, Jess," he told her. "Distasteful, maybe. But it's whoever set the thing that deserves the accusation of evil. The trap is just a horror doing what it's made to do."

She stopped to stare at him, dumfounded, eyes widening with appalled comprehension.

"You really think someone did this intentionally?"

He showed her what was written on the tag, closely watching her reaction.

Her body went completely rigid. "What does it mean? Why would someone do such a thing?" she asked, still struggling with the idea.

He shrugged and shook his head. "I don't know, Jess. These things have to be set with a purpose. Yeah—this thing was deliberately brought into your lot and set there. Whoever left it knew exactly what it would do, the mutilation it would cause, and wanted you to know it had been done intentionally—with malice."

Jessie started to shake her head, but hesitated as she thought it through.

"But who?" she breathed. "Why?"

Her face was pale and her hand trembled enough to slosh

tea as she picked up the mug. She clutched the mug close between both hands, elbows supported on the table, and brought it to her mouth.

"No idea," Alex replied. "I looked and didn't find anything. But in the morning I'm going out again, when I have lots of light, and I'll do another thorough search for signs of anyone coming into the back of the lot."

The edge of the cup rattled slightly against her teeth as she stared at him. Slowly, with great care, she lowered it to the table and spoke through stiff lips. Though barely a whisper, her questions sounded loud in the quiet room.

"It's not over, is it? You think whoever did this will come back, don't you?"

3

ffective as an alarm clock, the telephone woke them later
that morning. Thinking it might be the veterinarian, Jessie was
quick to answer it, but again found no one to answer her yawning "Hello." Once more, she heard only the same short burst
of complicated sound as the caller hung up.

"Another wrong number," she informed Alex with irritation, and headed for the shower.

Though it made her shudder to think about the events of
the night before, Jessie insisted on accompanying Alex when
he went back out to the dog lot after breakfast to make a more
thorough search for clues. As they walked again between the
dog boxes, she noticed that the temperature, as Alex had predicted, had fallen below freezing during the night and a thin
layer of ice covered the surface of each dog's water pan.
Nicky's blood had also frozen on the ground and straw in and
around her overturned box, retaining more bright red color
than it would have if it had dried in warmer weather.

In spite of the fact that Jessie was no stranger to cuts and injuries to her dogs, as well as herself, in the running and training of a dog team—the sport of sled dog racing was well-known for its hazards and accidents—this had been no misadventure. The wounding of Nicky had been accomplished with purpose and malicious intent that was aimed at Jessie as well. She stood looking down at the carnage on the ground for a long minute before swallowing some of the anger she felt rising again in her throat and chest, and turning to help Alex carefully go over the area foot by foot.

"Watch where you step," he cautioned. "I don't want to screw up prints or marks—if there are any—or confuse them with ours, though we already contaminated the scene last night."

Half an hour later, when they had found not a print or sign of any intruder to the yard—nothing to follow—Jessie swore under her breath.

"Hey," Alex told her. "Don't let it get to you. I didn't really expect to find anything. It would be unusual if anyone clever enough to leave that trap would be dumb enough to give us anything to identify them. Pulling this kind of a stunt wasn't a spur-of-the-moment thing. Someone put a considerable amount of thought into it ahead of time."

"I guess," Jessie admitted, still frowning. "I just hoped . . . The bastard. Wish I had a trap of my own to spring on his paw . . . let him see what it feels like."

As they headed back to the cabin, he put an arm around her.

"It isn't necessarily a *he*," he reminded her. "Most women are strong enough to set that kind of trap."

She nodded and grimaced.

"I just can't get hold of the idea that someone could dislike me that much. What could I have possibly done to anyone to make them feel like that? It's horrible."

"Careful, Jess," he cautioned, halting in the middle of the dog lot to turn her toward him, hands on her upper arms. "Don't assume things we don't know yet. You are *not* responsible for this. So don't start thinking that way."

They looked at each other for a silent space, before she agreed.

"Yeah, you're right. Some nut, maybe."

"Maybe. We'll do what we can to find out."

Climbing the front steps of the cabin, he gave her shoulders a squeeze, glancing at the diamond studs still in her ears.

"Hey . . . anyway. Happy birthday. It's not all bad."

"Thanks," she smiled—the first he had seen since the night before.

"I've got to make a quick run into the Palmer office this morning. You want to come along?"

"No, think I'll stay here—get that mess taken care of. But let's get some breakfast first."

"You've got it."

A phone call to the vet assured Jessie that Nicky was resting and doing well, her leg still attached to her body.

"It looks pretty good," the vet told her. "Wasn't quite as bad as I thought. Took almost two hours, but I got most of the damage repaired. She's going to be a bit lame, but she won't lose it unless some infection sets in. She'll need to stay here a few days till I'm sure."

Jessie agreed, relieved, and spent the next hour cleaning the dog lot, especially the area around Nicky's box. In the field beyond it, she built a small fire in a barrel and burned the blood-soaked straw. Several other dogs had straw that needed changing, so she dragged it out of their boxes and carried it to the fire. There was a rake in the shed near the cabin, but she knelt and used her hands to collect the straw. There were only a few boxes she wanted to clean, after all.

Three spaces from Nicky's box, she waffled, undecided on replacing the straw belonging to Darryl, a playful three-year-old she had included in her last Iditarod team. He and another male in the box next to him had come from the same litter and had been named for the brothers on *Newhart*: "My brother, Darryl, and my other brother, Darryl." Now they were simply Darryl One and Darryl Two, and had matured from their clownish behavior as puppies into solid dependable team members—two of her best—who also had sired good pups with sweet temperaments. This year she intended to train them together to run last in a team, closest to her racing sled. They were so much alike they seemed almost telepathic at times and would make a good pair of wheel dogs.

As Jessie assessed the straw in Darryl Two's box, wondering if it could be left for another week or so, she bent to greet the two with pats and affectionate rubbing of ears and backs.

"Good boys. What good dogs you are. Shall I give you new beds, or have you got the stuff arranged just the way you want it?"

They crowded closer, pleased with the attention, returning her caresses with much wagging of tails. Darryl Two lifted his muzzle to give her a sloppy lick on the nose.

"Hey, give me a break. I already washed my face once this morning."

Deciding to replace the straw, since she already had the fire going, Jessie stood up, wiped dog kisses off her nose onto a jacket sleeve, and moved to Darryl Two's box, where she pulled out the straw and walked across to toss it on the fire. On her knees in the door, she was reaching to pull straw from Darryl One's box when some instinct stopped her. For a second or two she froze, scarcely breathing, then cautiously drew back her hands, releasing the straw as she did so, and sat back on her heels. There had been a glint of metal from somewhere deep within the box.

Darryl One took her stillness as an invitation for more petting and bumped against her, pushing his nose against her wrist. She thrust him back with a sweep of her arm.

"No, Darryl. Back. Sit."

Both well-trained dogs obediently sat and waited, blinking in confusion at the oddly harsh tone of her voice. This was not enough for Jessie, however, who, feeling sick and incredulous, rose and unfastened them from their tethers. Gripping their collars tightly, she moved them to two empty boxes several yards away from their own.

She made a quick trip across the lot to collect the rake from the shed, then dropped back to her knees in front of the box and began to remove the straw with it, delicately, a layer at a time, taking care to avoid the metal she had glimpsed in the back—knowing already what she would find. As the space inside was emptied, the shape of the thing she dreaded became clear: another trap—this one's jaws still yawning wide and threatening. Her arms suddenly weakened, her hand trembled, and the rake inadvertently dipped into the circle of the gaping trap. With a sharp crack, it all but leaped from its resting place and clamped tightly to the tines of the tool, almost jerking it from her hands.

From a slightly fuzzy-headed, floaty feeling, Jessie knew she was hyperventilating. She forced herself to stop, and consciously brought her breathing under control. The knees of her jeans were wet and cold from contact with the icy dampness of the ground on which she knelt, staring horrified at the wicked thing in the box. She looked down and realized she was chafing her hands together, massaging them against each other protectively. She held them still and scrutinized them in minute, critical detail, as if they belonged to someone else. There was not a scratch—not a mark—nothing to show that only a fraction of an inch closer and this trap could have closed on her hand the way the other had crushed Nicky's leg the night before. Twice she curled her fingers into tense claws, then relaxed and straightened them, before she stood up, walked into the autumn dryness of the field behind the dog lot, and threw up her breakfast into the weeds.

When Alex parked his truck in front of the cabin an hour later, he was perplexed and troubled to see every dog box overturned and the straw they had contained scattered around the bases of them, as if a cyclone had hit the yard while he was away. Jessie was nowhere to be seen, though her truck stood where it had when he'd left.

Grabbing the mail he had retrieved from the large box at the outer end of the long driveway—a package and several envelopes—he climbed hurriedly from his pickup and up the steps to the cabin.

"Jess? Jessie? Where are you?"

At the door he reached for the knob to twist it open as usual. Solidly locked, it refused him. Frustrated and concerned, he pounded on it with his fist.

"Jessie! Are you in there? Open the door. It's me."

The deadbolt was turned and the door opened to reveal a white-faced Jessie, her eyes wide and anxious, a few bits of straw in her tangled hair, a knitted afghan around her shoulders. Tank stood silently alert beside her, as if he were on guard.

"What's wrong? What's been going on?"

Jessie turned and walked back across the room to the sofa—where she had evidently been sitting—pulled her stockinged feet up under her, and curled up against a pile of pillows, wrapping the afghan tight around herself and staring up at him.

Something was terribly wrong. This was not the confident, self-sufficient woman he was used to.

"There was another one," she said through stiff lips. She gestured toward the dog lot, most of which was visible through the large window in the northwest corner of the room. It was obvious that she had been keeping a close watch over her dogs from this seat on the sofa. Jensen's shotgun leaned against the arm of the sofa, within easy reach, barrels pointed toward the ceiling.

"Another trap, you mean?"

She nodded.

"Where?"

He dropped the mail on the opposite end of the sofa and sat next to her, intently awaiting an answer.

"In Darryl One's box—clear at the back, still covered with straw, and . . ."

She stopped, clenched her hands into fists in the fabric, swallowed hard, then gagged. In a swift movement, she stood up, the afghan sliding off her shoulders, half ran across the room and into the small bath beyond the bedroom. He could hear the sounds of her retching from where he sat, but did not follow, knowing from experience that Jessie had no patience for anyone foolishly inclined to assist her in being sick.

When she emerged from the bathroom, pale and shaken, Alex had the kettle on to boil for tea, and a box of saltines lay on the sofa next to the afghan he had retrieved from the floor.

"Thanks," she told him, once more cocooning herself.

In a few minutes he handed her a mug of steaming herbal tea.

"Hey, it's cold in here. I'll put some wood in the stove."

"Sorry. I didn't notice."

As soon as the fire had begun to spit and crackle, he sat down with his own mug and watched Jessie nibble crackers.

"Okay," he said. "Tell me what happened."

He could see the muscles work in her cheeks and neck as she clenched her teeth, and heard the deep breath she took before she spoke.

"It was in the back of Darryl One's box. I had a fire in the barrel to burn Nicky's straw and was reaching in to change Darryl's when I saw something . . . part of it . . . I think. Anyway, I stopped and took my hands out." She swallowed again and put her fingers to her lips. "I almost touched it, Alex. Another inch or two and it would have closed on my hand. But something made me pull back and take another look."

"And it was still set?"

"Yeah. I don't know why Darryl One didn't spring it. Most

of the dogs slept in their boxes last night, from the look of it. Maybe he didn't like the smell of it and stayed outside."

"Where is it now?"

"In the shed, with the other one . . . on the rake. I dropped the rake and sprang it."

"You didn't touch it?"

"No . . . and I made sure there weren't any more."

"I noticed." He grinned, trying to lessen her clear distress, and glanced toward the window, where the chaotic appearance of the lot could be seen. "You clearly left no box unturned."

"Well . . . I was a little desperate, and in a hurry. Then I came in here. I keep throwing up . . . thinking about it. You know how I feel about hands."

Early in their relationship she had explained her phobia about injuries to hands. "I don't know where it came from, but all my life I haven't been able to stand the thought of losing fingers or a hand. I'd rather lose a leg. That doesn't give me the bejeebers."

He knew it was true and that, though she tried to fight it, seldom let it show, she absolutely couldn't help it. She was a strong person, not easily frightened or intimidated: She stoically watched all the scary parts of the few horror videos they sometimes rented without nightmares or anything more than a surprised flinch—even, at times, got a kick out of snuggling next to him pantomiming apprehension. When he had smashed a couple of fingers in combat with the hood of his truck, she had applied first aid with no more reaction than a stiff upper lip, asking only that he not tell her the details of how it happened. But she hid her eyes when it came to sword slashes that severed hands on film, grew tense and refused to listen if conversations turned to tales of shop accidents or those involving sharp implements. "*Please!* I don't want to hear it." They had left a movie theater in the middle of *The Piano*— Jessie, caught completely off guard at the critical mutilation scene, in tears, apologizing all the way home. It shamed and upset her even more that she could not control her reaction.

"So it was meant for Darryl One?"

"Evidently. And Alex . . . it had another tag tied onto it—with another 'Happy Birthday Jessie.' "

"None of this makes sense, dammit. Oh, Jess, I'm so sorry you had to find this one the way you did—not to mention having to check out the rest of the kennel, feeling the way you do. It was shortsighted of me not to consider that there could be more *in* the boxes. I assumed they would have been set outside. Nicky's was probably set inside, too. Maybe she dragged it out trying to get away, then went back in, where, ironically, she felt safest."

Jessie sat up straighter, as her focus shifted to the problem of her dogs.

"I agree. It makes sense that whoever set them wouldn't want them seen before they did their dirty work."

"Well, we know now that there aren't anymore in the boxes."

He gave her a lopsided grin and aimed a significant look toward the dog lot.

She smiled a little.

"Yeah. I admit I went through it like Sherman through Georgia. I was scared to death another of the mutts would spring one of the things before I could find it. I'll have to clean up the mess or my guys won't have anyplace to sleep tonight."

"I'll help. It won't take long."

He picked up the package he had tossed on the sofa with the mail and reached across to lay it in her lap.

"Here's something to cheer you up—a package from my mom with your name on it."

Jessie tore off the brown outer wrapping from the package; the ends, covered with strapping tape, were impossible to rip. Bright birthday gift wrap covered the box and this she also tore off.

"Looks like she forgot something—maybe the card—and had to reopen it," Alex commented, noting the way the paper seemed to have been opened at one end and retaped.

Jess opened the lid to find a soft blue hand-knit sweater inside the box.

"Oh, how pretty. Your mom's so nice to remember me." She lifted it out and held it up, smiling, pleased.

"What do you think?"

"I like it—a lot." Alex reached a hand to feel the softness.

"Here's the card." She lifted it from the bottom of the box. "No, two cards."

The first was a humorous cartoon featuring Garfield the cat and enclosing a short, affectionate note from Keara Jensen. They read it together, smiling.

"What's the other one?" Alex asked. "Wonder why she sent two."

The envelope was sealed. Jessie carefully tore it open and removed a piece of paper folded like a business letter. Unfolding it, her smile vanished, and her face turned pale again.

"Alex?" she croaked, in a strange, frightened voice, and looked up at him helplessly.

He snatched it from her shaking fingers and read the few computer-printed words it held:

HAPPY BIRTHDAY, JESSIE. DID YOU FIND THE PRESENTS I LEFT YOUR DOGS? I HOPE YOU APPRECIATE MY THOUGHTFULNESS. WE WILL RUN THIS RACE TOGETHER, BUT THIS TIME I GET TO WIN.

4

"Listen, Cas, I know I asked you guys to meet us in Anchorage for Jessie's birthday dinner, but would you mind coming out here instead? We've suddenly got a very nasty situation. Some bastard is harassing Jessie, set traps in the kennel last night, and we really don't want to leave the place unguarded. We could really use your help. . . . Great. . . . No, not now. I'll fill you in when you get here. How soon can you make it? . . . Okay, see you shortly."

Jessie had categorically refused to leave the cabin for the special evening Alex had planned, and while he was in complete agreement, he was also in favor of salvaging something of her birthday celebration. He was also relieved for more than one reason when Ben and Linda Caswell readily agreed to the last-minute change in plans. It would be a good chance to get Ben's take on the problems and his assistance, but he also empathized with Caswell, friend and fellow trooper, who would suffer no disappointment at substituting a pair of comfortably worn jeans and shirt for the sport jacket and tie the more formal dinner would have required. Neither man truly enjoyed wearing dress clothes, though they appreciated the positive response of their womenfolk when they were persuaded to do so. He recalled Jessie's comment the first time she had seen him in a sport jacket and tie: "Hey, trooper, you clean up nice."

This evening, Jensen was satisfied not to have to make the effort, would rather concentrate on the circumstance of the traps and harassing note. In less than twenty-four hours three related incidents had occurred and escalated from confusion to actual threat. Alex had expressed only part of his concern to Jessie. Under the carefully controlled and thoughtful exterior he was trying to maintain, he was worried and apprehensive, fearfully aware that what had already happened should be viewed as a beginning and would probably, and quickly, get worse. What the hell was going on? Who was responsible, and why make Jessie a target? He had investigated this sort of thing before. It was unpleasant in the extreme, and he was maddened to have it happening to someone for whom he cared deeply. But, not ready to add to what was already considerably upsetting her, he kept his anxiety to himself.

The birthday present from his mother had clearly undergone some tampering, either in transit or, more likely, after it reached their roadside mailbox. Alex had bagged both the package and note for removal to the crime lab for investigation, but it was unlikely they'd find anything other than his mother's fingerprints and those of a few postal workers between Idaho and Alaska.

Leaving the phone, he turned to see Jessie standing at the window staring out into the dog lot with a look of bewilderment on her face. Crossing the room, he stood behind her and wrapped his arms around her waist.

"Jess . . . I think it would be better if you didn't stand quite so close to the windows."

As she frowned and gave him a questioning look over her shoulder, he added, "We don't know anything about this person, or what he or she is capable of, right? Better to be safe than sorry."

He walked with her toward the middle of the room.

"You mean they might have a gun, don't you?"

"I mean . . . well, I don't know. Oh, hell . . . yes. I guess there's no sense playing games with it. Whoever it is could as easily have a gun as a trap. But what I really mean is that it's time to be cautious. A lot of people are hurt just for making bad choices: putting themselves in harm's way when they could have done something else—been more careful."

She looked up at him, silent for a long minute, then put her arms around his neck and hugged him close.

"Thanks," she said in his ear. "Thanks for thinking for me, while I'm still trying to get my head around this."

She leaned back and looked up at him with a frown.

"I'm scared, Alex. I'm not used to being scared and I don't like it. But what I like least is feeling that somebody else is in control of part of my life."

"You should be scared, and that's not all a bad thing. It makes you more careful. We're both scared. It's a nasty, insidious situation."

"I'm sorry the nice dinner you had planned is spoiled."

"Hey, that's no problem. We can do dinner anytime. Rain check, okay?"

"Okay."

As she kissed him warmly, the phone rang and she flinched a little in the circle of his arms.

"What?"

"Nothing. Just all those wrong numbers."

"I'll get it."

The caller was Caswell, suggesting that he and Linda pick up pizza and beer on their way to Knik. "We'll stop in Wasilla at that great Greek place."

Later, however, as they shared the large pizza, thick with extra toppings and cheese, around the kitchen table, the phone rang again and, when Alex insisted on picking it up, brought only silence to his ear. He came back scowling thoughtfully.

"Jess? Did you hear anything but silence when you answered those other wrong numbers?"

"Yeah. For just a second or two at the end it sounded like someone took their hand away from the mouthpiece to hang up, and there was a short noise, like they were in a crowded place of some kind."

"Right. Music?"

"I on't know. Might have been. Yeah . . . maybe. It was so short."

"What's going on?" Linda Caswell asked, laying a hand on Jessie's arm. "You been getting obscene phone calls, too?"

"Not obscene—just no one there when she answers," Alex told her. "For the last two days."

"No, Alex." Jessie shook her head. "It's been longer than that. Three, or four days, at least. I think the first one may have been last Tuesday or Wednesday. Wednesday, because I had just come in from the grocery store in Wasilla. It was ringing as I came in the door. I had to put the sacks down to catch it."

"Tell me how it sounds to you, Jess. From start to finish."

"Well . . . it's like the line is open, someone there, listening and not saying anything. I say, 'Arnold Kennels,' like always, then, 'Hello,' but no one answers. Then, just at the last second, that little piece of sound, and they hang up."

Alex considered this, nodding.

Caswell leaned forward to claim the last slice of pizza.

"You're thinking the calls might be connected to this business with the traps?" he asked.

"Right. Could be another piece of harassment."

There was concerned silence for a minute while they all thought about the disagreeable situation. Jessie suddenly stood up to reach across the table, collecting empty plates, glasses, and discarded napkins—more comfortable with her hands busy.

Ben Caswell periodically worked with Alex, and socially he and Linda fit well with Alex and Jessie, for both couples enjoyed bridge, fishing trips, meals at one home or the other, and spirited conversation. Jessie and Linda planned similar small gardens in the late Alaskan spring, starting vegetables and flowers indoors from seed, sharing, and setting them out when all danger of frost was past in late May or early June. Cas and Alex had an ongoing, relaxed competition over who caught the most salmon each summer. The foursome had a relationship they valued and—like many residents of the farthest north state—viewed as extended family.

"Let's talk the whole thing over a little," Ben now suggested. "If we assume that the calls are part of it, you've had three different things: calls, the traps—with their tags—and the note. Anything else?"

"Not so far."

"Okay. Is there anything at all that may provide a clue to the identity of whoever's responsible? One at a time—calls first."

He laid a spoon down on the table in front of him to represent the phone calls.

"They all have that same scrap of sound at the end. It might be something the lab could identify if they had a recording and could slow it down . . . do their magic stuff."

"How about caller ID?" Linda asked. "You don't have it, do you?"

Alex shook his head. "Never had a reason to get it."

"What is caller ID exactly?" Jessie asked Linda. "Do you have it?"

"It shows the number and name of most of your callers, and lists them so you can see who's calling before you answer or before your answering machine takes over. It has a memory, so you can tell who called even if you're not home.

"We got it last year, when somebody got our unlisted number and kept waking us up in the wee hours. Turned out to be a teenager down the street with a dog that Ben had chased out of our yard several times before he threatened to call Animal Control. The next time the kid tried his get-even game we knew exactly who it was, and his father put a stop to it."

"You said *most*. Who doesn't it list?"

"Well, it doesn't list cellular phone identification or the ones from phone booths. It reads 'Out of Area' for long distance calls, but who's going to harass you long distance?"

Cas returned to his mental list and laid a fork down next to the spoon.

"The tags on the traps might turn out to be something, but from the look of them—and the traps—there's not a chance of fingerprints, as you said. The writing on the tags won't be worth much. Block letters, capitals, make handwriting identification very dicey—especially with such a small sample. Might be useful in combination with something else that you don't have yet."

"There's going to be nothing on this, either," Jensen anticipated, bringing the package box and wrappings to the table in its evidence bag. He laid the note, similarly protected, beside Caswell. "I'll take it in for testing just in case I'm wrong, but anyone capable of thinking something out this well is going to know enough to wear gloves. Television and movies have spoiled the fingerprint game."

"Well, DNA has replaced some of it," Ben noted. "This note is pretty unidentifiable—plain computer paper anyone could pick up anywhere. Could have come from one of thousands of laser printers in the area. Your mother addressed the package, so re-using the wrapping paper negated the need to write or print the address. Too bad. I'd like to see more of that block printing. Maybe there would have been something."

Thoughtfully, he laid a knife beside the fork and spoon—three different parts of the same puzzle.

Jessie suddenly sat up straight and looked at him, her eyes wide.

"What?" Alex asked. "You think of something?"

She got up so quickly her chair rocked on its legs, almost

tipped over, and returned to the floor with a thump. Crossing the room to the desk, she opened a lower drawer filled with file folders and searched through them until she found the one she wanted. Bringing it back, she spilled a pile of envelopes and letters out across the surface of the table.

The other three moved the bottles and silverware aside as the pile widened, spread by Jessie's searching hands. Flipping over several envelopes, she glanced at their addresses and put the ones that didn't interest her back into the folder.

"There's more?" Alex asked. "You got more notes from this person?"

He began to help her look through the assortment of mail.

Jessie Arnold was a well-known Iditarod musher. Though she had never won the race, she had come close, once taking second, and for several years she had placed in the top ten finishers. People from all over Alaska, as well as from places in the other forty-nine states and a few foreign countries, knew her name and often wrote her letters. She answered and kept them all, even the ones that were negative in tone, though frequently the people who wrote disapproving ones lacked the nerve to include their names or return addresses.

"Here." She lifted an envelope from the pile and handed it to Alex, who examined it as she went on hunting through the rest of the pile.

Cas and Linda leaned over to look as Alex took out a single sheet and opened it to reveal another computer-printed note with no signature.

GIVE UP THE IDITAROD. YOU'LL BE SORRY IF YOU DON'T.

The address on the envelope was on a label that was also computer printed.

By the time they had finished examining it, Jessie had found another with an address on the envelope so much like the first that it could have been printed at the same time. This one read:

STOP RUNNING DOGS IN THE IDITAROD OR YOU WILL
BE STOPPED.

"I knew that note in the package looked familiar," Jessie
said, scooping the rest of the letters back into the file. "These
were in the mail sometime in the last month. One is postmarked late in August, the other isn't postmarked."

"These don't sound quite like the first," Alex observed.
"No reference to a shared race."

"Which came first?" Caswell asked.

"The postmarked one. I noticed, because the lack of a postmark on the other made me wonder if someone local could
have put it in our box."

The postmark was, indeed, August, and had been applied
in Anchorage.

"We could find out where," Cas said. "But I'll take a guess
and predict that it was mailed at the big airport post office
that's open twenty-four hours a day—not at a local branch."

"Who is it?" Jessie pounded a fist on the table, making
silverware jump and an empty beer bottle fall over. "Why have
they picked me to badger? This just isn't fair. It leaves me
feeling helpless, with nothing to do—no way to respond."

"Unfortunately, Jessie, it doesn't have to be fair, and there
doesn't have to be much of a reason for it, except in the mind
of the perp. That, in fact, is the very idea of this kind of
harassment—to create fear that you have no way of responding
to directly."

Caswell picked up the note that had come in the package
and examined it through the protective plastic.

"This person seems to have some objection to your partici-
pation in the Iditarod or is using it as an excuse for some other
slight, imagined or real. Who knows? But each note seems a
little more sophisticated, but the threats are pretty clear."

Alex agreed, worrying one end of his handlebar mustache.
"I think that concerns me more than anything else about it."

Linda had been mostly listening to the exchange about the

notes. Now she turned to Jessie, and gave her a straight, serious look.

"I think you should consider getting out of here, Jessie. Go somewhere where this person can't follow you—let them cool off. Maybe our guys can find out who's responsible and clear it up. But you'll be safe—out of range. That's what I'd do."

Jessie stared at her, mouth open, and began to shake her head before Linda had even finished her statement.

"I couldn't—not just take off. There're the dogs to take care of. Besides, can't they catch this person just as well if I'm here as they could if I were gone? Alex? Ben? No. I won't go. This is where I live—my home. I didn't do anything, so why should I leave? Where would I go anyway?"

"How about a trip to Idaho?" Alex suggested. "I'd been thinking we should go maybe next spring. Why don't you go now? My folks would love to have you."

"Ale-e-x! Not a chance. Out . . . of . . . the . . . question!"

"Go ahead, Jess. Tell us how you *really* feel about it." Alex grinned at the Caswells.

Jessie was forced to laugh at herself, but it didn't discourage her from presenting one more rationale.

"If I left, the harassment would probably stop. Then how would you find out who it is? You've both all but admitted that you don't have enough evidence to identify anyone, really. You need more. How are you going to get it if I'm not here as the target?"

Alex was anything but happy at her choice of the word *target* to describe herself, though he knew it was accurate and, unfortunately, appropriate—also that she could be right.

5

The next day, Sunday, passed quietly, with no further suggestion of trouble, though Jessie and Alex were both watchful and uneasy. Individually and together, they had been up and down several times during Saturday night to check the dog lot from the window. Alex had disabled the motion detector so the floodlights remained on all night. Because light did not reach to the back of the yard, Jessie had moved as many dogs as possible closer to the cabin, within the bright circle.

"How could anyone have come into the lot without the dogs barking?" Jessie asked from her end of the sofa, looking up from an attempt to concentrate on the funnies in the Sunday paper. Without discussing it, they were attempting to fill the long morning, as usual, with breakfast, coffee, and newsprint.

"Wondered about that myself," Alex said, swinging his stockinged feet off the other end and opening the door to the pot-bellied stove to add another chunk of firewood. "I hate to suggest it, but there are a few people they wouldn't bark at. Could it have been someone you, or we—and they—know?"

"You know, someone might get past a person, but I don't think they could fool a dog that didn't know them," she agreed. "I can't think of anyone specific—anyone I'd want to accuse. There are a few people—mostly guys—who would rather women didn't run the Iditarod, but why pick on me? Besides, that kind of thing's sort of old news to come up this suddenly and viciously, isn't it? I've been thinking, and it seems to me there could be two other possibilities for how the traps were set—either it was done when neither of us was here or when the pups would naturally be making a racket about something else, using that as a cover."

"Okay, but we were here the whole evening before Nicky stepped in that first trap."

"Was there anytime during that evening when they barked or made a fuss? I'm so used to the sounds of the dogs that I might not have noticed something that might have caught your attention."

"It seems like there was something—just before we went to bed Friday night. Didn't someone stop by . . . or was it the night before that Fortis stopped in?"

"Night before." She shook her head, trying to recall. "But there *were* some lights that shone on the house from the road. A turnaround in the driveway. We thought someone was coming, but they just pulled in, backed out, and left. Remember?"

"You're right. And the dogs barked—they did."

"Yeah, and for longer than they normally would for that kind of thing. Remember? I was just about to go out and put a stop to it when they finally settled down and shut up."

"I'll bet anything that's when those traps were brought in. It would only take a few minutes to park on the shoulder of the road—or pull off where that trail of yours goes into the trees beyond the yard—slip into the back of the lot, and set them in two boxes. Has to be."

It gave them a possible answer for *when,* but told them

nothing more about *who*. The rest of the day seemed endlessly full of frustration and raw nerves.

They went out together and spent only the time necessary to feed and water the dogs. Jensen not only took the shotgun, but wore his off-duty Colt .45 semiautomatic, as well. There was nothing untoward, no hint of disturbance or further harassment.

"But it's not over, is it?" Jessie said quietly.

"No. If that first note came as long ago as August, there have been long spaces between incidents, so one day is nothing. The difference is that now we're aware of it. This person knows it and is just letting us stew and the tension build for something else, I think. These things usually escalate. Jess, are you sure about Idaho? This could—probably *will*—get worse."

She stood up from pouring water into a metal dish for a dog named Shorty, and gave him a long searching look. "Yes. Quite sure . . . for now. It would feel like quitting—like letting this S.O.B. win—and you know how I feel about quitting."

He looked down and scuffed the heel of one boot in a clump of dry brown grass.

"This is different from finishing a murderous race, you know. You don't have to prove anything here."

"I know. And I don't intend to be stupid about it. I promise that if I reach a point where I feel that I should or need to get out, I'll say so. Honest."

"All right. But you aren't used to having to gauge this kind of thing. So if I reach a place where I think you definitely should go—and I warn you, I'm close—I'll do the same. Fair?"

"More than fair. I'd trust your judgment."

"One other thing . . . for me."

"Yeah?"

"I don't want you to be alone out here. Will you agree to have someone here with you when I have to be somewhere else—at work?"

"Yes. I've been considering that, and I think it'd be a good idea. Not just as discouragement, but as a witness, too. Linda said if I wanted someone, she'd come."

"I meant . . ."

"No. No cops. That would make me crazy." Her eyes narrowed slightly. "Linda will be fine. She's smart, and quick, and can handle the shotgun as well as I can."

"Yeah, I know. Cas wouldn't have one in the house unless she learned to use it. All right. I'll have someone patrol out here during the day, and call you often to check. Keep the cell phone in your pocket, okay? And stay out of the lot as much as possible."

They spent another semi-wakeful night. Once, in the dark, Alex woke to find Jessie sleeping with her head on his arm, her back close against his side, as if seeking reassurance. He did not mention it when they got up, but, trying not to make her aware, he watched her carefully as she went through her usual morning routine. It was almost, but not quite, ordinary. Most people would have been fooled, but he noticed when she fumbled the toothpaste, informed her that she had put her sweatshirt on backward, and ate slightly scorched toast without comment.

Jessie said little, but was relieved, if not glad, to have him leave for the troopers' office in Palmer as soon as Linda Caswell pulled up at the cabin in her Blazer. Though she could tell he was trying hard to be unobtrusive, his constant, unspoken attention made her feel he could see the pressure she was feeling, even added to it. It made her feel clumsy, forced concentration on what were normally unconscious actions, and created awkwardness in their execution—water was spilled, silverware wound up on the floor, she bruised her shoulder on the bedroom doorframe. She found herself doing—and redoing—chores to keep her hands busy, so he wouldn't worry about her tendency to sit still, lost in thought.

She knew she needed to think, was convinced that whoever was doing these horrid things had to be someone with whom she'd had some kind of contact. There was certainly a chance it was just some unbalanced fan she wouldn't recognize face-to-face, but that chance, she thought, was small. It was much more likely that this fixation on her was the result of some encounter, however slight. To sort through her connections with other people, she needed time to sort through her experiences mushing and running public sled dog races. Before that, she would not have elicited this kind of focus, for who had known her then? If it didn't have something to do with the Iditarod, why would this person include that particular race in his or her threats?

But there were so many people over the last few years of racing and so much recognition of the state's premiere sport. How could she hope to pick out one among hundreds?

She waved good-bye to Alex and—glancing uneasily around at the trees and brush that could provide cover for many kinds of menace—forced a smile as she held the door open to welcome Linda into the snug log cabin. This evil had taken nothing of material value—except for injuring Nicky's leg which eliminated her use as a sled dog—but, she realized, it was rapidly stealing intangibles from her that she found more valuable than any thing she owned. It was a theft of trust, confidence, assurance—things she had always taken for granted—certainty, safety. What next? What else would be demanded of her?

She closed and carefully secured the deadlock on the door she usually left unbolted, and went to pour Linda a cup of coffee.

"'Happy birthday, Jessie. Did you find the presents I left your dogs? I hope you appreciate my thoughtfulness. We will run this race together, but this time I get to win.' And you say this came inside the package, after you found these traps?"

"Right. We found the dog caught in the first one and Jessie found the second the next morning. Almost got caught in it herself. Shook her. Seriously. And both tags said the same thing: *Happy Birthday Jessie.*"

"And the two other notes came in the mail in the last month."

"Yes. She didn't think enough about them to mention them. Stuffed them away in a file until last night."

Jensen and John Timmons, the burly assistant coroner, sat at a table in a central room of the Anchorage crime lab, examining the notes Jensen had brought in for testing. The traps—their tags removed for testing—lay on the opposite end of the table, one still stained with Nicky's blood. Timmons had rubbed at his fuzzy hair until it stood out from his head like a Brillo pad, and now he frowned down at the note in his hand.

"Well, we already know there's nothing here in terms of prints," he reiterated, "and it was sealed with water, not saliva, which says the perp may be significantly aware of DNA identification. As you said, there's a multitude of printers the notes could have been run out on. You're going to need someone who's more experienced than I am in the psychology of this kind of thing—Dave'll be back after lunch—but I'd say there are a couple of things at work here that might give you a start on the bastard."

He rolled away from the table in his specially built wheelchair toward a file across the room.

Paraplegic as the result of a skiing accident, John Timmons still managed to move faster than most people could on legs. His chair was equipped with a lift to raise him into a standing position. This, along with a set of braces he used while doing autopsies, or anything else that required him to be upright. The lift was unnecessary now, as he opened a lower drawer and took out a folder, which he brought back to the table. Though he was the assistant coroner, his interests reached beyond his job. The whole process of technical criminal investigation fascinated him, as it did Alex. Opening the folder, he laid out a list of soil types and where in the state they could be found.

"The traps aren't new—the first one even has some rust on it—but they're both dirty as hell, especially around the hinges. Tests may help us get some idea of where they've been used besides the kennel. Not much of a chance for anything vital, but who knows?

"The other thing you can do is start on the obvious Iditarod connection. The race people, or other mushers, might also have heard from this nut. You'll want to have them check their files for similar threats."

As Jensen nodded thoughtfully, a door banged open and someone came quickly through from the front office.

"Hey, there you are. They said you needed some help on some kind of harassment thing. Just finished the paperwork for the Coats trial. I'm all yours."

Jensen looked up to find Trooper Phil Becker striding toward him across the lab, an enthusiastic grin on his face.

The mood at the table improved with his arrival, for both the older men liked the young trooper, who wasn't long away from his rookie years on the force. He still reminded Alex of one of Jessie's half-grown pups, though he was convinced that Becker would exhibit this attitude when the hair that was always falling in his eyes had turned white. In his early thirties, Becker had close to six years with the post and almost three with the homicide group, under Jensen's direction. His interest in the detail involved in crime detection had initially brought him to Alex's attention, after which he had gone out of his way to work with Phil when the opportunity presented itself. The young officer had rapidly developed into a proficient team member.

Still, there were times when he had to tell Becker to put a cork in it, for the young trooper was inclined to think with his mouth. His main talent was his people skills: easy laughter, honest interest, and warmth. It was hard not to like Phil Becker. People instinctively trusted him, often enough to say more than they intended. Under his bright, greedy-for-facts exterior lay an increasingly efficient detection unit, capable of handling problem attitudes more easily than most, and defusing threatening situations with easygoing humor. Gulping information as fast as he could take it in, he could still be counted on not to let a crumb of it get away, and often made interesting connections between the bits and pieces he gleaned.

"Pull up a chair," Timmons invited. "We'll fill you in on this batch of *love notes* Jessie Arnold's been finding in her mailbox."

"Jessie? Damn, Alex. I thought you had her surrounded with our invisible shield that no one can get through."

"Not quite, I'm afraid," Jensen said grimly, handing the notes across to Becker. "Someone seems to think she's fair game for some rather nasty threats."

"Jeez, I'm sorry. She's a nice lady—doesn't need this kind of stuff."

"Well, who does?"

Quiet long enough to examine the notes and hear about the traps, Becker looked up frowning.

"Someone connected to the Iditarod in some way?" he asked.

"Maybe. Could be just an observer, for or against it."

"Lot of anger. No misspellings or glaring grammatical errors. Must have at least an average education. '. . . this time I get to win.' Could this mean there was a time when he, or she, didn't get to win?"

"Now, there's an interesting angle," Timmons commented. "Could it be a musher who came in behind her in some race?"

Jensen and Becker gave each other a haven't-we-been-here-before grin, remembering a case they had worked together.

"That idea will have to be considered, I suppose," Alex agreed. "But I think it's unlikely. However, Cranshaw's attitude was, too."

He referred, indirectly, to the Iditarod race where he had met Jessie, during the investigation of three murders that occurred early in its more than thousand-mile length. One of the suspects had been Bomber Cranshaw, a male musher who disapproved of women sled dog racers.

"Still," Becker said, considering, "it's an odd phrase to use in a note to Jessie. She's come close, but never won the race. What could 'this time I get to win' mean? It implies a sort of *my turn*—either *to win,* or to win *this time.* There's a difference, but it's subtle. Either suggests that this person has had prior contact, or thinks he or she has, right?"

"Right," Jensen nodded. "But where does that get us?"

"Nowhere, now. But it may make more sense later."

Alex's forehead wrinkled as he considered Becker's idea.

"It worries me. There's no way of identifying someone who only thinks they have prior contact. It could be anyone. People who develop this kind of fixation *can* convince themselves that their object either already cares for them, or will, if they are made aware of the admirer."

"Kind of a Catch-22 for the victim," Timmons said. "Damned if they do, and damned if they don't."

"Really."

Suddenly Jensen had had all the talk he could take for the moment. He wanted action, and there seemed little to be had.

"Come on. Let's make a run out to Iditarod headquarters," he said to Becker, as he shoved back his chair and stretched his long legs. "John, let me know if you get anything . . . anything at all on any of this, will you?" He waved a hand vaguely at the notes and traps on the tabletop and turned toward the door.

"Sure. We'll get right on whatever we can do. Priority for our own, and Jessie's one of them. She doing okay?"

"Yeah, Caswell's wife is with her. I'm checking in with her on a regular basis." He headed for the door.

Becker gave Timmons a nod as he shrugged into his coat and followed. "We'll most likely be in the valley, from the sound of it."

"Take it easy."

6

Headquarters of the Iditarod Trail Committee occupied a unique one-story log structure on Knik Road, closer to Wasilla than the cabin where Jessie and Alex lived together. Built of larger-than-usual logs, stained a warm reddish brown, it was impressive to visitors, including hundreds of tourists who came by the busload. It had been purposely situated near the route of the old historic Iditarod Trail that in the early 1900s had run from the docks in Seward, over a Chugach Mountain pass to the Matanuska Valley, where it joined the trail taken by the modern race north to the gold rush town of Iditarod. From there racers continued to Nome. During turn-of-the-century winters, heavy freight sleds had carried mail and supplies into gold camps of Interior Alaska and on to the coast, passing close to the present location of the current ITC headquarters.

The grass of a wide, green lawn that separated the building from a parking lot was now turning brown from nightly frosts, and baskets of flowers had been removed from their hooks on

the exposed ends of large log rafters, from which they had
hung throughout the summer in colorful decoration. As they
went up the walk, Jensen and Becker could see, through one
of the front windows, someone moving inside. The fame and
growth of the race had made its administration a full-time occupation for several people, who were kept busy not just the
first two weeks of every March, but all year.

The front door opened directly into a gift shop full of
mugs, T-shirts, books, and dozens of other Iditarod items.
High on the walls, and not for sale, was an assortment of
memorabilia from past races, and Alex knew that in a special
room to the left were trophies and other articles important to
Iditarod history.

A pleasant young woman greeted them from behind a cash
register. "Can I help you with something?"

Jensen introduced himself and asked for the ITC adminis-
trator, but she shook her head.

"He's at a meeting in Anchorage. Joanne's here. Would
you like to talk to her?"

"Hi, Alex," a voice called from within the offices to the
right. "Come on in."

He grinned, more than happy to settle for a conversation
with Joanne Potts, race director, who had worked for the ITC
since before Alex moved to Alaska, long enough for most people to automatically link her name with that of the race. If
there was anything going on that involved or affected the Iditarod, Joanne would know it.

A short, cheerful, brown-haired woman wearing glasses, she
rose from behind her desk as the troopers entered, offering
them chairs and a smile.

"Hey, Joanne. How's it going?"

"Quiet, thank goodness. We're drawing a well-earned
breath between tourists and the race madness that will gear up
after the holidays. Can I give you coffee?"

"No, thanks. Just need a little of your time."

He introduced Becker and explained their errand.

"I need to know if you've received any recent letters, packages . . . anything that would constitute threats against the ITC, the race, or mushers involved in it. Or if you've heard of anyone who has."

"Threats? Nobody's mentioned any. Of course, we get our share of strange letters—mostly unsigned—from the animal activists, and a few that are more general. But I can't say we've had anything lately—or against specific mushers. We do keep a file, though. Let me get it and we'll look."

She brought a handful of envelopes and letters to her desk and spread them out on the side closest to Jensen and Becker. "Here. Maybe you'll recognize it, if there's anything similar to what Jessie's been getting."

Jensen and Becker went through them all one by one, but found nothing.

"I think there're more archived somewhere," Potts told them. "But they're over five years old. Can't see how they'd apply now, but still we keep them, just in case. I'd have to dig them out of storage. They're not kept here: Space is limited, as you see."

"Don't bother," Alex told her. "That's too long ago. If we need to see them, I'll let you know. How about phone calls? You been getting any hang-ups? Anything strange?"

"No more than usual."

"Any mushers with particular attitudes about women in the race, or with a grudge against other racers?"

"Well, there's always stuff being said to intimidate the competition—part of the game plan. But it's not done with any serious intent to scare anyone—almost tongue-in-cheek, most of it."

"Well . . . let me know if you notice anything," Alex requested, getting up from his chair and offering his hand. "Thanks, Joanne."

As the troopers walked back through the gift shop, Becker stopped for a minute to take a look at a picture of several Iditarod champions that hung next to the sales counter. As he turned to follow Alex to the door, a tall woman in the gray-blue uniform of a postal worker came in and up to the counter.

"Hi, Jennie. Here's your mail." She handed over a pile of envelopes, large and small, held together with a rubber band, and went out the door.

"Thanks." The clerk didn't lay them down, but moved from behind the cash register to take them into the office the troopers had just left. As she passed Becker, he glanced at the collection in her hands and stopped short.

"Hey, wait a minute."

At the sound of his unexpected demand, both she and Alex swung toward him, startled.

"What . . ." she began.

"Let me just look at that top address."

She held it out in silence, a puzzled expression on her face.

Jensen took two or three long steps that brought him close enough to look over Becker's shoulder at the envelope. Joanne Potts stuck her head around the doorframe to see what was going on in the shop and raised her eyebrows in question.

The address label was printed in exactly the same font and size as those Jessie had received. The upper left corner, where a return address would have been, was empty. The postmark indicated that it had been mailed in Anchorage.

Potts came from her office and crossed the room to see what they were examining so closely.

"It could be anything," Jensen said. "Lots of people use this same kind of print."

"But it could be our guy."

"True. Better find out. Joanne, will you give us permission to open this one envelope? It looks just like Jessie's."

"Of course. You want me to do it?"

"I'd rather you didn't touch it before we know. There haven't been any prints, but you never can tell. Let's go back to your desk."

Using another letter to hold it down, he carefully slit the top of the envelope with an opener she provided, and with the metal tool lifted out and spread open the single sheet of paper. They all leaned closer to read the short vindictive message:

THE IDITAROD COMMITTEE SHOULD LOOK INTO JESSIE ARNOLD'S ILLEGAL TRAINING AND RACING METHODS. SHE'S NOT THE ETHICAL, EXEMPLARY MUSHER YOU THINK SHE IS. HEED MY WARNING, OR YOU WILL RE-GRET IT.

"Good God!" Becker exclaimed. "We were ahead of this, but not by much."

"Not when you consider that it had to be mailed yesterday or the day before," Jensen returned.

Potts leaned forward, both hands on her desk.

"This is awful, Alex. Can we do anything to help?"

Jensen thought for a moment before answering.

"What would you have done if you got it cold—before we got here to explain? How would you have reacted?"

"Well, it would have gone to Stan, of course, probably the board. We treat every accusation seriously, so we would have discussed it and made a decision about following up on it. We don't get many, but only a few are such obvious trash that we ignore them."

"And this one—if we hadn't come in?"

"We'd probably have gone to Jessie, checked her kennel and equipment, if she'd let us. Everyone's rights have to be respected, including hers. We're not the sled dog racing Ge-stapo, and don't intend to be, but she's registered for the next race, so that gives us some latitude and authority. We're not out to police mushers, just to keep the race as clean as we can make it."

"Then you should do exactly what you would normally. I'll take this—with your permission—to the lab and get you a copy to show Stan. Let's keep it tight—need-to-know only. Who-ever's doing this might anticipate that you would do something involving Jessie, be expecting it. It should seem that you are following through, as usual."

"Yes, I see. We can do that. Will you tell Jessie?"

"Of course. She'll go along with . . . whatever."

Phil Becker raised a hand, frowning as a new thought came to him.

"Do you think this person could be tapping Jessie's phone, Alex?"

They both turned to look at him—Potts with astonishment, Jensen with a nod, knowing how the younger man's mind skipped from point to seemingly unrelated point in the clues of a case.

"Possible, I suppose. Good thinking, Phil. We can find out easily enough. But if it is tapped, I want it left alone. Shouldn't alert the perp by messing with it. Joanne, if you call Jessie for any reason, be sure you keep that in mind. Don't say anything that would let a listener think you suspect there is a tap, but try not to sound unnatural, either."

"Right. I'll keep that in mind. And, of course, you can take that piece of garbage to the lab. Maybe it'll help somehow. Anything else?"

"Not that I can think of right now. I'll be in touch, okay? If you get any more of these, or if anything happens that I should know, call me."

"You bet—immediately. And Alex—thanks. This is important to us, too, you know. And, please, tell Jessie I'm here if she needs me and to hang in there."

"Thanks, Joanne. I sure will."

"Damn—damn—damn!" Jessie's anger once again had her pacing the room, after tossing a pillow furiously at the sofa. "This is too much, Alex. It never crossed my mind that this bastard would do something to involve the committee. It's monstrous—insulting. How dare he! I feel like I've been assaulted."

"You have. Don't kid yourself. Assault doesn't have to be a physical attack. Filth comes in all shapes and sizes."

He was in the process of attaching a recorder to the telephone, meaning to capture on tape the next hang-up call that came in. An expert from the lab had checked the line and the cabin for listening devices and found none, but he'd warned that if it were somewhere outside it might not be easily detectable.

"It could be tapped on an irregular basis—someone listening at specific times, for instance, or recording only when in use, like the one you're going to use."

The recorder Alex was installing would automatically turn itself on whenever the receiver was lifted in response to an incoming call.

"I want the techs to play with that short bit of sound at the end of these hang-ups. They can slow it down, massage it, maybe identify something we'd miss, and give us ideas on what it is. We'll get a trace going with the phone company, too. See where it's coming from."

He had also picked up a caller ID device, which, before the phone was answered, would show the identification of the caller—if it wasn't blocked, which he suspected it would be.

Jessie had left the few bills and junk mail in the mailbox as Alex had instructed. He wanted to pick them up as he turned into the long driveway. He had arrived early, to find that the day had passed uneventfully for her and Linda Caswell, most of it behind locked doors, planning what they would plant the following spring and how their gardens would be arranged. Linda had brought along a sweater she was knitting, and some extra yarn to show Jessie how to crochet a pot holder that required a clever fold in its construction.

Though Linda had completed a significant amount of her fluffy peach-colored sweater-in-progress, Jessie had found close work frustrating. Used to spending her days with her dogs, she resented being cooped up indoors and had been unable to sit still, making her friend nervous. Once, as they discussed the situation, she had burst into angry tears and threatened to go out.

"I *won't* live in a box. It's what he wants—to scare me silly. It's not *fair*."

But halfway to the door she had changed her mind and taken her temper and anxiety to the kitchen, where she threw together a large batch of bread and spent the next hour kneading it, punching it, pounding it—taking out her rage on it—then waited for it to rise and repeated the process. More plump loaves than she and Alex could eat in weeks now cooled on racks all over the room, waiting to be wrapped and deposited in the freezer. Several had now already gone home with Linda, and Alex cut large slices from both ends of one still-warm loaf and devoured them appreciatively with homemade raspberry jam.

"Yum-m. Best part. Have to make you mad more often if this is the result," he teased. "Great appetizer. What's for dinner?"

"Spaghetti, with sausage in green and black olive sauce. Some of what I froze last month."

"Wonderful stuff! I skipped lunch. Becker had a burger, but I wasn't hungry."

But he had something to do before dinner. He crawled out from under the desk once he had finished his installation chore.

"Now call this phone on the cellular, will you? I'll see if it's working right."

It was. The caller ID refused to give the number of the cell phone, as expected, and the recorder clicked on correctly when he lifted the receiver.

"Okay. Now we wait. Did you get any of those calls today?"

"No. But I jumped every time the phone rang. I let the answering machine pick it up and only answered when I knew who it was. There weren't any hang-ups."

Alex crossed to the sofa and sat down near the warmth of the stove.

"Come and perch for a bit. I'll tell you about the rest of my day."

7

onday night was long, wakeful, and completely quiet, with no further incident. Alex woke in the wee hours to find Jessie's side of the bed empty, and he was half aware that she had spent more time trying to find a comfortable position than sleeping. The air was chilly as he climbed out of bed and went to the door of the outer room.

"Can't sleep, Jess?" he asked the shadow that occupied the end of the sofa nearest the stove, from which he could smell the sweet scent of burning pitch and hear logs crackling as they came to life. She was sitting in the dark, facing the dog lot, once again wrapped in the afghan.

She turned her face toward him, and in the glow of the flames that shone through the glass of the stove door he glimpsed her weary smile.

"I'm okay, but I can't just quit trying to figure out who could be doing this. Sorry. I tried to be quiet."

"You were. I didn't hear you—just knew you weren't there and woke up."

"Get cold?"

"Nope, just lonesome."

He crossed the room and sat down close to her, inside the afghan that she held open for him. They watched the flickering fire in silence for a few minutes, until the wood blazed, increasing the glow.

"I had a bad dream," she confessed shortly.

"What was it?"

"I was running the race, the other side of McGrath. You know—where all the willow and snow machine tracks make the trail really hard to follow, and you can lose it if you're not careful? I couldn't seem to find it—kept going and going, and winding up back where I started. I knew I was lost. There weren't any markers, and there was no one to tell me where the trail was. Then there *was* someone, but they were following me and I couldn't see them. I knew it was someone who wanted to hurt my dogs, and no matter what I did, I couldn't get away. They kept coming closer, and—I could hear their phone ringing. . . . Then, all of a sudden there was a giant hole in the trail and I was falling into it—the whole team pulling us right in, they wouldn't stop—like they couldn't hear me yelling at them—and the phone kept ringing—and I woke up. Not very hard to figure out, huh?"

She was very still. He put his arm around her and could feel the tension in her body.

"It's okay, Jess. I'm here . . . right here."

She sat up straight and rigid for a second or two, before leaning back against him. "I *hate this*. Really, really *hate this*."

"I know. So do I."

"I'm so tired, Alex. Seems like every bone in my body aches and my mind won't stop. It feels like a bird that flies into the house and keeps frantically hitting the windows, trying to get out."

Alex and Jessie fed the dogs together the next morning and checked their condition.

"They need exercise," she said sadly, pouring warm food into the last bowl. "I should be running some of them with the four-wheeler until it snows."

"Don't even think about it. They're fine," he told her bluntly. "A few days without a run won't hurt them."

"Is it only going to be a few days?"

"I certainly hope so."

She stopped to pet a female that approached, wagging her tail in anticipation.

"Hey, Sadie. You just want a little sugar, don't you? She's going to have another litter."

"Great. She has good pups. How many of hers did you take along on the race last year?"

"Four, and I'm thinking of adding the Darryls this year, if they work well at wheel."

As they were bringing the feed buckets to the cabin for cleaning, Linda Caswell pulled up, the back seat of her Blazer full of grocery bags. She grinned at Jessie's questioning lift of an eyebrow.

"If cooking makes you feel better—we'll cook. It's a little early, but I thought, if you'd help, I'd get the fruitcake done ahead of time this year. We can test it at Thanksgiving."

They carried sacks of food into the cabin and Linda began to sort the supplies into piles on the table. Linda's fruitcakes were highly prized by friends and family, appreciated even by those who claimed to hate the traditional holiday confection. She refused to use the usual candied citrus, made them instead with dried apricots, peaches, dates, pineapple, cherries, pecans, and a generous amount of fruit brandy—before and after baking—prior to storing them away for a month or more to ripen. Preparing the ingredients—chopping and dicing—usually took her a day; mixing and baking the loaves, another. But with two of them working, she thought they might complete the job in one.

"Great idea," Jessie agreed, and began to fill the kitchen

sink with soapy water for washing the breakfast dishes—clearing space in the small kitchen.

"Be sure she doesn't get out the door with all of them, Jess," Alex instructed with a grin, and left the two absorbed in their culinary occupation of the day, pleased to see Jessie's mood lighten, even slightly. Nevertheless, when she accompanied him to the door and kissed him good-bye, she clung just a little, in an uncharacteristic way.

"Don't forget to call me," she requested as he put on his coat.

"I won't," he told her.

As he went down the steps toward his truck, he heard the deadbolt thump solidly into place in the front door. It renewed his uneasiness as he headed for Palmer, more determined than ever to track down the offensive cause of their tension. The longer this threat lasted, the more damage would be done to Jessie's self-assurance and confidence. Bound to affect their relationship, it was intolerable.

As his anger and resentment grew, he put his foot down a little heavier on the gas pedal, impatient with the time it took to reach his destination and some possible solution. He was so close to the situation, he felt he was blinded by the emotion of it, which added to his anxiety. As the truck rumbled over the railroad tracks and into Wasilla, he pounded the wheel with a frustrated fist, causing a woman headed the other direction in a van to give him a startled glance as she passed.

Jessie and Linda spent the morning slicing dried fruit and crushing pecans. By noon they were ready to take a break for lunch.

Looking out the window at the dog lot for the dozenth time, Jessie frowned.

"It's really warmed up out there," she said. "I should give the mutts more water."

"Is that a good idea?" Linda looked up from the bowl into which she was scooping apricot pieces from the cutting board.

"I can't take this out on the dogs—it's not fair. I'd normally water them. If we go out together and you keep watch with the gun while I do it quickly, I think it would be okay."

After thinking it over for a minute, Linda agreed, even though there was really no way to spot a sniper should one be interested in concealing himself among the trees and brush.

"Okay, but let's take the cell phone and lock the house."

From the windows, they cautiously examined everything they could see around the cabin before pulling on their coats and boots and going out onto the porch. Linda carried the shotgun and walked with Jessie as she poured water in the pan for each dog; both of them watched nervously as they moved through the lot. They had reached the last row of dog boxes when Linda's troubled voice stopped her friend cold.

"Jessie?"

From where she had been bending over in the farthest corner of the dog lot, Jessie rose and, bucket in hand, stood to watch a figure walking confidently up the long gravel drive toward her house. The two women stepped behind one of the boxes and stood silently examining the visitor. Linda rested the barrel of the shotgun on top of the box, pointed in the man's direction, ready for anything.

"Who is it? Do you recognize him?"

"No, not from here. Wait a minute—see what he does."

She appreciated it when visitors called before making an appearance, and they usually arrived in their own transportation. It was miles to Wasilla. Had this one hiked all the way? Hitchhiked, maybe, and been dropped off somewhere on the road? In either case, it was obvious that he had no wheels of his own, or had left them somewhere.

The figure, as he came closer, appeared to be a young man, from the way he moved and his slim build. He was wearing jeans, a jacket of characteristic Carhartt reddish brown, and a dark baseball cap pulled low on his forehead. On his back he carried a large green pack that looked crammed and lumpy.

He moved with a stride that created the impression he had been walking for some time and seemed used to the pack. Carefully avoiding puddles in the drive, he came steadily onward, stopping only when he reached the steps to the porch. There he shrugged off the pack, letting it slide onto the third step, where it would be easier to shoulder again. Raising both hands behind his head, he stretched his shoulders, then dropped his arms and turned to face the watching women.

"Hi—Miz Arnold?" he called.

Jessie could feel her heart hammering in her chest, and her mouth was dry. She saw Linda's hand tighten on the stock of the shotgun. Though she hadn't yet put a finger on the trigger, her right hand hovered close.

"Who are you?" Jessie challenged, hearing and feeling her strained voice almost break. "What do you want?"

The man—boy, really, she could see now as he took off his hat—stood staring at her with an unhappy, puzzled expression.

"But you said I could come. It's Billy . . . Billy Steward. Don't you remember? You said I could help with the dogs."

The relief was so intense that for a minute Jessie was afraid her legs would collapse under her, and out of her whirling thoughts came a phrase her Missouri grandmother had used: "The sand went right out of her." It was so appropriate that she barked a short, stress-releasing laugh and half choked on it.

Taking a moment to catch her breath, she laid a restraining hand on Linda's arm.

"I know him. He's one of the junior mushers I've been training."

Collecting the bucket she had dropped, she led the way across the yard, smiling apologetically at the perplexed young musher, who waited by the steps.

"It's okay, Billy. I'm sorry—I'd forgotten I said you could come and help. I've just had a few other things on my mind the last couple of days. What's in the pack?"

"Rope—and harness. You said you'd show me. . . ."

"Right. I remember. Come inside. We'll make a cup of tea and talk about it."

"I've got to get out of here, just for a little while," she responded to Linda's objections a little later. "I'm going to take him back to town. Can't let him work in the lot now, with this going on. We can all go in my truck and make a quick stop at the grocery store to get something for dinner before we come back."

"I thought you didn't want to leave the dogs."

"I don't, really, but I think it'll be all right for just a short time—maybe an hour? There hasn't been anything for two whole days. I'll call Alex and tell him we're going."

Alex answered her call from the lab in Anchorage and, after some thought, agreed to the quick trip to Wasilla.

"Don't be gone long," he cautioned. "And don't go anywhere but the Stewards' and to Carrs for the groceries. Call me as soon as you get back, okay? Watch carefully for anything suspicious, anything that you can't explain."

They locked the cabin and left the shotgun in its place on the wall, but Jessie took along the Smith and Wesson .44 that she carried with her when she was training or racing sled dogs. Moose were a hazard all mushers learned to avoid when possible, since they could devastate a harnessed team with their hooves if they weren't stopped. But more than that, the handgun was security. One very like it had saved her life once during an Iditarod race.

Linda and Billy were quiet as Jessie started her truck and swung it around in the wide space by the front steps. At the end of the driveway she stopped to wait for two cars to pass before pulling out onto the road heading south in the direction of Wasilla.

"I'm really sorry, Billy," she told her would-be helper, knowing how much he had looked forward to working with her at the kennel. "When things are better, you can come and spend a week if you want. I'll even put you on the payroll."

He nodded and grinned, his initial disappointment lifting.

"Do you have dogs of your own, Billy?" Linda asked, smiling.

"Yeah. I got two that I got from my dad. Lady and Totem."

"Totem?"

"When he was a puppy he looked like a bear on a totem pole when he showed his teeth."

"Good name," Jessie said approvingly. She turned on the radio and found a station that was playing rock and roll oldies. It was good to be going somewhere—away from what she was beginning to feel was a prison, even if it was the cabin that she loved and had helped to build.

The day was overcast, with pale clouds that hinted at snow soon to come, though they had brought a rise in the temperature. The wind, having plundered the gold from the birches along both sides of the road, had died, leaving the ground beneath the trees a mosaic of yellow leaves. Bare, their branches contrasted whitely against the black-green of scattered spruce.

She drove steadily along a straight section of the road, enjoying the hum of the tires against the macadam surface, tapping her fingers, in time to the music against the edge of the steering wheel. Ahead, the road made a sharp curve to the left. Jessie knew that it was poorly banked, requiring care and a slower speed. Though it was dry now, in the winter it could be dangerously slick with ice or snow. She touched the brakes lightly to moderate the speed of the truck before entering the turn.

The pedal plunged abruptly all the way to the floor under her foot. There was a brief, light resistance approximately half an inch from the floor when she could feel something take hold, just a little, but not enough to reduce their speed. She pumped the brakes repeatedly. Nothing.

"What's wrong?" Linda asked, frowning.

"No brakes," Jessie muttered, still trying to get them to work. "Haven't got any. Hold on."

Though she steered across into the empty opposite lane, in an attempt to stay on the road, the truck entered the curve at approximately forty-five miles an hour, and immediately she could feel the centrifugal force at work on the vehicle. Irrevocably it was drawn to the right, rocking off the ground on two wheels as she fought to keep it under control. The curve increased and as they came into the middle of it Jessie could see a car approaching.

To avoid a head-on collision, she was forced back into the right-hand lane and for an instant turning away from the curve lessened the tendency of the truck to roll. Having to steer to the left again to avoid hitting the shoulder worsened the problem. Once again both wheels left the pavement, thumping down hard as she wrestled with the wheel. They were going over the edge of the roadbed, one way or another. She knew it and tried to make a split-second decision. Would it be better to roll or to try to drive the truck off the road and down into the broad, uneven space that had been half cleared between the pavement and the thick stand of trees approximately a hundred feet away?

She heard Linda yell something as she made her choice and allowed the truck to drift onto the shoulder and, slowly, over the edge, attempting to retain some influence on its direction.

Any control she had was lost in an instant as the hood dipped alarmingly—dirt and rocks flying as the wheels dug into the steep graveled slope of the shoulder—and the truck began an uncontrollable sliding roll to the right.

The horrible, screeching sound of metal crushing and tearing and glass breaking went on and on as the truck revolved, throwing its three passengers violently back and forth against their seat belts. The bridge of Jessie's nose hit the top of the steering wheel, then her head struck the side window, a stunning blow. She felt Linda slam against her and heard a sharp cry of pain that was cut off as they turned over and seemed to hang upside down before continuing to roll. Then the truck stopped, rocked, and settled, driver's side down. Aside from the delicate tinkle of glass still falling, there was sudden complete silence.

Everything—everyone—was still for a long minute. Linda groaned and moved a little, and Jessie was groggily aware that both Linda and Billy were lying on her, mashing her against the door. She vaguely tried to think what had happened, why they were on top of her. Slowly, she brought her free right hand to her face, which burned; she felt something slick and warm, and when she moved her hand away, there was blood dripping from her fingers. Then everything began to look gray and fuzzy and she couldn't breathe.

8

After fading in and out of consciousness and finally falling into a deep sleep, Jessie opened her eyes early Wednesday morning to find herself in an Anchorage hospital and Alex sitting close beside her bed, holding her hand. She said nothing, but silent tears started to run down her face, neck, and into her hair. A dark, angry-colored swelling marred her left cheek and temple where she had hit the truck window and a butterfly bandage held together the edges of a cut on the bridge of her nose. Both eyes were beginning to turn purplish black, but aside from two broken fingers, pinkie and ring, on her right hand, a few minor abrasions, and some painful bruises, she had no major injuries.

"Linda?" she whispered. "Billy?"

They had been no luckier, though neither had approached critical condition. Linda had gone home from the hospital the night before in a cervical collar, with a cast on her fractured left arm. Three of Billy's ribs were broken and because one had punctured a lung, he was, like Jessie, still in the hospital.

Cautiously, with her right index finger, Jessie explored the damage to her face, winced when she found the bruise on her cheek, and frowned at the bandage on her nose.

"What's under this? Did they have to sew it up?"

Alex grinned, minimizing his response.

"They thought about it. But I figured you'd rather not have to go cross-eyed at needlework on your nose. The doc said you could have stitches or character. It'll only be a tiny scar, so I told them character would be fine. Okay with you? If not, they can still stitch it."

"Character's fine." She tried to nod and grimaced at the resulting discomfort.

"You're going to have a real headache for a few days; you have a bit of a concussion."

"When can I get out of here?"

"Well . . . tomorrow, probably. We'll talk about that."

"What happened? Why couldn't I stop? There weren't any brakes."

He was surprised that she remembered. Many people who have been involved in accidents, especially victims with head injuries, didn't recall the incidents at all.

"Do you remember all of the crash?"

"I think so. Until I blacked out, I think. I remember going over the shoulder and a lot of noise that seemed to go on for a long time. Then I couldn't breath, Linda and Billy were lying on top of me, and there was blood on my face."

She sighed and yawned, her eyes closing.

"It's okay, now. We'll talk later, love."

She was instantly asleep again as he stroked the back of her hand, laid it on the blanket, and stretched to relieve the ache in his back. Friends and family had come and gone through the hours, but he had taken only a quick break or two to gulp something to quiet his growling stomach, though he had no idea what he had eaten. His eyes felt full of sand. He had rubbed at them with his knuckles and discovered that the unshed tears weren't all exhaustion.

The door opened to admit a nurse, who, noticing his emotional condition, crossed the room and laid a hand on his shoulder. "It's going to be all right, you know?"

"I know. I just hate hospitals and having people I care about in them."

"It can be scary, but she's going to be just fine."

Leaving Jessie in her care, he went to find Becker, who was waiting to give him an automotive report.

The truck, a crushed and crumpled total loss, had been claimed by the troopers for an immediate and thorough examination, the result of which Becker now related to Jensen.

"The brake line wasn't cut. It was punctured with something sharp and pointed, like an icepick, maybe a little bigger. If it had been cut, she would have known she couldn't stop before she left the lot, the first time she stepped on the brakes, because all the fluid would have drained out. You might even have noticed it under the truck. This way it was a ticking time bomb until the truck was on the road. She had to step on the brakes several times to pump out all the fluid, then it must have been just suddenly gone. It wasn't just chance that it happened on that particular curve, or another one like it, because that's where she would normally use the brakes. They were all damned lucky it wasn't worse. Whoever punched a hole in that brake line didn't care who was hurt—or killed."

"And any one of them could have been. We've got to get this asshole, Phil."

"You're right about that. It's gone way past harassment now."

"First I want to get Jessie out of here—out of the area, I mean. I want her safe—somewhere out of danger, where this crazy can't get at her."

"Where?"

"Idaho? I can send her to my folks in Salmon."

"If she's in a safe place, we can focus on what has to be

done. You won't have to worry about whether she's okay or not. I think that's a good idea, but will she go?"

"She promised she would, if the time came that I decided it was necessary. Well, I've decided. It's now."

Jessie agreed, as Alex knew she would, but not to Idaho.

"I've been thinking about it," she told him, sitting up to spoon lime Jell-O into her mouth from a bowl on her lunch tray. "First I want you to know how much I hate the idea of going away and leaving someone else to take care of something that's my problem."

"Jess, it's not just . . ."

"I know, but . . ." She paused, then it came bursting out. "Not much scares me, Alex. You know that. But this does—because there's no way to see it coming. It's like trying to see in the dark, when it's all shadows and no substance. I hate it—detest being afraid."

"Jess," he told her seriously, "sometimes the better part of valor is to *run like hell.*

"You know that as long as you're here, you put both of us in danger, not just yourself. Think about it. You're in jeopardy because he can get at you—one way or another—and there's no way we can intercept his attempts because he keeps changing his angle of attack. I'm in danger because I'm focused on you—when I should be focused entirely on him. It's not letting him win to put yourself beyond his reach. It's smart, and defeats the game he's playing. You stay—nobody wins, and you may lose. You go—he has no chance of winning."

"You're right," she said. "I know you are. Okay, I'll go. I said I'd respect your professional judgment, and I will. Disliking it—feeling guilty—is beside the point really. I can see that."

He nodded. "That's right."

"However, somebody's going to have to take care of my dogs . . . and you're going to be too busy, I think."

"Already got that fixed. Don Morgan's moving them to his kennel in Willow this afternoon."

"All of them? What a friend. He's got his hands full with his own—has more than I do."

"You've got more friends than you know. All your junior mushers have volunteered to help him out—except Billy, of course."

"How's Billy? Did you see him?"

"Yeah, he's doing fine, considering. Going home in a day or two. Said to tell you you're not off the hook about him helping—when you're both well and up for it."

She smiled weakly. "He's a good kid. I'm just sorry I got him and Linda hurt. What about Linda's fruitcakes?"

"This wasn't your fault, Jess. You didn't put a hole in the brake line—"

"And the fruitcakes will get done—when they get done," Ben Caswell told her, coming into the room. "Linda says to tell you this is a hell of a way to get out of helping."

"Sounds like she's gonna be okay. How's her neck?"

"Just strained a muscle or two, thankfully. They did an MRI and there's nothing torn or broken. But she aches all over—says she feels like someone put her in a wooden box with you and Billy and rolled you all down a long, steep, extremely bumpy hill."

"Tell her she's not alone. Even my toes ache."

"Glad her neck's okay," Alex said. "Now help me out here, Cas. I'm trying to get Jess to go down to my folks's place in Idaho, but she's got some other idea."

"Hey," Jessie corrected him. "I said I'd go—somewhere. I just don't want to go out of state. There're places here where I could drop out of sight just as well as if I went back to the old country."

"Where? Name one where no one would recognize you and let something slip."

"I told you I'd been thinking about it. How about Niqa Island in Kachemak Bay?"

Alex stared at her, shaking his head.

"Bad idea. There's no one out there this time of year, Jess."

"That's just it. No one out there would be no one to mention that *I* was. It's isolated, private, and, best of all, not a place I often go or am associated with. How could this awful person possibly find out I was there? I know Millie would let me use her beach house and wouldn't breathe a word— to anyone."

"She's right, Alex," Caswell said. "It's not really a bad solution."

Alex frowned, exhibiting a stubborn streak. "I like Idaho better. It's farther away, and my folks would be around to help."

"Alex, the idea isn't how far, but how well hidden— safe—right?"

She finished the Jell-O, curled a lip at the broth-pretending-to-be-soup, and waved a cracker at him.

"I'll take Tank, the shotgun, and my .44, food for a couple of weeks—catch up on the reading I've been meaning to do. No one will know where I am. Additional benefit? I won't have to see everyone I know while I'm looking like a raccoon, or keep explaining that you didn't beat me."

Caswell grinned and nodded, noticing she had, unconsciously or not, slipped from *would* to *will*.

"I don't really think your looks are at the heart of the issue, Jessie, but . . . We could fly her down in my plane, Alex. Set it down in the cove and taxi right up to the beach, like we did last July. It works. I like it."

Alex chewed his lip, still unconvinced.

"What I don't like is that you'd be down there alone. There would be no help if you needed it."

"There's the radio and half the bay to hear me if I used it. I can take my cellular."

"It's not secure, either. Anyone could listen."

"So? They wouldn't know where it was coming from unless we mentioned it, would they? We could check in at specific

times so you'd know I was okay. Niqa's not that far from
Homer—about half an hour by boat. And it's only two hundred and twenty-five miles from Anchorage . . ."

"Less by plane," Caswell noted.

". . . so you could be there fast, if I needed you."

Alex only partially capitulated, but they both knew he was
weakening—running out of objections.

"Well . . . call Millie and ask her. I'll think about it. Now
get some rest. If you're not going to eat the rest of that, I'll
move it."

"I'm not. Oh, *ple-ease*, bring me some real food, okay?
Pizza—tacos—even a Big Mac. I don't care, but I'm going to
starve on this." She rejected the bland contents of the tray with
a dismissive flick of her fingers. "There's nothing wrong with
my appetite."

"She's better," Alex told Cas, with a straight face. "Getting
pushy and demanding."

"Yeah. Linda's like that, too." Cas grinned. "You'd think
she broke an arm or something. I think Jessie'd be pretty capable of taking care of herself on an island."

"Yeah, I guess you might be right."

"I'd be okay, Alex. Really, I would."

"And if you weren't?"

"Then you two will be my knights in shining airplane."

"I don't like it," Jensen told Caswell as they walked out of the
hospital a few minutes later. "I'd rather have her a long ways
away from here—or where I could keep track of her every
single minute, and that's not possible. Even if I could, it
wouldn't make her completely safe and might just get us both
killed. This guy seems to be a real loony tune, but an extremely
cautious and clever one."

"We could send someone with her—one of ours—or . . .
Listen, I've got a friend with the Air National Guard Para-

rescue. Those guys are awesome, better than guerrillas any-where—really know their stuff. This guy I'm thinking of can turn completely invisible on a patch of scorched earth—and also be deadly, if necessary. I'd rather one of them guarded Linda in a bad situation than me, if I had the choice."

"Naw, it won't work. You know Jess. She's already refused a 'baby-sitter,' as she called it. She said she wouldn't go if we insisted on sending somebody along—even you or Phil. She's so damned used to doing things alone, by and for herself."

Caswell picked up a paper cup someone had dropped in the parking lot and tossed it into a trash can.

"Let me kick it around a little," he said contemplatively. "I might be able to come up with something. Now let's get you something to eat before you seize up on me. You need some-thing to take back to Jessie, too. Then we can figure out how to get her out of town as quickly and inconspicuously as possible."

9

On Thursday afternoon, Jessie had gone from the hospital to Alex's truck, according to regulations, in a wheelchair. Though she felt much better, she was still sore from the battering she had taken in the rolling truck and had been exercising in her room to alleviate the stiffness and the slight depression she was feeling.

"Don't leave this room," Jensen had cautioned her. "There's an APD officer outside, screening whoever comes in, and I've had a word with the nursing staff. Let this loony think you're still incapacitated."

It made sense, and Jessie had found she was glad to comply—grateful, even, for the guard at her door.

"I can walk from here," she told him Thursday as he wheeled her toward the hospital doors.

"But you won't. I want you to look as pathetic as possible. If this guy's watching, I want him to think you're hardly able to sit up, let alone protect yourself. He needs to think you're going home and right back to bed—won't be up for a week or more, from the look of you."

"Oh, I see. Good plan."

She slumped in the chair and suppressed a nervous giggle as she tried to look pitiful.

"I'm so glad to be getting out of here that it's hard to take this seriously."

"Do it anyway. Just think of the cause of the wreck and Nicky."

Her snigger disappeared instantly, and he was sorry to have been the cause, though he felt it was necessary.

"We've been saying *he* ever since the accident. Have you decided that it's a man now? Why?"

Cautiously sweeping the parking lot with his eyes, Alex thought about that.

"I guess I'm making an assumption. Tampering with the brakes on a truck seems more like something a man would do, though that doesn't really make sense. A woman could do it just as easily—you just have to know where the line is and how to puncture it. I'm not sure, but I'm going to say *he* till I find out differently."

She allowed him to lift her into the passenger seat of the truck, where she continued her weak-sister act as he drove directly to the Caswells' in Eagle River.

"Great! You look terrible," Linda—aware of the pantomime—told her, opening the door so Alex could carry Jessie in and set her, finally, on her own two good feet.

"Thanks a bunch. You don't look too fantastic yourself. Oh, Linda, I'm so sorry."

"What for? This wasn't your fault."

"I feel like it was. It's me he's after, not you—and not Billy."

"Well, you can forget it. You think I don't feel guilty for agreeing to that drive into town? Now that we've both got that out of our systems, let's put it away and get this trip to the island planned right. Dinner's about ready. Ben'll be home soon and we'll talk about tomorrow morning while we eat."

"Wonderful. Something besides institution food."

"Hey," Alex reminded her. "Who's spoiled you rotten with gourmet takeout for two whole days?"

The next day, very early on Friday morning, Alex and Cas flew Jessie and Tank southwest to Kachemak Bay, following a plan of action that had been arranged carefully, discreetly, and with uncommon care.

"Why don't they have alleys anymore?" Jessie complained as she and the two men drove out of the Caswells' garage and onto the street. "We ought to be slipping out the back of the house, to foil anyone watching from the front. I feel like a spy or a secret agent leaving a safe house."

"Well, they don't need 'em these days," Alex answered. "Garbage trucks come to the curb instead. I'm watching. There's nobody following us that I can see."

Getting up while it was still dark, they had eaten a quick breakfast and were headed for Anchorage in Linda's Blazer, from which Alex was keeping a close eye on the traffic around them.

"Don't fret," Cas assured Jessie. "Even if he were following us, he couldn't get any farther than Lake Hood. The last thing he'd expect is for us to get into the Maule and fly off."

The day before, to confuse anyone watching or following, Ben Caswell had flown his plane from its space at the end of Wasilla Lake to Lake Hood near Anchorage International Airport, where he had landed and sat watching people and planes come and go for half an hour. Seeing no one suspicious, he had left his Maule M-4, filed a flight plan for the next day, and gone home for dinner.

When they reached Lake Hood this morning, while Caswell prepared the plane and ran through his preflight checklist, Alex hurriedly loaded supplies, the shotgun, Tank, and Jessie, then climbed in himself, closely followed by Cas. Jessie wore her .44 in a neat holster on her right hip, having found it difficult, with her two broken fingers taped together in splints, to reach under her jacket to her usual shoulder holster, but possible to hold and shoot the gun if necessary.

"Can you use that?" Alex asked, watching her put it on.

"Yes." She demonstrated. "It's a little awkward, but using the other hand to steady it, it'll be fine."

He had hoped she wouldn't have to try it, but said nothing more.

The sun had begun to turn the peaks of the Chugach Range gold around the edges as they took off, circled, and headed east.

"This isn't the way to Homer," Jessie commented from the rear seat, where she sat hemmed in by supplies and Tank. The husky lay on the floor against her feet—alert, and doing as he was told. He had flown before, but was never sure how to respond to the unusual experience of being airborne and feeling the surface on which he lay move under him.

"Right," Cas agreed, "and with my best planning. To anyone watching, we're heading for Glennallen, or anywhere beyond—Fairbanks, Tok, the Canadian border. We'll swing across the Chugach when we're out of sight and head down the Kenai."

"Good thinking."

"Just making absolutely sure this is done right—no slips—jumping through all the hoops I could think of, necessary or not, so no one knows where we're going. Taking good care of you."

"Thanks, Cas."

The long valley where the Knik and Susitna Rivers flowed into an arm of the sea drifted by beneath them, discernible in the rapidly increasing light, and in a few more minutes the sun began to cast its light between the spires of the mountains in long golden fingers. Looking down, Jessie recognized the landmarks she was used to seeing from ground level: the communities of Palmer and Wasilla, the road leading out of Wasilla to her own cabin, Pioneer Peak rising between her and the rising sun. It looked peaceful, benign, and safe as it slid away below.

She could see that new snow had already dusted the tops of the ridges, as Cas swung the plane to the south to cross their western end. From Anchorage, what appeared to be a large wall of mountains was really just an edge of the Chugach Range, which stretched beyond her sight about a hundred and fifty miles directly east until it came to an end at the Bagley Ice Field in the Wrangell-Saint Elias Wilderness. Intense morning sun added such brightness to some of the white, reflective surfaces of the snow on peaks and glaciers that they were too brilliant to look at without squinting.

It took only a few minutes to fly over them and reach Turnagain Arm, where Caswell turned the plane a little more southwest above the Kenai Peninsula, which was full of small lakes and muskeg and more mountains off to the left. Looking down, Jessie could see the highway, the only motor route that ran all the way down the peninsula, ending at the community of Homer on Kachemak Bay. Examining it carefully, she noticed a few vehicles, including an eighteen-wheeler headed up the long road to Anchorage from the port. A few puffy clouds had drifted in from the south, and as they flew through them, the plane bumped and jerked slightly for a moment or two in the turbulence.

"Alex. There's a moose . . . look, down there."

He craned his neck to see where she was pointing and saw a brown speck, very tiny but recognizable, browsing for breakfast in the reeds of a lake that looked like a silver puddle.

Jensen enjoyed flying with Caswell, though his tall frame never fit comfortably when it was doubled into the small Maule M-4. Seeing some part of Alaska spread out under him gave him a feeling for its enormity. Mountains that rose like giants from the ground—which he saw every day and forgot about most of the time—now looked much different, though they still towered impressively. It always surprised him that the coastline of the south-central part of the state was so rugged and uneven, with its deep arms and channels of ocean. From above, it was possible to understand that it was really a new, sharp mountain range, still forming—that these mountains were twice as tall as they looked, because at least half of each one was below the surface of the sea.

Looking ahead, he could now see the wide reach of Kachemak Bay, running northeast to southwest, and nestled beside it the small community of Homer. Pointing southeast from the town, at a right angle to the shoreline, was a three-mile-long protrusion of land—the Homer Spit. Too narrow to be a peninsula—hardly wider, in a place or two, than the road than ran its length—this finger of land had been the original reason for the town's location and was the focus of much of the area's business. In summer, the road, with a single lane in each direction, actually created traffic jams of tourists, who came by the hundreds to park their tents, motor homes, and trailers on the sandy, oceanside beach of the spit. Now it was deserted, shops and charter services closed, and Jensen could see foam blowing from the caps of wind-whipped waves on the unsheltered ocean side.

"It looks rough," he commented. "Glad we're not going across in a boat."

"Weather service says there's a storm predicted in the next couple of days," Caswell said. "Jessie, you can expect to be stranded till it's over. I can land in this much wind, but not in a big blow. Better make sure you have lots of dry wood indoors." He banked the plane a little to the left and headed south over the end of the spit, toward the other side of the bay. Jessie looked down to see the harbor, where containers were off-loaded from the ships and barges that traveled to and fro between Homer and the Pacific ports of the contiguous forty-eight states and foreign countries, bringing half of what was necessary for life in the Far North—from the down clothing that kept many of its people warm to the duct tape that seemed to hold everything together. They had already passed over a large public and commercial marina where dozens of boats were moored when they were not somewhere out on the waters of the bay, taking fishermen for the trip of their lives—if they could hook onto the bay's enormous halibut—often several hundred pounds apiece.

Kachemak Bay, over thirty miles long, ran from Cook Inlet to the Fox River Flats. From three miles wide at its navigable upper end, it widened to twelve between Homer and Tutka Bay on the opposite shore. Scattered a mile or two offshore at the mouth of Tutka were a number of islands that partially sheltered it from the furies of the sea. They ranged in size from a mile or more across to so small they were not even large enough to hold a picnic at low tide.

It slowly became possible to make out a few tiny houses on the mainland of the peninsula, around the mouth of Tutka Bay, and that of Sadie Cove immediately to the east of it. The latter was responsible for the name Jessie had given to one of her female puppies, after her first visit to Niqa Island.

As she watched, the group of islands grew larger until she could make out the channels of water between. Jessie named some of the larger ones.

"There's Cohen Island, Yukon, Hesketh, Herring, and Grass Island—the funny one that always reminds me of a loaf of green bread." It was a grass-covered hump in the water, sides rising straight up as tall as it was wide, which wasn't much. "And there's Niqa."

She grew silent, watching it come closer.

Alex looked back to measure her mood.

"You still sure about this, Jess?" he asked. "We could get you on a southbound plane tonight instead."

She gave him a long, pensive look that ended with a short nod.

"Yeah. I'm still sure. It'll be fine, Alex. You'll see. Just go catch this guy, okay? Let me know when it's over, and don't forward my mail."

Well, that answers that, Jensen thought, exchanging a quick, conspiratorial glance with Caswell. They would not tell her about the new message from the stalker that had appeared at the hospital, in an envelope bearing Jessie's name. With it had come a vase containing a seriously inappropriate arrangement of white lilies.

A nurse had brought it to the patrolman on duty, who was checking every get-well card and floral offering before it went into Jessie's room and had passed it on to Jensen, when he saw what the envelope contained:

GET WELL SOON, JESSIE. I'M WAITING.

What had made Jensen even more furious were two snapshots folded in with the note. Each showed Jessie and Linda in the dog lot at the cabin—Linda carefully keeping watch, Jessie watering her dogs. The photographer had obviously been standing in the grove of trees just beyond the yard, close enough to clearly show both women in the pictures.

He and Caswell—who had expressed himself excessively in four-letter words—had taken the photos to the crime lab.

"Not much we can tell," John Timmons had informed him later. "Kodak paper, ordinary size and film. Could have been developed anywhere—probably the local Carrs grocery, or Costco, where they get hundreds of jobs a week and wouldn't pay attention to anything unless it was really unusual or pornographic. Crank 'em through a developing machine and send 'em back for pickup. No prints, but we expected that."

"Dammit. He was close enough to shoot them both—and not just with a camera," Jensen complained.

"And won't come back to that spot again, I'll guarantee you."

"Gives us nothing to work on."

"Yeah, well. Keep trying. Search the spot he took them from. Nobody's perfect. There'll be something eventually."

"Eventually isn't soon enough. He'll figure out that Jessie's not here and quit, or go hunting for her. I want something to get him before he does."

Alex turned now to glance at the woman beside him. She needed to recover, physically and mentally, in a calm, safe, quiet place—to be invisible, silent, and unreachable. And she would be—on the island they were approaching.

10

Niqa Island rose from the salt waters of Kachemak Bay near the outer edge of the island group, exposed to weather from the mouth of Cook Inlet, which widened and opened, through Kennedy and Stevenson Entrances, into the Gulf of Alaska. On a clear day, Augustine, one of the active volcanoes of the Aleutian Range, could be seen periodically releasing steam and, infrequently, ash and cinders from its fiery core. Approximately a square mile in size, from above Niqa appeared a rough triangle—an arrowhead aimed at the Homer Spit. The scalloped, irregular line of its base was formed by the crescents of two shallow coves, separated by not quite a half mile of wooded area at the top of a fifty-foot cliff that put its feet in the water at high tide.

Aside from two open meadows near the coves, around which Millie's family members had built several beach houses, the island was almost completely covered with large trees and brush. Not really intended for winter occupation, the compact

structures were uninsulated and lacked electricity. Batteries ran
a radio communication system, and a generator was infrequently used to power tools for working with wood or metal.
Propane stoves were used for cooking, and the houses were
heated with wood from the beach, cut and split. Water was
carried from freshwater springs, or jerry-rigged into kitchen
sinks with the aid of gravity and hose, or plastic pipe.

Caswell set the Maule down gently in the waters of the
western cove and taxied to the rock-strewn shore that was half
exposed by the falling tide. Above the rather steep beach that
was washed by the ocean twice a day was the house that belonged to Jessie's friend, Millie. It was a low building, twice as
wide as it was high, with a broad, open deck across its entire
length. Built of rough unpainted lumber that had silvered over
the years, it blended in well with the natural colors of the
island.

"We can't stay here long," Cas warned, "or the bird'll be
high and dry until the next high tide."

"Aw-w, we could *lift* this bird back into the water," Alex
teased.

"Obviously you've never tried to shove it more than a few
feet, let alone lift it. Besides, the longer we're parked, the more
likely it is that someone will notice we're here. A plane on the
beach isn't exactly invisible. Let's get this stuff up to the
house."

Using the floats of the plane as bridges to dry land, they
carried off several boxes of human and canine food, an ice
chest, Jessie's duffel and sleeping bags, and the rest of her gear,
then gazed unenthusiastically at the uphill stretch of rocks the
size of melons, across which they would have to transport the
supplies they had piled in a sizable heap.

"Don't panic. There's help," Jessie said, starting up the
slope toward the deck of the house. She came quickly back,
pulling a handcart with two large wheels, into which they grate-
fully loaded everything. While Cas checked to make sure the

plane was secure, Alex slowly pulled the bumping, jolting barrow to the top of the beach.

"Let me do it," he said, when she started to help. "You're still sore and gimpy."

As the cart jerked along, the rocks gradually grew smaller until the way was paved with gravel. Mixed among it were broken pieces of shell, drying kelp, and other remnants of the sea.

"I thought beaches were supposed to be sand," he grunted, when he paused to catch his breath at the foot of the ramp that led to the deck.

"Yeah? Well, this one isn't."

"No kidding. You'd better *eat* all this food. I'm not carrying it back down when it's time to take you home."

"Listen," Jessie suggested. "Let's just leave this stuff in the cart. I have the rest of the day to sort it out, and Cas is right, you should really get out of here."

Alex nodded as Caswell joined them.

"That's not a bad idea. Let us carry the ice chest out to the back. You'd have to unload it to move it."

The men each grabbed a handle of the large chest and took it up the ramp and along a walkway on the east side of the house.

A small stream of potable water wandered down from a spring high on the hill to the west side of the house, where it formed a shallow pool that drained onto the beach. Sheltered from the sun by trees, the back of the building remained quite cool, aided by the nearby trickle and rain that fell often in this part of Alaska, especially during the winter months. Vegetables and other perishable foods were stored either in a small screened box that hung from the wall or in ice chests like the one they had brought full of meat and dairy products. They set it against the house, below the pantry box, and returned to the deck.

Caswell pulled back his jacket sleeve to glance at his watch.

"Ten minutes—pretty good. Let's get the bird off the beach."

Alex looked at Jessie, who was gazing out across a mile of salt water at Hesketh, the nearest island, and, hesitating, suddenly saw her more objectively than usual. Slim, her hair a short, honey-gold tumble of waves and curls, attractive even with both gray eyes bruised black from the accident, the cut on her nose healed enough to dispense with the bandage, she stood tall, independent, and confident, with Tank at her side. He was suddenly more than a little reluctant to leave her here alone, however capable she might be.

She turned and saw the equivocation in his eyes.

"You know . . ." he began.

"Don't, Alex." She held up her hand, last two fingers in their splints and tape. "It's all right. I'm going to miss you, too, but I feel safe here. For the first time in a week, I feel safe. You know?"

" 'Bye, Jess. Stay well." Caswell walked away toward the plane, leaving them to say their good-byes in private.

"Thanks, Cas."

He raised a hand in salute without turning, ambling clumsy-footed over the uneven rocks toward the water.

Alex sighed and gave it up.

"Okay. Eight in the morning—eight at night. You call me on the cellular—which you keep with you at all times, right?"

"Right."

"Shotgun goes in the house—handgun stays with you, right?"

"Right." The ghost of a smile twitched her lips.

"Anything goes wrong . . . call Homer—troopers' office, right?"

She couldn't keep her grin from breaking through.

"I've got it all written down, along with the numbers, right?"

"Right." He smiled sheepishly.

"Okay. Give me a hug and get going."

He held her for a long minute, kissed her thoroughly. "I love you. Take good care of yourself."

"I will. Love you, too. Go catch the bad guy for me, trooper."

He reached a finger to touch her cheek, and noticed a glitter in the morning sun.

"You've got on your new earrings. Pretty fancy for an island."

"Yeah—well—so I like 'em."

A swift pat for Tank, and he was off down the beach in long strides, negotiating the rocks with cautious arms lifted to maintain his balance. Ben revved the engine as Alex pushed the plane from the shore, then clambered along the float and up into the passenger seat. Both men waved out their windows as the plane roared away and lifted from the water. The wings waggled once before it disappeared behind the trees that topped the cliff at the end of the long curving beach.

For a minute or two, Jessie stood listening as the sound of the plane grew faint and died away. It felt a little strange to be so abruptly alone. Since Alex had moved in to share her cabin in Knik, they had seldom been apart for very long, and when they were it was usually Jensen who was traveling as a part of his homicide investigations, or other duties as a sergeant with the state troopers. Most of Jessie's trips were involved in sled dog racing during the winter months and, with the exception of the Iditarod or the Yukon Quest, were only two or three days in length and full of activity. Training runs sometimes took her out overnight, but during the last winter she and Alex had planned and taken several of these together, as he learned to enjoy driving one of her teams. She had been contentedly, self-sufficiently alone before she met him, knew she was capable of being so again, but her unexpected reaction to his birthday gift now crossed her mind again, and she wondered how she would feel about marriage, if next time it were a ring. Maybe this solitary time would be a good test.

Later, she thought. I'll think about it later. Closing her eyes, she tipped her face up to the warmth of the sun, appreciating the freedom to stand outdoors after being cooped up in the hospital and the cabin on Knik Road.

If a storm's coming, I should spend today outside, while I can, she thought. But first I'll get the rest of the stuff off the beach and out of sight.

Several trips later, she had put the cart away and stood in the beach house, sorting supplies to see what she had. Her duffel of clothes and personal items she had stashed with her camera bag in a small alcove bedroom set off by curtains from the main room.

The central room was approximately twenty feet square, with a bay of three large windows that faced the deck and the beach and cove beyond. Two chairs, a worn upholstered rocker and a captain's chair beside a low circular table, allowed a wide, southern view of the beach, neighboring islands, and faraway mainland, with its tree covered slopes below the sharp, snow-covered grandeur of the Kenai Range. On the walls were pictures drawn by family and guests, photographs of vacation gatherings, and maps of the Kachemak Bay area. Windowsills held casual collections of shells and stones picked up along the south-facing cove which attracted the family beachcombers like a magnet, especially on sunny days. The whole room reflected lazy days isolated from the bustle and stress of everyday urban life. Jessie could almost hear voices and laughter as she stood looking around her with half a smile.

The kitchen, along the rear wall, had a high window that presented a rectangle of the hillside's lush green. It had no walls, but was simply a sink, gas stove, and counter, arranged in a line under shelves that held dishes, pots, and pans. Another curtain separated the kitchen from a passage lined with tall storage shelves for everything from canned goods to paper products, all of which had to be brought to the island by boat from the Homer Spit. At the end of this passage were two small rooms that were used for extra storage, but which also held bunk beds for visitors and family members who did not have their own houses.

On the east wall, an outside door opened into the main room opposite the bedroom, behind a partition into which a series of large nails had been driven for hanging outerwear—coats, hats, rain gear. There, too, were shelves of collected hand tools, and several flashlights required for trips to the out-house after dark. A large wooden picnic table that stood under a window in the front corner of the room held most of the boxed supplies that Jessie had moved in from the beach.

In the center of the room was a bench that helped define the kitchen area and was long enough for two or three people to sit facing the bay windows and a fire pit that lay beyond a waist-high table made of a large slab cut from an enormous log that had washed up on the beach. A small wood-burning stove took up most of the pit. The rest was convenient for warming cold feet or drying kindling.

A day's supply of firewood was piled against the wall be-hind the stove, next to a second bench, but Jessie told herself to remember to bring in enough from under the deck to last through the anticipated storm. Even better—maybe she could find some on the beach and chop it to replace some of what she would use during her stay.

With a list from Jessie, Linda Caswell had shopped for and packed the supplies Jessie now sorted on the picnic table. In the middle of the first box she found a loaf of last year's fruit-cake, with a note saying, "Hang in there." Grinning, she opened it and broke off a chunk to snack on while she worked.

There was a flash of something moving on the deck, and she looked up to see one of the large blue jays that hung around looking for a handout and gobbled up scraps in competition with the local ravens. How did they know someone was in residence? She hadn't even started a fire. Must be some kind of winged telegraph that passed the news along from bird to bird. Another jay floated down to land close to the first and the two sat expec-tantly on an outside bench, looking in through the bay window, heads cocked to one side. *Okay—where's the food?*

Amused, Jessie paused in her sorting and went to sit in the

rocking chair by the window to watch the birds watching her. There was plenty of time to get organized. She looked out at the sunny day, relieved and pleased to be settling in a place she loved. It was true—she did feel safe here. The island, with its beach houses, was the source of pleasant memories of previous visits, familiar and welcoming. She knew the way it worked—where to get water, search for a chocolate lily; when to trim a kerosene lamp, find thimbleberries; how to make the woodstove work efficiently, use the radio, follow the trails. But what had made the place especially dear to her were the people who owned it, had hand-built it, and so generously shared it with her and others.

Millie and her six grown children were a large, close family, that came and went from Niqa as their jobs and busy lives allowed. They relaxed on the decks, caught up on conversation, and brought Millie's grandchildren to fill the otherwise peaceful place with shouts and laughter, skin their knees on the rocks of the beach, exhaust themselves running back and forth on the trails between the two coves, and keep a long rope swing in constant motion. Though they were seldom all there at once, each Fourth of July was a crowded weekend reunion to which was added a host of invited friends who camped out in the meadows and on the beaches of both coves, sharing meals, fireworks, and campfire songfests.

Jessie had been part of the camaraderie and fun for a number of years and hated to miss the traditional extended-family gathering. For the last Independence Day celebration, she had brought along Alex, Linda, and Ben, who had flown them all from Wasilla. Now it seemed odd not to have a multitude of people around and she found herself half listening for the sounds of absent friends.

What am I doing still inside? she thought. Springing up, she found her camera, grabbed her jacket, and, cellular phone in her pocket, handgun on her hip, went out the door into the sun-filled morning, with Tank for company.

11

The flight back to Wasilla was pleasant and uneventful for Jensen and Caswell. In a sharp assessment of the surrounding air and water, they saw no boats or planes that might have observed their takeoff from the Niqa Island cove. Alex heaved a great sigh of relief as they passed back over the Homer Spit and started up the peninsula.

"Now," he said, "I can get on with catching this bastard."

"How are you going to go about it?" Cas asked. "He's given you nothing to work on—no prints, no clues to his reasons for all this. Where are you going to start?"

"I sent Becker and a team to search the area where those photos were taken. Maybe they'll turn up something. I reminded him of that old theory that at a crime scene there's always something left and something taken away. We might get lucky.

"Then I'm hoping to catch that phone thing on the recorder. That first time—when you and Linda were there—I heard the same sound Jessie heard, just before the hang-up. Now he knows my voice, and when I answer the damn thing, the receiver goes down immediately on the other end. So I had Jessie record a few hellos and I'm going to play them when it rings. If it fools him into the same sort of response she's been hearing, I'll get it on tape. We can have it checked and maybe be able to tell something about where he's calling from. It doesn't show on the caller ID. Could be a pay phone or a cell phone that doesn't give a number."

"Might work at that. Any results on the soil samples Timmons was trying to get a lead with?"

"Nope. Nothing except the dirt from the dog lot. There wasn't enough to make a definitive analysis of anything else. There was some old animal blood—wolf, wolverine, who knows? He says he may be able to use it later as a comparison, but not to pinpoint a definite location."

"It's worth a try. Is that rookie, Tannerly, still going to play Jessie this evening?"

"Yeah. I'll pick her up at your place after work. She's going to wear a blond wig and ride back to the cabin with me. If he's watching, he won't be close enough to tell the difference if I carry her in and he doesn't see that she's shorter. The most important thing is to keep him from knowing Jessie's gone, if he doesn't already. Moving the dogs may have clued him in, but we might have done that anyway till she was well enough to take care of them. He might have followed us to Lake Hood, even though we didn't spot him. How could we? We don't know what he looks like and there was enough traffic on the road for him to disappear in if he was there."

Caswell frowned in concentration. "What concerns me most is that we have no idea *why* any of this is happening. Did Jessie come up with any possible names?"

"No one she could really imagine doing this. And you're right. If we could just get a handle on the motive behind this, we'd have a good chance of figuring out the who. I can't help wondering about that ex-boyfriend of hers. She never says much, but the reason she finally left him was that he tended toward abuse. When it turned physically violent, she wasn't having any. She expressed it to me as, 'Hit me once, shame on you. Hit me twice, shame on me.' She got out and he wasn't at all happy about it."

"Sounds possible. But why would he have waited till now? Is there something that might have set him off?"

"Not that either of us could think of. He's had a live-in girlfriend for a couple of years now. It's a long shot, but worth checking, maybe. There are other possibilities that seem more likely to me."

"I agree. Something related to the Iditarod makes the most sense, I think."

"It seems like it. But the fact that someone sent the committee a negative letter doesn't prove the sender is related in any way to the race or the mushing community—just that he knows she is. Could be someone who's watched her, even on television, and used it as a means of harassment. I doubt it'll be the last note received by someone that slanders Jessie."

But the next bit of depravity did not arrive in anyone's mailbox. Returning home Friday evening with Caroline Tannerly, the rookie trooper who was impersonating Jessie, Jensen was confronted by a furious neighbor, parked and waiting in front of the cabin. He climbed out of his pickup and stomped across to wave a fist in Alex's face.

"Dammit. I don't care if you're the law. You're gonna pay me for the nanny them damn dogs of yours savaged. A 'gee whiz, we're so sorry' note tacked onto my shed just don't cut it."

"Whoa, Jim. What note? Slow down a minute and tell me what you're talking about. Nanny? You mean one of your goats?"

"You better fuckin' believe it. My best milker. Hadda be

your damn dogs. No others around I know of. Whatcha gonna do about it, huh? What?"

The older man was so angry, his face so red, that he looked near a heart attack, and was almost ready to hit something or somebody. Alex knew him enough to remember that Jim Bradford treated his goats almost like the family he didn't have. His animals always won prizes at the state fair in Palmer, were extremely well cared for, and he always had a waiting list for the high-quality milk they produced.

"Well," Alex told him sympathetically, "whatever it takes, we'll make it right, Jim. Now let's go inside and have a beer while we talk it over. There are some things going on that you don't know about."

Settled with a Killian's at the kitchen table, Bradford calmed down and related his tale of disaster.

"I took the truck to town yesterday, just after noon, to pick up a roll of fence wire—gotta weak spot in it, out by the trees. When I come back the goats was all up by the shed, crowded up like they was scared of somethin'. I looked 'round and didn't see Gertrude, so I hiked on down to the end of the field. And there she was, layin' on the ground, her udder and flanks all tore up, and there was dog tracks all over the place 'round her. Thought I'd hafta put her down, but the vet came in a hurry and took care of her. Says he thinks she'll be okay when she heals up, but might be crippled in one back leg.

"So, what else but your dogs? Hadda be. . . ." His face grew pink as his temper took over again.

"Wait a minute, Jim. This happened yesterday afternoon?"

"Yeah. While I was gone to town."

"Well, it couldn't have been Jessie's dogs, then. We had them moved to Willow on Wednesday."

"Willow?" The old man frowned. "Then why'd you leave the note?"

"Have you got that note?"

He hauled it out of a pocket of his red Woolrich jacket and

laid it on the table, slightly crumpled and grubby from handling, but readily readable. White paper—computer-printed:

SO SORRY ABOUT WHAT HAPPENED TO YOUR GOAT. YOU
SHOULD BUILD BETTER FENCES, OR NOT KEEP THEM SO
CLOSE TO A KENNEL. AFTER ALL, YOU CAN'T BLAME A
DOG FOR BEING A DOG.

JESSIE ARNOLD

"Jim, Jessie never wrote this. She's been in the hospital
since Tuesday afternoon."

"What the hell happened?"

Bradford turned to the woman Alex had carried into the
cabin and whom he had assumed was Jessie. In his distress,
he had never really looked at her; now he could see that it
wasn't her at all.

"This is a trooper who's helping me out, Jim. I'll tell you
what's been going on, but you've got to promise to keep it
to yourself."

The old man nodded—so thunderstruck he forgot to close
his mouth—then turned back to stare and listen as Alex began
a somewhat abbreviated explanation.

Jim Bradford had no more than disappeared down the driveway when Phil Becker came to the cabin from the trees at the
far end of the dog lot, where he and a forensics team had been
searching the woods for clues.

"I didn't see any vehicles. Thought you guys must be
gone," Jensen said, letting him in.

"Nope. Couldn't get here early this morning. Had a robbery in Palmer we had to cover first. We parked off the road
farther down, and there's indications that someone else's been
off the road there with a truck of some kind. No tire tracks
we can identify, but at least we know it's been used. There's

something else—in the trees. Get your jacket and come on out. You'll want to see this."

Estimating the area from which the pictures of Jessie and Linda had been taken, the search team of three had sectioned off the perimeter with yellow crime scene tape and concentrated within it. Becker led Jensen to a spot behind a screen of brush. One trooper examined the area for clues and another was on his knees with a camera, taking flash pictures of the ground beside a birch. Alex nodded to them.

"You said he'd leave something," Becker said. "There it is. Love to know what he took away."

"He took the pictures. Doesn't look like he was too worried about leaving these, though. Why not?"

Beneath the tree were several boot prints, surrounded by the paw prints of a dog, or—from the number of them—more than one.

The trooper with the camera lowered his camera and looked up.

"Didn't care because there's not much to learn from them. It'd be extremely difficult to tell one dog from another, though I'm sure there were two of them and that they were big dogs— Rottweilers, maybe. The boots are Red Wings—common as the dirt they made prints in . . . well-worn, from the look of them. You most likely couldn't tell them from a thousand others on Alaskan feet in this part of the country."

"So there's nothing that helps?"

"I didn't say that. Just that the prints are probably no good for specific identification. We'll do a thorough workup for specifics at the lab, but don't get your hopes up.

"He's been here more than once. There're two more places that look like someone spent some time—and both gave him a good view of the cabin and dog lot. There's no fiber, no human hair that we can find, but some canine. To stay here any length of time without being spotted, he'd have to wear something that blended in well with this environment. I'm wondering if he might not have worn some kind of camouflage. Wouldn't take much in the right colors—browns, grays."

He pointed to another part of the taped-off ground.

"There was a very small amount of blood smeared at a low level on a tree over there. Looked pretty fresh. I cut it out for testing."

Jensen could see the pale blaze marking the birch the trooper referred to and shook his head.

"That's just about the height of a dog. I think you'll find the blood's from our neighbor's goat. This guy's branching out. Looks like he sicced his dogs on a milk goat and left a nasty 'so-sorry' note tacked to a shed door. Tore the nanny up pretty badly."

"Nice guy," the cameraman commented wryly. "There's one other kind of odd thing about these tracks. Don't know if it means anything, but the weight of this guy seems to be distributed oddly."

"Oddly?"

"Well, you know how a bare footprint looks. It has a heel mark, a ball of the foot and toe mark, but only a slim impression from the outside edge of the foot—no print under the arch, which lifts that part of the foot away from contact. In a shoe or boot it's hard to tell, of course, but these prints seem to have made a heavier impression on the inside than on the outside of both feet—like he was walking very badly knock-kneed."

"What the hell would cause that?"

"It might be the result of a symmetrical physical deformity—or he might have been wearing some kind of insoles that threw his weight to the inside, but it's something you hardly ever find on *both* feet. Odd. We'll take casts of these. Along with some photos, they might be of some help later."

"Thanks. Anything else?"

"Not so far. Sorry."

The search team spent the rest of the afternoon combing the woods and dog lot, but found nothing else. Jensen left the cabin a couple of times, but stayed mostly indoors with Tannerly as they waited to see if the phone would ring and give them a chance to record the mystery caller. It remained silent except for two condolence calls from friends of Jessie's. Alex told them both that she was resting and couldn't come to the phone, but appreciated their good wishes.

When they finished working the scene, Becker and the other two troopers came in and, after a few diversions between car and cabin, Caroline Tannerly left with them, wearing a cap instead of the wig, and walking on her own two feet. If the stalker had been watching, Alex hoped he wouldn't notice and would think Jessie was in the cabin.

As it grew dark, he turned on the lights, stoked the fire, and set about making himself some dinner. It seemed terribly quiet in the cabin without Jessie, especially since there weren't even the usual small sounds from the dogs outside. In the back of his mind, he kept feeling that he had forgotten to feed them, then remembered they were gone. Normally he would have brought Tank in to keep him company, but even the affectionate, dignified lead dog was off with Jessie on the island. He wondered if the two of them had eaten dinner yet.

Tossing a foil-wrapped potato into the oven to bake, he seasoned a small steak to broil, and absent-mindedly made a salad that was much too large for one person. Running out of cooking chores, he retrieved a Killian's long-neck from the refrigerator, switched on the television, and sat down to watch the news.

Jessie called at eight and, in the brief couple of sentences they had agreed would be best, let him know she was fine and missed him. An hour later, he had flipped through the TV listings, discovered a rerun of *The Great Escape,* a favorite, and settled on the sofa to watch Steve McQueen and his compatriots tunnel their way out of captivity. The movie claimed his interest through dinner, a quick kitchen cleanup, and half a cup of tea. He watched McQueen bounce his baseball off the wall of his solitary confinement cell, but dozed off, warmed by the woodstove and pleasantly full of food, while the escape was still in its creative stages.

Something obnoxiously loud and full of Chuck Norris fighting a conglomeration of shadowy ninjas had replaced World War II when the telephone brought Alex back to consciousness. Stabbing awkwardly at the off button on the TV remote, he staggered up to answer it. The caller ID indicated that once again the call was unidentifiable, so he started the recorder before lifting the receiver and waited silently for Jessie's voice to say, "Arnold Kennels. Hello . . . hello?"

It worked. There was silence on the open line for perhaps ten seconds, then the short sound he had wanted to catch—as if the caller had taken his hand away from the mouthpiece to hang up the phone and allowed the background noise to be heard for a second or two—sounds like those that would be made in a crowded place by other people—a bar, maybe, or a restaurant, a gathering of some kind. The receiver on the other end of the line went down and the sound changed to that of a closed line.

The recorder he had attached had automatically clicked on. He was able to play it back and assure himself that he had captured an example of the harassing calls that could be analyzed and might possibly lead somewhere.

Satisfied, he went to bed, anxious to make an early start to the Anchorage lab the next morning.

It was almost two o'clock in the morning when a fist-sized, note-wrapped rock shattered the window that overlooked the dog lot, sending shards of glass flying across the outer room.

Alex unwrapped the note:

I'LL GET YOU NEXT TIME, BITCH.

Well, at least he thinks Jessie is at home, Alex decided, assessing the damage with disgust.

12

Jessie spent the afternoon outdoors, enjoying the sunny day, but though she felt safe and relieved to be away from the harassment, she found that a significant part of her mind and emotions was still very much attached to Knik. She couldn't quite relax and allow herself to let go of the wary watchfulness that had so quickly become a part of her everyday life. There was also a niggling thread of guilt at leaving Alex to solve the mystery of the mysterious stalker—a feeling that she should be doing something herself, not hiding out. But it had been clear that he would do a better job without her to worry about, and there had been little choice, really. Well, she decided, it will take some time. By tomorrow I'll be able to let more of it go.

From the boxes of groceries she took three slices of wheat bread and, tearing them to pieces, scattered them along the bench on the deck for the opportunistic jays. But while she watched them greedily gobbling up the offering and took several pictures, using a zoom lens to fill the frame with the cocky birds in their brilliant plumage, she couldn't keep herself from occasionally lowering the camera to glance around, checking to make sure she was alone. Aside from a small boat with a red canopy that, made tiny by distance, sped across the open water of Eldred Passage heading for Tutka Bay, there was no sign of anyone at all. The day was warm, fingered by a gentle breeze that rippled the surface of the cove, holding only the natural sounds of birds and water washing the larger rocks of the shingle as the tide continued to go out.

When the bread disappeared, so did the jays, though two squirrels chased each other up the trunk of a nearby evergreen and a large, inquisitive raven perched on the wooden handrail to watch her closely and assess the possibility of additional scraps. Ignoring it, she called Tank, who had been exploring new and fascinating smells between the pilings on which the house was raised, and they walked slowly west along the sweeping crescent of the beach, avoiding the big rocks, keeping to the pebbles and sand above the high tide line.

As she walked, Jessie examined the varicolored, water-worn stones and white pieces of broken clamshell, picking up a few pieces, pocketing one of a smoothness particularly pleasing to her fingers. Bleached pure white by the elements, the shells reminded her so much of skeletal remains that she had always called them beach bones, and on each trip to Niqa, she took home a handful to add to a gradually filling glass jar on her desk. She also looked carefully for small flat stones with notches chipped in two opposing sides, for, hundreds of years earlier, they had been shaped by Native fishermen to use as sinkers for their lines and could sometimes be found, though she had always been remarkably unsuccessful in her attempts and retrieved none now.

Over the edge of a low rise above the beach, the meadow spread out: a wide-open space full of tall grass, and beyond, dense forest met it at the bottom of a steep slope, full of brush and all but impassable. Along the water side of the rise, huge logs had washed in, driven by a combination of winter storms and high tides. A few were piled atop each other; others lay half buried in sand and had been there so long that runners of beach peas had thrust their way up to cling and camouflage sections of the pale, sea-silvered driftwood with their bright green foliage and purple blossoms.

Among these, Jessie found a gap where two logs lay together in a V, forming a deep, sun-warmed space carpeted with sand and affording a view of the north side of the nearest island across the waters of the cove. Here she sat, wiggling her hips to make a comfortable depression in the sand, then leaning back against a log to watch an eagle draw lazy circles overhead as it searched the waves for fish.

Tank abandoned his olfactory examination of a drying pile of bull kelp the tide had abandoned, flopped down beside his mistress, stretched his jaws in a huge yawn, and laid his muzzle on his forepaws for a rest that soon turned into a nap.

It had always seemed to Jessie that time on Niqa was somehow different from time anywhere else. It passed too quickly, filled with the comings and goings of people who enjoyed each other's company. She had never been alone on the island before, and wondered if the time would stretch out without conversation and activities to fill the days. She also wondered briefly what Alex would be doing with *his* time, how he would go about finding the person who had upset her life—both their lives—so completely. Involuntarily, she felt her body tighten as if a fist had clenched inside her. Part of the reason she had lost her appetite, had not been able to sleep well or lower her guard in the last few days, had been a constant feeling of weight and pressure in her upper chest and throat. She laid a hand flat against her breastbone and, taking two deep breaths, felt the sensation lessen slightly.

Leaving the beach house, she had borrowed a faded, billed cap from one of the hooks by the door. Now she purposely pulled it down to cover her eyes, ignored a stab of concern at not being able to see what was around her, and closed her eyes. Stubbornly, she refused to contemplate any danger and chose to think instead about the coming winter's sled dog racing schedule and what preparation her dogs would need to be ready for it, what gear she would need to acquire or repair, what events she would enter this year.

She was considering the possibility of entering the state's second premiere distance race, the Yukon Quest, as well as the Iditarod, feeling that she finally had enough well-trained dogs to field two teams. The Quest took place in February, however, and her own physical recovery time between the races would be critical, for both were exhausting endurance tests. There would also have to be someone at the kennel to keep up the training of her Iditarod team to get them ready for her return from racing between Fairbanks and Whitehorse in Canadian Yukon Territory. In the twenty-five years since it had started, the Iditarod had changed and become a more professional event, with highly technical equipment and training methods. The Yukon Quest was close to the same length, but more like sled dog racing had been in the Iditarod's early days. It had fewer checkpoints and longer runs. Though both races took mushers through difficult wilderness country in winter weather, temperatures during the Quest were usually colder because its course ran through interior country far from the coast.

As she had mentioned to Alex, the two Darryls were becoming good wheel dogs, and they would work well in a team for the Quest, both of them heavy through the chest, wiry and strong enough to work just ahead of her sled, managing its weight in the turns, keeping the lines tight. She planned to take Tank as lead dog on both races, for he would recover much more quickly than she and, barring the unforeseen injury or illness, would be eager and ready to go, for he loved to race—would be disappointed, even insulted, if left at home.

He whined slightly at her side, causing her to peer through her lashes to see that he had turned onto his side and, though he slept on, all four legs were in motion as if he were chasing a moose through his dreams. A cloud or two drifted across the blue sky, casting shadows that alternated with the sunshine, lightening and darkening her cozy nook in the logs, a condition she half noticed when she closed her eyes again. But as she considered her dogs one by one, mentally selecting teams that would work well for each race, the warmth of the day helped her to drift off into a nap and a dream of her own.

In the middle of the Iditarod was a seventy-mile stretch between Eagle Island and Kaltag on the Yukon. When she raced this flat, frozen section that followed the wide river's graceful curves, if the weather was good Jessie usually put on her headphones and played favorite tapes. Now she dreamed she was there and the music she was listening to was classical, full of the delicate trills of a flute.

She had no idea how long she had slept when a sharp movement and breathy sound from Tank brought her drowsily back to the present. As she opened her eyes to see him on his feet and attentively staring at the dense forest on the hillside west of the meadow, she thought she heard a few notes of the thin echo of the flute in the soft sigh of the breeze that whispered past her ears. The sound was not repeated, and she reached out to lay a hand on Tank's shoulder.

"What is it, guy? You see something? Hear something?"

He relaxed and turned to give her wrist a sloppy, affectionate lick.

She gathered herself up, sudden adrenaline waking her completely, and sat very still, waiting . . . listening intently. Nothing but the wind. What had it been? Left over from her dream—or the inspiration for the flute music she had imagined on the Yukon? Standing up, she considered searching for the source of the odd sound, tension and pressure once again a lump in her chest. Her breathing altered and resentment filled her mind. If it was real, it was unwelcome and disturbing.

Before she could decide to move, there was a sudden shrilling from the trees, and an eagle rose from it and flew out over the open space, clutching a still faintly shrieking squirrel in its talons. Tank's attention turned quickly to the bird and they watched together as it circled and disappeared toward the east.

Jessie sank to her knees and gave him a good rubbing of ears and throat.

"Well, old mutt, you're a good pup, but we're still kind of flinchy, aren't we?"

A rumble of her stomach reminded her that it had been a long time since her early breakfast, and she picked up her camera as she spoke again to the dog.

"You hungry, buster? Let's go find something to eat, okay?"

Recognizing the familiar words, he dashed playfully around her, scattering sand and pebbles as they headed back along the beach. She picked up a stick of driftwood and tossed it for him to fetch until they reached the ramp to the deck, where she laid it on one of the huge logs to save for a future game.

Looking to the west, Jessie noticed that a bank of clouds was drifting in and would soon steal the warmth and glow from the day. It was dark and probably full of the storm Ben Caswell had predicted. Before she went inside, she checked the firewood that had been split and piled under the deck. Finding there was plenty, she remembered that she had planned to drag some in from the beach for cutting. Taking a large armful, along with some kindling, she lugged it up the ramp and into the house. She could collect driftwood another day.

By the time she had fed Tank, made a sandwich, and heated a can of soup to fill a large mug, the sunshine had disappeared and the wind was making waves of the ripples in the cove. So she retrieved a new Father Brad Reynolds paperback that she had brought along and settled in the upholstered rocker, with her stockinged feet on the table, to enjoy one of her favorite inactivities—simultaneous food for mind and body.

Except for pauses to make mugs of tea and locate a package of oatmeal cookies in one of the half-sorted boxes, nothing disturbed the peace and quiet of Jessie's reading for the remainder of the afternoon. When she finally noticed that the house was becoming uncomfortably cool, and dark enough to qualify as gloomy, she laid aside her book and took Tank for a quick trip to the beach, while a fire she had started in the fire-pit stove took the chill off the room.

It was lighter outside, the wind was stronger, and the tide was coming up the beach with enough strength to create a rattle in the medium-sized rocks that it reached with each surge. She spotted a gray harbor seal riding easily on the white-capped waves of the cove, with its large round head raised out of the water, seeming to watch her walk across to the front of the deck. From a distance, lighter coloring around the eyes made it appear to be wearing a pair of enormous spectacles. With barely a splash, it slipped beneath the surface, reappeared much farther from shore a minute or two later, then vanished for good.

Jessie took Tank back into the house and out of the wind, which so far had brought no rain—a condition that could clearly change at any time.

The fire had done its work and the room was rapidly growing warm. She lit a kerosene lamp, wondering briefly if it was a good idea to advertise her presence with a light in a supposedly empty house. But there would be no one to see it from the water or the other island, which had no houses on its near side—not even a tent camp of sea kayakers this late in the year. She made herself a cup of hot chocolate and another sandwich and, cutting a slice of Linda's fruitcake, went back to the rocker and resumed her reading as it grew darker outside the large windows. Soon all she could see was her own reflection in the broad panes of glass.

At eight, she called Alex in Knik for a reassuring check-in. By nine-thirty, fire banked in the stove, Tank snoozing on a rug beside the bed, she was snug and warm under two blankets and a quilt, oblivious to the growing storm outside, and—for the first half of the night, at least—sleeping better than she had in a week.

13

Jensen was poaching eggs and making toast shortly after seven the next morning when Ben Caswell and Phil Becker arrived.

"What the hell happened to your front window?" Becker queried, examining the duct tape and plywood that filled the gap and darkened the front room.

Jensen told them about the middle-of-the-night stone-throwing incident, laying the rock and the note on the kitchen table.

"Damnation," Cas said. "You hear from Jessie? She okay?"

"She was last night. It isn't time yet for her to call this morning. I'm not so worried. It worked. He's obviously still here."

"You know, Alex," Caswell mused, frowning, "it might not be the best idea in the world to let this guy go on thinking that Jessie is here in the house. This is getting serious. He might as well come right in after her—you, now—as throw a rock."

"That occurred to me about two-thirty, as I was hunting through the shed with a flashlight for plywood," Alex agreed.

"I had the feeling he was out there somewhere watching me, and it wasn't a sensation I'm particularly fond of."

"I'll bet." Caswell glanced at Becker, who had accepted a cup of coffee and taken a bright red chair at the table. "But we didn't come all the way out here just to share your breakfast."

"Damn." Alex grinned. "With all that bread Jessie baked the other day, I thought I had help getting rid of some toast. There's raspberry jam we made last summer."

"Nope, sorry. Already ate. But I did some thinking after we got back yesterday, and there's a couple of things you might want to reflect on."

Jensen brought his plate and the coffeepot to the table, where he nodded and poured salsa on his eggs.

"What've you got?"

"You know what I said on the way back about a motive for this harassment?"

"Yeah."

"Well, it seems to me that there's a couple of possibilities that could help us out along that line. Why, I wonder, would anyone focus so completely on Jessie? What kind of a grudge could he have? It would have to be personal and relatively obscure, because no one else seems to be able to think of anything that comes close to explaining it. Jessie's thought through everyone she can and come up empty—well, maybe the ex-boyfriend, but that's a stretch. The Iditarod committee has no ideas. You're doing no better than we are.

"It would also have to be something pretty significant—at least to this guy who's throwing rocks, poking holes in brake lines, and setting traps for dogs—or people. Those things aren't just harassment. They're malicious attempts to hurt— and I think we classify the truck accident as attempted murder or manslaughter, right?"

He now had both troopers' serious attention, though Alex almost automatically refilled both his and Becker's coffee mugs.

"What could inspire that kind of hatred? Doesn't seem like

it would be a small gripe, but none of us has come up with anything large enough to fit, anything that seems worth it."

"It could be something so personal it's only in his mind and wouldn't seem important to us," Jensen suggested.

"True. I'll grant you that it's got to be very personal. But doesn't it seem like we should be able to come up with something—even if it's wrong—that connects to Jessie . . . unless it doesn't?"

"What do you mean, *doesn't?*"

"Well, think about it. What if she's the medium—the message—not the target?"

"You mean . . ."

"I mean, what if it's you—not her—he's aimed at? These things do fit if you look at it from that angle. Last night, I was watching Linda struggle to put toothpaste on her toothbrush with her arm in a cast, and feeling unreasonably guilty for having allowed her to get involved in all this—like I had a choice. Then I thought how frustrated you've been about Jessie, and it suddenly occurred to me that, in a very real way, it's worse for you to watch her being harassed than if it was directed at you. So . . . what if that feeling of failure is exactly what this bastard intends for you—that helplessness?"

He stopped, giving Jensen a chance to consider it.

"The worst way to threaten anyone who cares about his family is to threaten that family," Becker added slowly.

It was true, Alex admitted to himself. Having Jessie hurt or killed would be the worst thing he could think of that could happen to him. He remembered her phobia about injuries to hands, and realized that the idea of some kind of horror being perpetrated on her caused his mind to flinch in just the same way. It was unendurable, intolerable—the very concept was almost worse than reality would be—a torture of the mind. It would be as effective a way to inflict mental agony on him as anything he could imagine.

He looked up at Caswell, who had silently watched the theory play itself out on Alex's face.

"When you take time to kick something around, you don't do it by halves, do you?" he said.

"Well . . ." Cas shrugged, and half smiled at his friend. "It occurred to me that it might be useful."

"If this is true," Becker asked, his mind racing ahead, as usual, "what can we expect? Will he switch to you, Alex, when he finds out Jessie isn't here?"

Jensen nodded. "He might. Or it may just stop. He could decide to wait for her to come back, knowing she will have to, eventually."

"So . . . what do we do now?"

"Several things, but first you said you'd thought of two things, Cas. What's the second one?"

"It's not such a big deal. Becker called last night to tell me what they found in your trees yesterday and mentioned the boot prints."

"Yeah, the weight of the person who made them was distributed oddly."

"Right, but that's not what seemed inconsistent. If this guy set the traps in those two dog boxes, doesn't it seem funny that there were no prints in the lot? Why would he be careful not to leave tracks near the traps and not care how many he left at his lookout sites?"

"Didn't want us to notice them before they'd done their dirty work? Thought we wouldn't look in the trees? Figured we couldn't identify that particular pair of new boots?"

"Maybe—but that last one might not be true with a really good print. There's almost always some anomaly. How could he be sure? Maybe there's some other reason, if we can find out what it is. This guy seems to be terribly careful not to leave fingerprints on anything he sends—has to be wearing gloves. It's a curious discrepancy for him to ignore his boot tracks, and even more incongruous to leave them in one place and not another."

"You're right. It may give us something to work on."

The phone rang.

"Jessie," Alex said, glancing at the clock, and went to answer it.

He was back in a few minutes, with the report that she was fine and sent greetings.

"That recorder came on when you picked up the phone. Are you recording your own conversations, too?" Phil asked.

"I'm recording everything. Seemed like it might be a good idea to have anything that could possibly concern this case on tape, admissible or not."

"Yeah, you never know."

Jensen turned back to Caswell. "You know, you could be on to something with this idea that it's me he's really after," he said. "Have you got any more ideas?"

"No, but we should go through the files to see if there's anyone you put away who's been sprung recently. Or somebody who might have been carrying a grudge for any other reason, for that matter."

"That's not going to be easy."

"Time-consuming. You may want to take a look at your own case notes for the last few years."

"I can do that. But I don't think it would be smart to make any assumptions on this one. We keep looking at things that would tie it to either me or Jessie, right?"

"Absolutely. It's just an idea—not carved in granite. A question, not an answer."

Although it was Saturday, the troopers' office in Palmer was busy when Jensen sat down with Ivan Swift, his detachment commander, and asked to be relieved of his other cases in order to work on Jessie's case full-time.

"If you hadn't asked, I was going to call you in today," Swift told him, rocking back in the office chair behind his desk. "Sure you don't want someone else working this one? Can you stay objective about it?"

"Yes, sir, I think so. And if we're looking for someone out to get even with *me*, I may be able to put a finger on it faster than someone else."

Swift nodded thoughtfully. "I understand that you and Caswell got Jessie out of the area yesterday."

"That's right. After the wreck last week, we decided it was time to find her a safer place, but she refused to leave the state."

"Why doesn't that surprise me? You certainly picked yourself one with a mind of her own, Jensen. Hope you value that quality."

Alex grinned. "Don't have much choice, but I'd just as soon she thought for herself."

"Well, take the time you need. I'll assign one of the clerks to search the records for anyone recently out of jail who might be hell bent on revenge. Who was that kid who swore he'd get you a couple of years ago? That drive-by shooting conviction. Remember?"

"Calvin Porter. Nasty piece of work, but he's still in prison out of state, and won't get out till long after the year 2000."

"There's always others. Don't neglect the relatives, either. I seem to recall a distraught mother or two shouting things in court through the years. People get emotional at verdicts—but most cool off later. It's the few that carry a grudge we have to investigate."

"Believe me, we will."

"We're not too overloaded at the moment. So use Becker and Caswell where you can. I'd like to see this one solved quickly. We all like Jessie. Proud to have her as part of the family, so to speak, and I hate to have this happening to her."

Alex left the commander's office with relief and a grin, appreciating Swift's regard and concern for Jessie, and glad to be working with people who were also personal friends.

Though Caswell and his plane were tied up on a short run for another case, Jensen and Becker spent the day going through records of past cases, making lists of the names of anyone who might have had a grievance or might have exhibited a strong inclination to seek revenge for perceived injuries. At the end of the day they had sifted out three.

One was the kid Ivan Swift had asked about that morning, Calvin Porter. Though Alex didn't see it as necessary, Becker insisted on putting his name on the list.

"There was an older brother involved. He got off, remember? We couldn't prove he'd been in the car. But he swore to a reporter that he'd get even for his little brother's conviction. He threatened the judge and jury, just about everybody in the courtroom—including you personally, as I recall hearing it. We kept tabs on him for a while till he left the state. So I don't care if the younger kid's still in jail, I think we should take a look at the older one—find out where he is and what he's doing."

Alex agreed, but his focus was directed at the other two names, one of which he remembered more clearly than usual for a nine-year-old case.

James Robert "J.B." Moule had been a troublemaker with a sheet several pages long whom both the troopers and police in several Alaskan communities had been glad to see convicted and given a twelve-year sentence. He had been only twenty-four at the time of his trial, but his crimes had been many and most were violent—armed robbery, rape, assault, theft of all kinds. In an argument over a six-pack of beer, he had assaulted another young man with a baseball bat and had crippled him for life. His vicious temper had driven away all his family members, except his father, who had testified for him, supported him throughout the trial, wept when the sentence was handed down, and clearly encouraged his son to blame Jensen's testimony for his conviction and incarceration.

Alex thought it very possible that by now Moule might be out of prison, and decided it would be a good idea to check, for in this case as well, threats had been made during and after the trial. He couldn't quite believe that incarceration would rehabilitate this vindictive individual. It usually worked the other way around.

The third suspicious person was a woman. There was no doubt in the law enforcement community, given the evidence that the crime lab had collected and processed, that, five years before, nineteen-year-old Mary Louise Collins had brutally stabbed her next-door neighbor to death for a television set and a few dollars' drug money. A legal technicality had forced a reluctant judge to dismiss the case halfway through the trial, after a full afternoon of Jensen's testimony. Though Alex had tried his best to forget it, it rekindled fury and frustration every time it crossed his mind. His long and careful effort to build a clean case had been wrecked by a rookie policeman who, innocently enough, contaminated the most important evidence, leaving less than enough to convict Collins. To make it worse, she had taunted Jensen with an angry, contemptuous comment as she shoved past him on the way out of the court.

"Fucked up, didn't you? Well, don't think it's over. Someday I may decide to make you sorry—or dead. And you'll never know when or where it's coming from."

Could one of these three be responsible for Jessie's harassment and stalking? Had one of them finally found an insidious way to get even with him? Tomorrow he would begin the involved process of finding out.

14

At three o'clock Saturday morning the storm broke over Niqa Island, wind howling as the sea, which had once again turned tide, roared and growled on the rocks of the beach. Rain swept in, pounding like a waterfall on the roof and deck of the house, startling Jessie awake. When she sat up in bed, Tank raised his head from his paws and cocked his head in mute question.

"It's okay," she reassured him and herself. "It's only the storm."

Snuggling back into the warm, comforting bed, she lay listening to the fury of nature, glad she was not exposed to it, and actually enjoying its clamorous barrage. The beach house had once again cooled and the air smelled fresh, but the bed and its covers had acquired the luxurious body temperature that always made it hard for her to get up on winter mornings. Smooth with many launderings, the sheets and pillowcase felt like silk against her face. Rolling over, cocooning herself, she was drowsily amused at her own tactile pleasure and indulgence. She had always appreciated the sensation of being protected from the elements—warm and dry. Though she loved being outdoors in good weather or bad, there was a distinct pleasure in watching a storm do its worst from within a shelter.

Got to get some sleep, she told herself. But immediately after it came another thought. No, I don't. I can do anything I want to—get up, build a fire, make some tea, watch it rain in the middle of the night if I like.

With that, she drifted off to sleep again, secure in her own independence.

Tank put his head down again, but remained awake and listening for a long time after his mistress was breathing in small half-snores. There was something he could almost hear in the wind, far away and overpowered by the rousing sounds of the storm. With his ears perked, he waited and listened intently, finally going back to sleep after moving just a little closer to the bed in which Jessie serenely slept.

She woke again just after seven in the morning, to a feeling of well-being and a steady, but gentler tattoo of rain on the roof of the beach house. Rubbing sleep from her eyes, she reached an arm over the side of the bed to give Tank a good-morning pat.

He gave her hand a very small lick and, with infinite dignity, padded away into the outer room, where he sat by the door.

"All right—all right. I'm getting up. I know you want out."

Taking off the oversized T-shirt she had slept in, Jessie pulled on sweats and stuffed her stockinged feet into a pair of tennis shoes. Stretching her arms to relieve the soreness that still lingered from the wreck of the truck, she shivered in the chilly air. The fire was dead and the house had cooled considerably as the wind slipped fingers in through cracks and crevices to steal what was left of the heat.

Crossing the room, she opened the door, let Tank out, and went to build a new fire in the stove. While it began to warm the place again, she put a large teakettle on the propane stove to heat water for coffee and hot cereal, and, borrowing a rain slicker from the hooks by the door, made a quick trip to the outhouse that was hidden behind some brush a dozen yards from the door.

When she came dashing back, holding the slicker over her head, Tank was waiting for her by the door, ready to go back inside. Opening it a crack, she looked down at his wet coat and instructed him sternly, "Shake yourself. Shake."

Water flew as he complied, familiar with this request, and they both went in quickly before the rain could drench them again.

"Not too great a day out there, huh? You hungry?"

She put a can of dog food in a bowl for him, made herself some instant oatmeal, and they ate breakfast together near the crackling fire, Jessie with her feet in the pit near the stove. He finished first and sat quietly beside her as they both looked out the window at the rain.

The waters of the cove were dark and uninviting, but the wind that had driven them into white froth during the night had calmed for the time being, though Jessie doubted it was gone for good. No boat, person, bird, or animal was to be seen, and the neighboring island was all but invisible in a bank of fog—a dim gray outline against a barely lighter gray sky, across the arm of water that separated the two.

The jays did not appear on the deck to commence their morning solicitation, but a single, courageous raven coasted in to strut up and down the bench, casting accusatory glances through the window to express its displeasure at not being fed. It was hard to tell if it was the same bird that had appeared the day before, since all of them looked alike: feathers, feet, eyes, bill—pitch-black.

Ravens had always amused Jessie with their antics, for they seemed the jokers of the Arctic world, and indeed were so designated in many tales of Northwest Coast Native cultures. In them, Raven was the Creator, the Trickster, the Shape Changer, who stole the Sun, Moon, and Stars from their hiding place in a great carved wooden chest and fled across the sky, where he was forced to abandon them, bringing light to the world. Legend said he had once been white, but the angry Magician, from whom the bright glitter had been snatched, sent fire after Raven that scorched his feathers black and reduced his beautiful voice to a rough croak.

As Jessie watched, the bird ruffled its damp feathers, scattering tiny drops of rainwater, cast one last disgruntled look, spread its wings, and sailed away toward the shelter of the trees.

With a smile, she got up to refill her coffee mug.

With rain on the menu, Jessie spent the better part of Saturday indoors, finishing the book she had started the day before. It was quiet and peaceful, and the patter of rain on the roof made her feel safe and secure. Gulls, riding the wind over the cove, caught her eye several times, and two fishing boats ran through the passage between the islands in the early afternoon seeking shelter by the shortest route they could find, for the waves grew larger and more threatening as the day wore on.

Although she enjoyed caring for the dogs in her kennel, training and running them, it was good to feel unencumbered by daily chores. A completely lazy, slothful day seemed just what she needed to revitalize her flagging energy and alleviate the fatigue she had been experiencing since the accident. She had to giggle when she caught sight of herself in the mirror, for both eyes were black and looked as if she were wearing an excess of stage makeup. Around three o'clock she baked a chicken and ate with her fingers, relishing the freedom from plates and silverware as well as from designated mealtimes. There was something satisfying about the solitary privilege of greasy fingers—like drinking milk directly from the carton—that, however childish, made her feel more independent, gave her back control of her life.

When she had eaten her fill, she noticed that the rain had almost stopped. Taking Tank, she went for a short walk on the beach. The west end of its crescent ended in an interesting section of rock, part of which had fallen away, exposing the structure of a hill. It was distinctly volcanic, layer on layer, but these layers had been shoved and twisted until they looked like loops and folds of huge gray ribbon. While she examined them, Tank explored the tide pools between the rocks and found a small crab that skittered off under a stone when he sniffed at it, startling him into a half bark. When Jessie turned to see what had inspired it, he gave her an embarrassed look and trotted off to pick up a piece of driftwood that he brought and laid at her feet.

"Another game?" she asked him, and threw it for him to retrieve. They played until it started to rain again and they were both getting wet through.

He carried the driftwood back to the beach house, where she added it to the one from the day before.

"We'll be able to keep track of how long we've been here, if you keep carting in sticks," she told him.

Warm and dry again, she started another mystery, feeling luxuriously indulgent, for it was seldom she got to read a whole book in one or two sittings. She ate the rest of the chicken, smearing grease on most of the first dozen pages, and finished up with cookies and tea.

Tank snoozed on the floor beside her until she was ready to call it a night, then he rose and moved to the rug beside her bed.

The night was not quite as serene as the previous one had been. Two or three times Jessie woke in the dark to hear Tank moving around the house, sniffing at the floor and windows, but he didn't seem to want to go out when she got up and went to the door.

Must be an animal of some kind, she thought, and went back to bed, knowing he would let her know if there was anything to worry about. He came, each time, and lay back down on the rug, chin on paws, making himself comfortable.

Sunday morning dawned to similar weather.

"If the storm's going to get worse, I wish it'd get on with it," Jessie told Tank as she gave him his breakfast. "I'm getting bored with this constant drizzle."

She refilled his water dish, along with her coffee cup.

"Well . . . I'm not staying inside all day, but we'll wait awhile and see if it lets up," she decided.

Lacking a shower, she washed in some of the warm water left from breakfast, brushed her teeth, and combed her short hair. Changing into jeans and a warm sweater over a turtleneck, she strapped on the handgun in its holster. Dressed and ready for the day, she used the last of the warm water to rinse out the few dishes she had used, left them to dry in the rack by the sink, and quickly sorted the rest of the groceries that were still in the boxes on the large table.

"Hey," she told Tank, "Linda was thinking about you, too."

A rawhide chew had been included in the bottom of the last box.

"You want this?"

The husky came across the room and raised his muzzle expectantly, but waited without begging, retaining his self-respect—pleading was for puppies. Jessie gave him a pat, along with the prize, which he took back to a spot near the stove and began to gnaw.

At eight o'clock, as she had done the morning before, she called Alex to speak for a few minutes. He mentioned that

Caswell and Becker had dropped in for a conference but he had nothing to tell her, except that they had a couple of new theories. The cell phone, crackling with storm-induced static, finally forced a frustrating end to the call.

Jessie put it down with an uneasy, troubled feeling. There had been something about the tone of his voice that made her wonder if he was telling her everything. Of course they had agreed to keep their telephone contacts brief and avoid speaking of specifics in case they were overheard, but it seemed more than that. Maybe she was just letting her imagination run on overtime.

At ten o'clock, she had finally had enough of the solitaire she had been apathetically playing on the table by the front windows. Her book held no appeal, and she had done all the small, make-work chores she could think of. Resolutely, she got to her feet and searched through the rain gear hanging near the door. Donning a pair of waterproof pants three sizes to big for her, she cinched them up around the waist with a belt and retrieved a dark green slicker that proved a better fit. Measuring her feet against several black knee-high rubber boots, she selected a pair and pulled them on, tucking in the too-long pants.

"Okay," she said to Tank, who, sensing an outing, had positioned himself by the door. Double-checking to be sure she had the cell phone in one slicker pocket, she dropped a handful of ammunition for the .44 in the other, along with a ring of keys for various buildings on the island, drew the hood up over her head, took a machete for clearing trails from its nail on the wall, put the shotgun over her arm, and opened the door. "Come on. Let's go. We'll hike over to the other cove."

Behind and to one side of the beach house, two trails rose sharply up the hill. One rambled in curves that made it longer but less steep, while the other ran farther east, more directly up the steepest part of the slope. Jessie started up the latter, Tank dashing back and forth ahead, pleased to be out and given a chance to run. From one of the trees, a squirrel objected loudly to their invasion, and the dog stopped to watch it twitch its tail in time to the *chit . . . chit . . . chit* of its warning call.

There was a third trail that ran from the eastern end of the beach along the top of the cliff. But taking it would mean a longer walk that was more exposed to the rain still steadily falling. It was also possible to walk the beach at low tide, from one cove to the other, but below the steep rocky precipice it was a maze of large rocks, slippery with seaweed over jagged barnacles, and a mistake in timing could strand a hiker. In only one place was it possible to climb the cliff from the rocks. In a narrow indentation a rock slide had opened an abrupt and highly difficult opportunity to reach the ground high above, if one was exceptionally careful—and desperate. Though the tide was once again on its way out, the length of this route would have exposed Jessie to the rain, and she had not even considered it.

For about five minutes she climbed the trail she had chosen, watching where she put her feet: the large, gnarled roots of the evergreens made it uneven, at times almost creating steps to clamber over. Finally it leveled out a little, and she paused between three large spruce to catch her breath and look out over the tops of trees below to the waters of the cove. The fog was lifting slightly and glimpses of neighboring islands faded into temporary view, only to disappear again the next minute. It looked like a long day of bad weather was in store, the beginning of a system that would probably last for several days.

The beach was empty and colorless compared to Friday afternoon's brilliant sunlight. She visualized Caswell's plane, where it had rested on the stones, rocking gently against the shore, and suddenly felt solitary in a different way—a little lonely for the first time. A gull floated into sight below her and glided in to land on the roof of the beach house. Following it, a raven—possibly the one she had already seen—coasted silently out of the trees and perched on the deck. It marched the length of the bench in its characteristic swagger, swaying back and forth, foot . . . foot . . . foot—making her grin in spite of herself. Ravens were such clowns.

Still smiling, she went on up the trail that now crossed ground that was more level and soon joined the other path, which had meandered its way up a less demanding route.

The machete now became useful, for this part of the way to the other cove had been cut directly through a dense thicket of salmonberry that grew rapidly in season, constantly attempting to reclaim the trail with long, thorny runners. Here and there, Jessie swung the heavy knife to cut the ones that had overreached themselves and intruded into the way. It would have been easier without the shotgun, but, hanging it over her shoulder, she soon found a rhythm with the blade. At first she could feel the ache and pull of bruised arm and shoulder muscles, but as she warmed to the physical activity, that soon lessened.

On one runner she found a few late berries, past ripe, somehow missed by the birds, but still clinging to the vine like rubies that shone in the half-light under the trees. The seven or eight that dropped into her hand were swiftly conveyed to her mouth, their sweetness bursting on her tongue. She gathered enough of the youngest leaves to steep later in the day, for they made a pleasantly flavorful tea.

The rest of the trail ran without impediment, curving back and forth, up and down through the forest, until it began a definite descent toward the eastern cove. Broad expanses of devil's club, flat leaves turned skyward, filled the open spaces between the tall trees—drums for the soft tapping fingers of the rain.

Jessie and Tank came to open ground high on the bluff above the cove. Beneath one of the last trees, she paused to look out across the broad expanse of Eldred Passage to the south and east. The heavy overcast hid the sharp peaks of the Kenai Range and fog shrouded the mainland around Tutka Bay, but much of the arm of ocean and its islands was visible

and obscurely beautiful through the curtain of mist and rain—
like a pencil sketch on soft gray paper.

Still following the path, they went down between tall
grasses, crossed a tiny bridge over the trickle of a creek, and
passed between a small, dark, shuttered house that belonged
to one of Millie's daughters, and a large garden space with a
tall wire fence to discourage the island's animal residents. On
the opposite side of the building was a berry patch, similarly
fenced.

Beyond these, a long weathered stairway led forty feet down
to the foot of the bluff. Between it and a ridge of sand and
driftwood where the beach began lay a wide space full of grass
still green in the damp weather. Within this open space was a
large multiple-use building, the ground floor of which, Jessie
knew, was a shop and storage area for tools and equipment.
The upper story held two rooms of living space—a combination kitchen and dining area, and a more open room with a
woodstove, bed, and work space. On the east end of the rectan-
gular building, behind the shop, a sauna and deck had been
added.

"Let's go check the wood and water supply for the sauna,"
she said to Tank, and started down the steep stairway. "Maybe
we'll come over later, or tomorrow, and heat it up. Not you.
You'd hate it, buddy. But me—for sure. Steam out the rest of
the sore spots and get really clean."

As they went around the back of the shop building, she
searched in her pocket and found the keys, but upon reaching
the door to the sauna she was surprised to find it unlocked,
the hasp hanging open, its usual padlock nowhere to be seen.
Split wood was piled neatly under a tarp on the deck and two
buckets stood just inside the door in the empty outer dressing
room, where a bench ran around two sides and towels hung
from several pegs on the wall. An overlooked bottle of sham-
poo lay on its side on the floor. The scents of heat, soap, and
damp wood hung in the enclosed air.

"Hey, somebody forgot to lock up. I'll bet the lock's upstairs. We'll go up and find it in a minute and have a cup of tea before we start back, okay? Let you dry off?"

She opened the door to the inner room of the sauna itself and was surprised as a breath of warmish, damp air hit her face. Frowning, she looked in. Light from two tall slender windows allowed her to see that the room was empty and the wooden ledges, used for sitting or reclining in the heat, were dry. A half-filled bucket of water stood near the woodstove that supplied heat. Positioned in a box full of beach rocks, the stone opened to the outdoors so wood didn't have to be carried in, and had a chimney that ran up through the roof. As it heated the rocks, water could be splashed directly onto them, creating the rejuvenating, luxurious steam. Water could also be heated in buckets placed on the stove or stones—in fact, one sat there now.

Jessie stepped closer, dipped her fingers into the water it contained, and immediately jerked them out again—not burned, but startled.

It was lukewarm! Not hot—but almost warm—when she had expected cold.

She stared at her hand, disbelieving. Then, slowly, she laid it against the cast iron of the stove.

This was also warm—slightly warmer, even.

What the hell was going on? She was supposed to be the only one on the island. But someone had clearly been here—used the sauna—and quite recently. Not this morning, she calculated; in the warm room, partially insulated by the rocks it lay among, the stove would have been warmer now if that were the case.

But last night. Someone had been here, soaking in the steam, *last night*.

Who?

15

Jensen went to work on Sunday as if it were a workday, having spent a quiet, but not restful night at the cabin on Knik Road. He had not put new glass in the broken window, but had taped and nailed several plywood strips across the outside of it. His priority was making progress with the case, not taking the time for repairs. He locked the door and headed for the Palmer office.

If this loony wants in, he'll get in, whether I change the glass or not, he decided.

"Porter's still in an Arizona prison," Becker told him, when the young trooper arrived to help just after noon. "Incarcerated in Florence, about sixty miles south of Phoenix. Won't even come up for parole for a long time yet."

"And the brother?"

"Harold Porter. From all we know, he moved to Phoenix to be near Calvin when he was transferred and hasn't been back since. I put in a call to the PPD and they'll check him out for us—at least see if he's still in residence. Considering that he did a couple of years here for a drug deal and has a sheet almost as long as Calvin's, they may have something on him there."

"Those letters were mailed in Anchorage, not Phoenix. If he's still there, we can probably eliminate him from the list, right?"

"Well . maybe," Becker said, frowning. "Let's wait and see what we get back. How about Moule?"

"He's out, like I thought, and still in the area. Don't know exactly where yet. I'll call his parole officer tomorrow and find out, but there've been no additional arrests, so he may be behaving himself."

"Or just hasn't been caught. Going to give Mary Lou Collins to Caswell?"

"I told him not to come in. Linda needs help getting around at home, and we can do without him today. I thought I'd see if I could get a line on Collins—see if she still lives next door to the old lady she *allegedly* killed—though she probably moved. The neighbors were pretty upset."

"You tried the phone book?"

"No listing. She may have left town. If we can't track her down, we'll try Anchorage."

He was right—she had moved. The door was opened by a small boy of two or three wearing nothing but damp training pants and a grubby T-shirt. The floor of the cluttered room behind him was littered with Matchbox cars and oversized Lego blocks, amid a spilled scattering of dry cereal of some kind. A large orange cat sprang down from the back of a couch to vanish behind it.

"Hi, there," Becker said, crouching down to be on the same level. "Is your mommy home?"

The child shook his head from side to side.

"Then is your daddy here?"

Again the slow negative shake.

"Is someone taking care—"

"Simon? *Simon?*" an exasperated voice called from somewhere in the back of the apartment. Close behind it, a thin, frowning young woman came out of what appeared to be a bedroom, a baby in a disposable diaper balanced on her hip.

"I told you *not* to *open the door.*"

Grabbing the small boy by one arm, she pushed him toward a green chair with worn upholstery. "Sit there and be quiet."

He hadn't uttered a word, and didn't now. He also didn't sit, as instructed, but stopped just short of the chair and continued his inspection of Jensen and Becker.

"Who are *you?*" the woman demanded.

Alex introduced himself and showed her his identification. She gave him a harassed look and did not invite them in.

"So—what do you *want?*"

"We're looking for a woman who used to live here, Mary Lou Collins. Do you know her? Is she still here?"

Her scowl grew even more pronounced.

"I don't *live* here. I'm just the baby-sitter for these two rugrats while their mother is at work in Anchorage. She's a waitress at the Sourdough Mining Company, and Sunday's big. She works lunch *and* dinner today."

"Is her name Collins?"

"Not *even* close. Nancy Stilton. You'll have to ask *her* about that other name. She'll be back at about nine tonight."

He started to thank her, but the door slammed shut before he finished, and they could hear her voice full of shrill irritation, berating young Simon for his transgression.

"How many times have I *told* you, *never* . . . *never* . . . *never* to open . . ."

Becker raised his eyebrows as they turned away from the apartment. "With that every day, he might welcome strangers. The restaurant?"

"Let's try this apartment next door," Jensen suggested, having spotted a twitch in the curtains of the unit to the right.

A knock on this door solicited a prolonged hesitation, as if whoever lived there was pretending not to have been eavesdropping, or didn't want to answer. After a second knock, they heard the sounds of a safety chain being withdrawn from its slide and the door opened halfway, exposing a frail old man with a shock of white hair. He leaned heavily on a cane, his body bent so far forward he had to tip his head back to look up at them.

"Yes?"

Alex again produced his identification.

"Come in." The old man beckoned with a bony finger. "Come right on in. My name's Williams. Fred Williams. Sit down. Make yourselves comfortable."

With surprising speed, he moved in a sideways hobble to the center of a neat, sparsely furnished living room and waited for them to catch up.

At a glance, the space was pleasant, with plump pillows that lay in the corners of the couch and a pair of small ceramic birds occupying a place of honor on the coffee table in front of it. One wall held several pictures that were clearly of family members, among them an alertly smiling middle-aged woman with graying hair standing beside a similarly aged Fred Williams, each with an arm around the other.

It was obvious where the old man spent his time. A brown recliner with a small table beside it faced a large-screen television set. The table was partially filled with a pile of crossword puzzle magazines, a thermos next to a coffee cup, and the remote control for the television lying on the week's program guide. A pile of library books five or six deep stood beside the chair, carefully lined up with spines out, one facedown on the arm of the chair.

The troopers took seats on the edge of a green couch with a cheerful yellow afghan spread smoothly across its back, and waited as Williams settled himself in the recliner. The television, sound low, was tuned to a football game. He switched it off with the remote, reclined in the chair, and turned to them with a smile of anticipation.

"Now . . . how can I be of service to you, gentlemen?"

As he answered, Jensen could sense Phil Becker's suppressed amusement.

"Have you lived here long, Mr. Williams?"

"Oh . . . my, yes. Eight years this coming December. Since before my Eva died." He waved a hand at the picture on the wall. "Then I just stayed right here, and we'd been here three years before that. My daughter does for me now, you see. Comes once a week with the groceries—keeps the place clean. Bent up like I am, I'm not much good at that, but I can keep myself fed okay."

"Do you remember the woman who lived next door to you three years ago, sir?"

The pleasant expression disappeared from Williams's face, and a look of distress replaced it.

"Oh, my. Yes, I certainly do. That Collins woman, you mean? You're looking for *her*?"

"Yes, sir."

"It's just about time. Have you got new evidence? Can you get her now, or has she done some other terrible thing?"

"No, sir. Not that we know of. We're just trying to locate her. Do you know when she left here—where she went?"

The old man sighed in disappointment before he answered.

"Well . . . it wasn't much after the judge threw the whole thing out . . . maybe a month. I almost moved, myself. Daisy—my daughter, you know—was worried about me, so upset that that Collins girl was allowed to come right back here, where . . . It was *so awful*," he burst out angrily. "We all knew she killed

Mrs. Post. Horrid. It was just *horrid.* She went in and out, giving everyone those nasty looks. We all kept our doors locked all the time. Daisy took to coming in once a day after work, just to make sure I was okay. Why didn't you put her in jail, officers? It was so unfair."

He gave the arm of his chair two weak thumps with his fist and came to an emotional halt.

Jensen's stomach lurched with his own familiar anger, and he had to wait a second or two before he could answer.

"We just didn't have enough to convict her, sir. Sometimes that happens. We weren't happy about it, either. Do you have any idea where she went?"

Another sigh. "Nope, I don't—nor do I want to. I was just glad she was gone and my daughter could stop being afraid for me. Nobody ever said where she went. None of us cared."

He hesitated, then smiled. "But that's all over now. Can I get you boys a cup of coffee? A beer, maybe? I still drink one now and then. There's some in the refrigerator."

They thanked him but refused.

Resignation and disappointment showed plainly in his eyes, but he smiled and insisted on shaking hands with both of them before they went out the door.

"You won't mind if I don't get up? Sorry I can't be more help, but if there's anything I *can* do, come on back. I'm always here, except from two to four o'clock on Wednesday afternoon, when Daisy takes me to the library."

The troopers returned to Jensen's truck and climbed in.

"Must get pretty lonely, living like that," Becker commented as they drove out of the parking lot. "Wonder why his daughter doesn't have him with her."

"I got the feeling he wanted to stay where he was—where he and his wife had been—didn't you? It may be lonely, but he's got his independence, and that can be a lot, especially at his age."

"Well, back to the drawing board. Where now?"

"Let's call it a day. I think I'll pick up some glass and repair that window before dark. It has to be done, and might as well be now. We'll get back on it in the morning, okay?"

After dropping Becker off at the office to pick up his car, Alex stopped by the local building supply store and had a pane of glass cut to fit the broken window. Heading home, he realized that he wasn't looking forward to another solitary evening.

He backed in toward the porch and lowered the tailgate, ready to unload the glass. Collecting the tools he needed from a box welded to the bed of the truck, he climbed the stairs to get the repair done before he lost the late afternoon light.

To his surprise and fury, he found the plywood had been ripped from the now-open hole that still held sharp fragments of shattered glass around the edges. The wood now lay on the ground beyond the porch. He carefully scanned the interior of the house, which was silent and empty as far as he could tell.

Retrieving his off-duty Colt .45 semiautomatic from the cab of the truck, he cautiously unlocked the front door and turned on the lights as he entered the large, open room. He searched all the rooms and found no one, but his anger grew as he moved through the house.

It had been systematically ransacked. Papers from Jessie's carefully kept files covered the floor, the recording devices and telephone had been ripped from their cords, books lay where they had been tossed from their shelves, and three of his treasured mustache cups were shattered. The kitchen was a mess of pans and cookware that had been dragged from their usual spaces to lie among broken crockery and food from the refrigerator. Flour covered everything and a bottle of catsup had been dumped over a small collection of cookbooks.

A single word, "BITCH," had been scratched into the surface of the kitchen table with the point of a knife that lay on it, along with a sheet of white paper with computer printing.

The vandal had left *him* a message this time:

THE TELEPHONE TAPES WERE INTERESTING, JENSEN. WHERE IS JESSIE? TELL HER THAT I MISS HER AND IF SHE DOESN'T COME BACK HERE *RIGHT NOW* SOME OTHER BAD THINGS WILL HAPPEN THAT SHE WON'T LIKE AT ALL.

16

Jessie stood staring at the stove that should not have been warm, her stomach in knots, mind whirling with apprehension, trying to think who could have been making use of a sauna supposedly locked against intruders. Oh God, what if it was the person who had been harassing her in Knik? Could he possibly have followed them and somehow found out where she was? Was it starting again? If so, what would he do? What could she do to protect herself?

Taking a deep breath, she forced herself to stop making panicked assumptions and think this through. There were other possibilities besides the one that sent adrenaline pumping through her. Perhaps a tourist kayaking in the passage had landed on the beach, discovered that the cove was currently uninhabited, and broken into the sauna, thinking no one would ever know who was responsible. It might also have been some resident of the Tutka Bay area, or from Jakolof Bay, a little farther to the west. On their way past the island, anyone could have pulled in and taken advantage of the sauna.

Had it been broken into? She made herself move, go to look at the hasp and the eye that fit through it. The lock was missing but the door was not damaged, leaving only two options she could think of: either it had been cut off or whoever removed it had a key. Neither prospect pleased her, especially the first. It was just possible that Millie's daughter had given someone a key and permission to use the sauna. In that case, where was the lock? Was the visitor still around? Was there a boat of some kind on the beach?

Refusing to ask herself any more questions, Jessie went back around the building to the steep flight of stairs leading up to the top story of the building. Pausing with one hand on the railing, she examined the door that she could see on the upper landing. A lock was clearly visible, but she couldn't see if it was fastened or just hanging there. Slowly, aware of every sound and motion around her, she climbed the stairs, Tank padding up close behind her. At the top she relaxed a little when it was apparent that the lock was clasped: a firm guard against unwelcome entry. Taking the keys from her pocket, she sorted out the right one, opened the door, went in quickly with Tank, and shut it behind her.

The overcast day provided minimal light through three large windows that faced the cove, but it was enough to see that both rooms were empty. The air was chill, the woodstove cold. She shivered, moved to a kitchen window that provided visibility along the whole curve of the shallow cove, and looked carefully up and down its entire length. Empty—it was absolutely empty of any boat or sign that one had landed.

Knees suddenly weak, she sat down abruptly on a bench at a large table that filled one end of the room. A sigh of relief escaped her, attracting the dog's inquisitive attention.

"It's okay, guy. Whoever it was must be long gone by now and forgot to lock the door—or ruined the lock and couldn't."

But in the back of her mind a small voice worried about

the outside chance that the trespasser could still be somewhere on the island. Unlikely, she thought, for in that case a boat would be at the beach—and the beach was empty. Still . . .

"Come on, Tank. We're going back to Millie's."

It's warmer there, she rationalized to herself. I won't have to build a fire, and it's time for lunch anyway.

Refastening the lock, she hurried down the stairs and returned to the sauna, where she put a stout stick through the eye, to hold the hasp closed and keep the door from blowing open. Before she went back to the top of the bluff, she checked the big double doors of the shop to see that they were safely locked as well. The small house on the bluff was also tightly closed, but she cautiously rattled its doors, front and back, to be sure.

They went swiftly back across the trail they had traveled earlier, skipping the shortcut for the gentler route down the hill to the beach house this time. The wind increased as they hiked, till tossing trees and brush were shedding sprays of water, though the rain had all but stopped. Jessie was glad she had worn foul-weather gear, and smiled once when Tank paused, braced his feet in the trail, and shook himself vigorously, only to grow wet again as they continued. Most of the brush was at his level.

Reaching the house, Jessie unlocked the door and went first to add more wood to the stove. Before taking off her waterproof suit, she went out to bring in two or three armloads of firewood.

She had just carried in a load from under the deck when she heard the sound of an engine entering the cove. Turning, she watched as a medium-sized boat came around the point at the eastern end of the beach and proceeded directly toward her. Watching nervously as the craft came closer, she recognized it as a water taxi that ferried people back and forth from the Homer Spit to various parts of Kachemak Bay, and, with a sinking feeling, knew who would be behind the wheel. Laying down the wood, she started across the long space emptied by the tide, toward the edge of the water that was just beginning to flood in again.

Damn, she said to herself. How could he have known I was here? But then, how does he know anything?

"Hey, it's Jessie Arnold. How're you, Jessie? What're *you* doing here?"

The figure that walked around the cabin and onto the covered bow as the boat bumped the beach rocks was tall and also wearing rain gear—yellow.

Ted Carver—solidly built, a pair of glasses slipping down his nose beneath a stray lock of straight brown hair on his forehead—had been an area resident all his life, working a variety of water-related jobs: fisherman, charter boat hand, bay-tour guide, and now skipper of his own floating transportation service. Jessie had traveled to and from the island aboard his boat in the past, and wasn't particularly glad to see him. He was pushy and one of the bay's biggest sources of information about other people. Her temporary residence on Niqa was now no secret, for half of Kachemak would know it by nightfall. Dammit, anyway.

"Hello, Ted. I'm fine—just taking a break from the big city."

He waited, grinning, obviously hoping she would elaborate on the reason for her presence.

"How did you know I was here?" she asked instead.

"Oh, I saw smoke from the chimney and thought I'd better check to be sure it wasn't some trespasser. Obviously, you're not one."

"Nope."

"That one of your dogs?"

She turned to see that Tank had followed her over the rocks to the water's edge.

"Yes. My leader."

"Going to be here long?"

"Just a few days."

She thought of asking him to keep her occupancy to himself, but realized it would only ensure that her wish for privacy would become a more significant part of his gossip. *Hey, Jessie Arnold's out on Niqa Island for a few days, but she doesn't want anyone to know. Kind of makes you wonder why, doesn't it?*

Ted stood, feet apart, legs braced against the boat's motion from waves that were strong enough to rock it.

"You got any coffee on? I could use something hot."

Hell. If he came ashore, she would have him and his infernal nosiness on her hands for at least an hour.

"No coffee. Sorry, Ted. Can't help you out," she told him firmly.

"Oh . . . well, it wouldn't have to be coffee. You got hot water? Tea would do."

"Not even that. Stove cooled off while I was across on the other side. I just got back and I've got . . . ah . . . some chores to do . . ."

Just in time she kept herself from mentioning the wood she had to move, which he could insist on moving for her.

". . . so I really can't take time right now, but it was good of you to stop. Thanks a lot."

He frowned and shrugged, hesitating.

"Well, if you're sure you don't want company."

"Yup. Some other time. But, again, thanks for checking."

"Okay. See you again . . . maybe tomorrow."

Not if I see you coming, she thought, and the smile she forced herself to give him felt grim.

Still frowning, he went back to the boat's cabin and roused his idling engine. In a minute or two, the craft was rapidly diminishing in size as it whipped through the waves on its way to Tutka Bay.

Relieved, Jessie went back up the beach to her load of firewood, concern for the smoke from the chimney foremost in her mind, feeling dumb for not having thought about it. If Ted had noticed, then anyone could. It was a pointless consideration, however, for she had to have heat—especially with a storm on its way.

*   *   *

Through the rest of the afternoon the idea of someone using the sauna—someone on the island that Jessie had no way of knowing about—bothered her. Smoke from the chimney was a giveaway she had not considered. What else had she missed? Anyone could have come and gone from the west cove while she was either on the other side or walking through the woods between the two, and she would never have known.

Even if there was no one else on the island, she no longer felt secure, but maybe that wasn't such a bad thing. She had stepped onto Niqa and allowed herself to feel safe without questioning the reliability of it. It would be a good idea to be more alert, more suspicious, but she hated the idea of going back to what she had experienced in the preceding week. Okay, what should she do? How should she be proactive, rather than just responding to whatever came along? What if the S.O.B. really did manage to find out where she was? What could she do to make her safety more difficult for him to shatter?

The beach house had seemed like a haven, but in reality it would be easy to just open either door and walk in. And if she weren't close enough to the shotgun, all she had was the handgun at her belt. It might not be enough in a moment of surprise and adrenaline rush—too easy to miss with a first shot, which could then be her last.

She didn't like the idea that both the doors opened out and could only be locked from outside. Anyone could come in while I was asleep, she thought, be inside before I was aware of it. Tank would hear them, but would he hear them soon enough? Was there a way to remedy that situation? She decided there was, and that, under the circumstances, Millie wouldn't mind a temporary and fairly minor addition to her house.

On a flat shelf on the hillside, almost hidden in the trees between the beach house and the meadow, was a large shed.

Once used as living space while the house was being built, in the years since it had become a storage place for odds and ends of tools, bits and pieces of equipment, furniture, and things that no longer fit into the island houses. Potentially useful, too precious to throw away, or simply forgotten, objects found their way to this building that also housed a shop with a workbench. A section of the front of the shed was sectioned off by several walls of shelves that held hundreds of books collected by family members. An old upright piano, badly out of tune and with a few dead keys, stood in one corner, and a couple of cast-off, but still comfortable, chairs with faded upholstery filled the rest of the space.

Late in the afternoon, Jessie walked the short distance up the hill and let herself into the shed. Passing between the book shelves into the shop and storage area, she searched the workbench and a few boxes until she found the tools and materials she needed. One by one, she clamped four pieces of foot-long rebar upright into a vise attached to the bench. Then, slipping a long piece of pipe over the free end for additional leverage, she bent a right angle in each piece about four inches from the end.

Back in the beach house, she pounded heavy nails into the doors, top and bottom, and bent them over, forming slides for the rebar. With a hand drill, she made holes in the doorframe into which the rebar pieces could be inserted by sliding them with the four-inch extensions. These improvised locks, she calculated, could have been ripped from the doors if the doors had opened inward and force could be applied against them, but would be extremely difficult, even impossible, to dislodge by pulling on the doors. If nothing else, they would give her warning—plenty of time to reach the shotgun or escape from the opposite side of the building.

Feeling more secure with these slides engaged, she put the tools by the back door, ready to return them to the shed in the morning. Making herself a cup of tea, she sat down to further analyze her surroundings and watch the light fade from the waters of the cove. It went quickly, already half dim because of the overcast and rain, and the house was soon almost too dark to see anything but shapes. She lit a kerosene lamp and quickly tacked up two blankets over the large windows to keep the light from shining out, and was glad the chimney's smoke would be invisible in the dark.

At eight o'clock, after she fed Tank and had eaten dinner, she called Alex and, through static that was even worse this time, told him about her day, though she found it hard to tell without mentioning anything that would give away her location to an unwelcome listener. It was easier for him to tell her about the destruction he had found in the Knik cabin, but he revealed little about the ongoing investigation. They were both frustrated by the time they had picked their way through as much information as was possible, the reception fading in and out, and having to repeat themselves often. He was anything but pleased to hear that some unknown person had been in the sauna.

"But, I'm . . . I'm fine, Alex . . . eally. I'm sure . . . was only a tempo . . . intruder."

". . . can't know that."

"Maybe not, but . . . obviously it wasn't wh . . . trashed my cabin. No one . . . once."

"What?"

"Nobody . . . be in two plac . . . once."

". . . less there's mo . . . an one. . . ."

"Is there . . . indica . . . of that?"

"No . . . just . . . *what if*."

"Did . . . ou repla . . . window?"

"Yes . . . but it's li . . . closing the proverb . . . ba . . . n door."

"How . . . mutts doing?"

"Fine. I call . . . on them. Tank?"

"I'm glad I . . . him."

"So . . . I. He's a good . . . atch-dog."

There was little else to say and, after hanging up, Jessie found herself feeling torn between missing him and being glad she hadn't been there to see the vandalism of their possessions and living space. She knew it must have been worse than he had told her and, this time, didn't so much mind his tendency to protect her from unpleasantness. Still, she would always rather be informed of everything, however disagreeable, for how could you be prepared for things you didn't know about?

For a minute she frowned, hating to be protected, her mind slipping back to the quandary of her relationship with Alex— remembering her reaction to his birthday gift. What *would* she do, if and when he did offer her a ring? Why was she so sure it would happen? Part of it, she knew, was her sure and instinctive knowledge of his rather traditional values. They fit well together, enjoyed each other's company, were good friends, all of which counted for much. But did she want to marry him— to marry anyone? Somehow it felt like letting go of a large part of her independence. Living with Alex was one thing, marrying him another. Why was it different? Was it all in her mind?

"Well, I'd better decide, before it comes up," she said aloud. Then she consciously forced her thoughts back to the situation at hand.

It was reassuring to know that whoever had been in the sauna the night before could not have been her stalker—to know it must have been someone who had come and gone without realizing her presence at the other cove. If she had not happened to walk across and lay her hand on the barely warm stove, she would never have discovered the person had been there at all. She would be feeling as safe and confident as she had the day before . . . well, except for Ted and his big mouth. Maybe saying nothing to him of the reason for her visit would keep his speculations from running rampant. After all, Millie loaned the use of her house periodically, and it was not especially unusual for someone who was not a part of the family to be there.

Oh, to hell with it, she told herself, tired of her own concern. I've done all I can, given the circumstances. "Don't trouble trouble unless it troubles you," she said to Tank.

He looked up, waiting: company, at least—dependable company.

With that, she banked the fire, changed into the shirt she slept in, took the lamp to the chest of drawers beside the bed, and got in with her book and a handful of cookies, to read and forget about the whole thing. The sheets felt damp and cold, so she got up again, heated some water, and filled a hot water bottle to put between them. With her feet on it, the rest of the bed was soon comfortable. An hour later, she had blown out the lamp, listened for a while to the wind and the lulling monotony of rain on the roof, and gone easily to sleep. The shotgun was now within reach between the bed and the chest, and once again Tank slept on the rug beside the bed, carefully guarding his mistress.

Something woke him in the darkest part of the night. The storm had swept in again, this time in earnest, the wind creating a host of large and small sounds in and around the building. A metal wind chime clanged irregularly, tossing to and fro, and something rattled on the deck. A corner of a plastic tarp covering a small generator outside the front door had evidently pulled loose and crackled as it flapped. Knowing these were natural sounds, the husky discounted them and listened alertly for another—different—sound he had heard.

Quietly, he got up and, toenails clicking softly on the wood floor, went into the larger room, where he lapped a little from the water dish Jessie had put down for him. Then he moved slowly through the whole house, from door to door, and into each room, listening and searching for something he felt was not normal to the environment. Between the gusts of wind, he heard the odd sound again, faint and far away, before it was again overpowered by the stronger roar and clamor of the rain.

Hesitating, he waited till it was repeated once more, then

went back to the bedroom, put his forepaws on the bed next to Jessie, and whined.

Instantly, she was awake, turning over and reaching for the flashlight she had left on the chest. Aiming its bright beam at the ceiling to give the room a dim, diffused light, she sat up and swung her feet over the side of the bed.

"What is it, Tank? You hear something?"

As she rubbed his ears and under his chin, she listened, heard nothing, and asked him again.

"What is it, guy? Show me."

Dropping back to the floor, he padded into the outer room while she followed silently in her stockinged feet. He led her to the back door, where he paused, cocking his head to wait for the sound. Watching him, she listened, too, identifying the chime, rattle, and crackle among the sigh of spruce branches and dull growl of heavy waves washing high up the beach to tumble the smaller rocks and pebbles as the tide flooded in.

The wind died slightly, as if it were taking a deep breath, and suddenly there was a hint of music beneath its suspiration—upbeat notes of music, almost too far away to be heard—simple treble notes over a plinkety-plunk bass. The melody faded and disappeared as the wind rose to overwhelm it. But Jessie had recognized the song, as well as the instrument—knew what made it, if not who.

Someone, on the ancient piano in the shed above the beach house, was playing a half-familiar song—an old, out-of-date favorite of her mother's.

She could even remember some of the words:

See the pyramids along the Nile.
Watch the . . . da-da . . . on *a desert isle.*
Just remember . . . da-da . . . da-da-da . . .
You belong to me. . . .

17

Jessie's heart turned over as fear flooded in, turning her skin clammy with the sensation of being hot and cold at the same time. She drew one horrified, shuddering breath, then suddenly was furious, as well as frightened, and a little contemptuous.

Who the hell was playing the song? Who would dare? "... *you belong to me*"? ... Was she reading meaning into the lyrics and title of that particular piece of music? But, most of all, who was playing the old piano, and was it for her benefit?

Two choices lay open to her. She discarded the first immediately—stay where she was, keep the doors locked, barricade the doors, and wait to see what would come next. Unacceptable. She knew she could not tolerate the stress and apprehension of closing herself in the beach house, crouched in the dark, with the shotgun clutched in icy hands for the rest of the night—let alone the following day or days—without identifying the cause of her anxiety. The preceding week had shaken her confidence considerably, but she was suddenly determined to have it back. She would have to go and find out who was in the shed. But she would not go carelessly, without making sure she had as much of an advantage as possible, for what if that sound was meant to lure her up the hill?

Should she call Alex before she went, just in case? She considered and decided against it. A phone call would wake him in the middle of the night for something she couldn't explain and he could do nothing about. Best to cautiously assess the situation, find out what was going on, and wait to call him when she had facts instead of fantasies to report.

Quickly dressing and buckling on the .44 in the dark, so no beam from the flashlight would betray her through some crack or window of the house, she put on the rain slicker, but left off the oversized pants that would make it impossible to move silently. Pocketing the flashlight and adding some shotgun shells to the ammunition she had put in earlier for the handgun, she took the shotgun and the keys to the house and, sliding back the jerry-rigged locks, opened the front door, which put the house between the shed and herself.

Tank didn't usually bark when they were together, but she warned him anyway with a tap on the nose.

"Quiet, boy. No barking."

Together, they slipped out, and she used the key to lock the door. No sense in providing an opportunity for . . . *whoever* . . . to hide or use the beach house for an ambush.

Cradling the shotgun across one arm, she stepped around the corner of the house. Wind-driven water instantly hit her in the face and began to soak her hair. With her free hand, she pulled up the hood on the slicker, found it impossible to hear over the roar of rain hitting it, and shoved it off again. So she would be wet—she could get dry later.

It was dark, but not quite as dark as it had been inside. She could differentiate shapes, which was all she needed; she was familiar with the route she would take. Like a shadow, she moved almost silently around the back of the house and across the plank that was laid as a bridge over the small stream of fresh water, Tank behind her. As she gained the opposite bank and started up the steeper part of the path, she heard the sound of the piano again—a few notes of a tune she did not recognize this time—before the wind, whistling in the spruce, whipped it away. Pausing to wipe her face and take a deep, even breath, she felt her hands tremble.

The shed was perhaps a hundred yards away. Looking up between the trees, she could barely distinguish its dark rectangle. The wall facing her was windowless, but as she moved up the hill, she could detect a glimmer of light shining from one of the shed's front windows onto a nearby tree trunk. The tinkling of piano keys came again, louder as she approached, then faded away. The crash and thunder of the waves on the shingle of beach was louder, too, as she neared the top of the rise and drew close to a twenty- or thirty-foot dropoff that fell straight down to sand and driftwood invisible below. Though the sounds of the storm disguised any small noises she made, they were also a hindrance to her own ability to hear.

Cautiously, carefully, she crept up and around the corner of the shed, and now, mixed with the thunderous music of the storm, she could plainly hear what was being played. Another tap on Tank's muzzle to remind him to be still, and she moved forward, toward the glow of what had to be a lamp that shone from the nearest of the two windows on either side of the closed door. Abandoning popular tunes, the pianist had shifted to classical, for Jessie recognized Debussy's *La Mer*—how appropriate—and how odd. The player was accomplished, but the dead keys and out-of-tune condition of the piano gave the music a strange and ominous funhouse quality.

Focused on the lighted windows she was about to reach, Jessie didn't realize she had lost her night vision until she stumbled over a half-buried rock. Pitching forward, she dropped the shotgun with a clatter and instinctively threw out her hands, which landed with a thud against the wall just under the nearest small square window. The advantage of surprise lost, she scrambled from her bruised knees back to her feet, ignoring the sharpness of a splinter in her palm, in time to see the light go abruptly out. Then she heard the dull pounding of feet on the wood floor within the shed as the phantom pianist dashed for a second door at the back of the building.

"Dammit!" Jessie swore under her breath, then grabbed the shotgun, snatched the flashlight from her pocket, and leaped to the door. Throwing it open with a crash, she raced through the library and workshop to the rear door, which she found swinging emptily wide on its hinges, and cast the beam of the light back and forth in a wide sweep across the trees and brush on the hillside.

The heavy flashlight was an exceptionally bright and far-reaching variety used by law enforcement, which Alex had given her for use in wilderness sled dog races. Halfway through its arc, she caught sight of a human figure in motion as it vanished into the trees behind the beach house, headed east. In that brief glimpse, she noted a tan jacket over jeans and what appeared to be gray hair pulled back into a braid at the nape of the neck.

Without hesitation, she followed, running when she could, fighting her way through brush and over irregularities in the ground, hurdling the narrow creek to land with one foot in a patch of mud, which staggered but hardly slowed her determined progress. Wet branches whipped at her, stinging where they hit her cold face and hands. There was no time to think, only to pursue.

Thrashing sounds guided her into a particularly dense clump of devil's club. As she thrust her way through it on a ragged path in the large leaves shredded by her quarry's passing, she felt the spiny thorns tear at her clothing and bare hands. But the person she tracked had taken the worst of the wicked stabs and was slowed a little, for the desperate sounds of flight were a bit nearer when Jessie broke out into the open space beyond, which held a familiar trail. Rather than take what she recognized as one of the two paths that went up behind the beach house, the person had dashed across the paths and back into the brush on the other side.

She paused for an instant to listen, soaking wet from the waist down and the neck up. But as soon as the sound of her advance died, so did that of the fugitive she sought, and once again there was nothing but wind in the trees, pouring rain, and the roar of the surf to the right. Tank started forward, but she caught his collar and they both waited, listening hard. There was nothing for a long minute. Then a stick cracked from the weight of an incautious foot, farther along and up the hill. The sound suggested the pianist was headed almost directly up the steep hill she had climbed on her way to the other cove.

Rather than crash on through the undergrowth, advertising her position, she swiftly elected to go down one trail to Millie's then cut back up the other. Shielding the light with her fingers so that only a thin beam showed her where to step, she went quietly along it and was almost to the intersection of the two trails when another sound stopped her. There was a crash, a thud, and the noise of a fall, accompanied by an involuntary cry of pain or surprise as a body hit the ground and, from the sound of it, tumbled, until stopping with a grunt loud enough for Jessie to hear from where she stood.

Immediately she was running up the hill toward it, shotgun held barrel skyward, without concern now for the flashlight's beam, Tank a swift, dark, eager shape at her side. Reaching the area where she estimated the sound had originated, she stopped, and shone the light in a circle around her. Trail, spruce needles and cones on the ground, brush, tree trunks, and . . . a boot below blue denim, under a bush against the large stump of a fallen tree. Over the sound of her own heavy breathing, she could hear someone gasping, trying to catch limited breath. Evidently the collision with the stump had knocked the wind from the tumbling figure.

Cautiously, keeping herself behind the beam, she took a few steps toward the person on the ground, and, extending the barrel of the shotgun so it could be seen, moved the light to the man's face. As it hit his eyes, he closed them and threw up an arm to deflect the brightness—or the threat of the gun.

"Don't . . . shoot. Please . . . don't," he said breathlessly. "I won't . . . move."

"Hush," she told Tank, silencing his low growl.

The man on the ground was probably in his late sixties. A tanned face bore the traces of years spent in the outdoors—a myriad of wrinkles and creases that were exaggerated with tension in the blinding light. Receding gray hair had widened his forehead, and as he squinted, trying to see who was confronting him, Jessie caught a glimpse of eyes the color of the bay on a day of scudding clouds: gray-green. She moved the flashlight beam a little to one side so she could examine him as he relaxed his face.

"Thank you," he said, and his breathing eased.

He was clad in the jeans and tan jacket she had already seen; under the jacket he wore a blue-plaid flannel shirt, open at the collar, with a plain brown sweatshirt over it. She could tell he was short and spare of flesh, though his shoulders were wide enough for strength, and he did not appear frail.

"Who the hell are you?" she demanded.

"Rudy. I'm just old Rudy Nunamaker. It's all right. I won't hurt you."

"Not likely. Not while I've got a shotgun pointed at the middle of you, anyway. What are you doing here, playing the piano in the middle of the night and running away from me?"

"You scared me. Can I sit up, please?"

"No. You stay right where you are and answer my questions."

He sighed. "Really, I can't hurt you. I just come here sometimes when there's nobody home. I don't hurt anything. Just like to spend a day or two, then I go back."

"Back where? Where did you come from?"

He squirmed uncomfortably.

"There's something sticking into my back," he told her. "Could I please just sit up?"

"Okay, sit up, but keep your hands where I can see them, and don't do anything stupid. I know how to use this, and I will—in a heartbeat."

He used a branch of the bush to pull himself to a sitting position, kept his hands on his thighs, and looked up at her silhouette behind the light, sighing this time with relief. He didn't look dangerous, but rather disturbed and leery of the gun she held steadily pointed at him.

"That's better, thanks. Now . . . I have a little place up at the end of Jakolof, built it myself back in the woods, before so many people moved over there. But a couple of times a year I go across the bay to Homer for supplies. Then, if nobody's here, I usually stop for a day or two on my way back. I don't hurt anything— just use the sauna and play the piano. Millie knows me. She knows I come over—leaves a key to the sauna where I can find it. Sometimes, when she's here by herself, I stop in to see her."

"Describe her."

"Nice lady—medium build, brown hair turning white, good smile. Comes down mostly in the late spring or summer for a week or two at a time. She likes gin and tonic—or, once in a while, a martini. Fell on the beach rocks getting out of a boat a couple of years ago and broke her arm."

It was Millie, all right. He knew her, and Jessie thought it unlikely her stalker would. Still, she was not absolutely sure. She paused to think for a minute, half soaked with rain dripping off her hair and down the neck of the slicker. She could smell the salty, iodine odor of the sea on wind that blew water from the nearby trees into her face. She was tired, wet, and the hand with the splinter was pulsing with a sharp, annoying pain. She needed to ask another question or two, however.

"So, Rudy, it was you in the sauna, night before last?"

"Yes, I used it. How'd you know?"

"You forgot to lock it and the stove was still wa— Never mind. How long have you lived there—in Jakolof?"

"Oh, must be almost thirty years now." He half smiled, remembering. "Let's see . . . I came in '69, and . . . "

Jessie lowered the shotgun. This old man was no threat that she could discern. She felt weak all over as relief took the place of anxiety. Then she had to smile.

"So, I scared you, huh?"

"Yeah. Why'd you hammer on the wall of the library like that? Gave me a real turn."

"I didn't mean to. I tripped on a rock and hit it as I fell."

"Well, I had no idea who it was in the middle of the night, so I skedaddled. Better to be safe than . . . you know."

"Yeah, I *sure* do. You about scared me silly when I woke up and heard your music in between the gusts of wind. Really spooky. Gave me a nasty few minutes—then a chase through the woods that beat us both up. Are you okay? Oh . . . you can move now, by the way."

He got to his feet, moving his arms and legs, checking to be sure they worked, rubbing a spot where his ribs had evidently come in hard contact with the stump. He would be stiff and sore for a day or so, but there didn't seem to be anything broken or seriously damaged. He completed his inspection, tested the side of his head over his left ear, and grimaced.

"Ouch. Got a pretty good bump swelling up. Must have hit it on something on the way down the hill. A limb or something rolled under my foot and flipped me on my keester. Knocked the breath right out of me."

"Can I see your head?" Jessie asked, stepping up with the flashlight.

He turned obediently. There was a swelling with an abrasion oozing a little blood into his gray hair.

"Let's go down to the house where I've got some first-aid stuff and can see to clean this. I'm soaking wet, and we could use a cup of tea. There's even a little apricot brandy, I think."

Rudy agreed and they were soon ensconced in the chairs near the woodstove, drinking hot tea laced with the promised brandy, and chatting like friends.

"Where do you sleep when you stay here, Rudy?"

"Oh, anywhere, really—sometimes up in the shed behind the library."

A grin spread across his face and suddenly he looked like an impish small boy with a secret.

"This time, though, I've been two nights in the old A-frame on the other side of the lagoon."

"A-frame? In what lagoon?"

"Well, it used to be a lagoon a long time ago. It's the meadow now, since it dried up. You know—that way." He pointed to the west. "The A-frame's on the hill on the other side."

"I didn't know there was anything but trees on that hillside."

"Yeah, most people don't. And it won't be there for very long. It's been empty for years and it's falling apart. Still, what's left keeps the rain off my head. The basement part of it's still pretty watertight and snug, if you have a good sleeping bag—and I do."

Jessie remembered that there was a trail of sorts along that particular hillside, but much of it had caved away and she had never seen any sort of building. It had to be almost invisible.

"Long way from the piano in the shed."

"Oh, not so far. I like it over there. When it's stormy, like it is now, with all the trees blowing, it feels like flying, or like a ship at sea, everything in motion from the wind."

She chuckled. "I guess it would, in this blow. Where'd you learn to play the piano so well?"

Rudy took a long drink of his tea and reached to adjust the position of his damp jacket, which was hanging on a railing by the stove to dry. He frowned a little, thinking, and a faraway, slightly nostalgic expression flitted across his face.

"Well . . . you see, I used to play before I came here— worked gigs in bars and hotel lounges for a living, back when people used to like to listen and sing along—before there was so much of this recorded music. I haven't really played in years—couldn't now, anyway, with my old hands—just on the old clunker here, now and then."

"You were playing Debussy."

"Oh, yeah. My favorite. I like some of the classical pieces, just for myself. That one seemed appropriate tonight."

"I thought so, too." Jessie had a sudden thought. "Do you play any other instrument?"

"I have a recorder that I taught myself to play after I came here and didn't have a piano."

"Were you playing it on Saturday around noon?"

"Yes, I was. It helps pass the time. Did you hear it?"

"I thought it was part of a dream I was having. Where were you?"

"In the A-frame. I saw you land, then come out for a walk, but thought you'd gone down the beach. I was playing very quietly. Surprised you heard me at all. But then, I thought the wind would drown me out on the piano, too. Have to be more careful."

"Oh, don't . . . please. I like it—a lot. Now that I know it's you playing, I won't *worry* about it."

He looked at her closely, assessing the underlying tone of her voice.

"Why did it frighten you so much?"

She hesitated, finding it hard to explain the reasons for her fear, then gave up and told him about the stalker and why she was on Niqa. She found the story pouring out of her in a flood of words and feelings that she hadn't even shared with Alex— her anger and resentment, the trapping of her sled dog, the horrible idea that someone had purposely caused the wreck of the truck, the threats, phone calls, leaving Knik. She talked for ten minutes, and Rudy didn't interrupt or comment, just nodded and listened carefully until she ran out of words and drifted into silence.

"The things people do to each other. No wonder you were after me like a bloodhound," he said sympathetically. "Courageous—the way you stood over me with that shotgun barrel steady as a rock. I must have scared you half to death. I'm sorry, Jessie, but you were heroic, as I think about it again—a strong, brave lady to come right out after me, when you could have just cowered in here, panicked."

Jessie had relaxed back into her chair from the rigid position she had assumed on its edge as she related her tale of harassment. She realized that now that it was all out, she felt better, as if a spring had unwound inside her. At his words of commendation and apology, tears began to run down her face without warning. Then she was coughing and sputtering to control them as it all caught up with her: the whole, taut week, the wreck, this night's strain and apprehension—it was too much.

But in only a minute or two she was over and beyond it— drying her face, blowing her nose with a matted tissue from her pocket, and smiling at her own emotional response. He was right. She *had* taken care of it; had gone after what terrorized her, and knew she could do so again, if necessary. That knowledge was empowering, or would be when she wasn't so exhausted.

"Will you come down for breakfast in the morning?" she asked Rudy as he was going out the door in the slicker she had loaned him from one of Millie's hooks, heading for his sleeping bag on the other side of the meadow. He was limping a little stiffly and there was no doubt he would be sore in the morning. She had offered him one of the bunks in back, but he politely refused, saying that he liked his windy hillside perch among the tall spruce. Resisting the smile that tempted her lips, keeping her slight amusement to herself, she realized that there was a streak of chivalry in him that made sleeping under the same roof unacceptable.

"Breakfast? Sure." He grinned. "I'm bribable. You have any sausage?"

She nodded. "And eggs, toast, cereal—whatever you want."

"I'm a pushover for sausage. I'll be down, but not too early. You should get some sleep."

"You, too."

In less than five minutes, she had followed his advice— after sliding her improvised locks into place on both doors and propping the shotgun once again beside the bed.

18

"I can't tell her any more than I already have," Jensen replied with irritation the next morning to Caswell's suggestion. "Besides, if I talk about it over the cell phone, I could give away too much of our investigation, let the bastard—if he's listening—know that we've got some leads. He'd be able to make it harder for us or disappear. But I really don't like the idea that there's someone else down there on that island with her. Haven't talked to her yet today; the storm's screwed up the phone."

"Give it a little time. Maybe it'll clear. She's right, you know," Ben cautioned. "It was probably someone totally unrelated to any of this—someone who never even knew she was there—who's gone now. How could it have been *our* guy, when he was here trashing the inside of your place?"

"I know. Dammit. But that doesn't make me any happier."

"What'll make you happier is to catch this creep. So let's get on it. You want me to check on Moule? Call his probation officer?"

"Yes, thanks. I want to know where he is and what he's doing—exactly."

"I'm on it."

"Yesterday didn't net us much. I still want to find out about Collins—where she is and what she's up to. I'll get in touch with Nancy Stilton, the woman who's living in Collins's old apartment. Maybe she knows something that will help, but probably not—since she moved in after Collins was gone."

"Department of Motor Vehicles? She doesn't seem the type to be registered to vote."

"Right. Work I can do on the telephone. Let's get at it."

A few minutes later, Alex put down the telephone with a frown and a shake of his head, the result of a trail gone cold. Nancy Stilton, as he had anticipated, knew nothing at all about Mary Lou Collins, except that there had been at least two other tenants in the apartment before she moved in with her children.

He called the DMV, but there was no record of an automobile of any kind registered in Collins's name.

"Doesn't mean she doesn't have one—just that it's not registered, or belongs to someone else. In any case, it won't help us with an address," he told Caswell, who was waiting with a troubled expression when he hung up again.

"I told John McIntire we'd come in to see him in about an hour," Ben said. "I think we'd better go talk to him about Moule. There's some complicated stuff going on with this guy. It seems he didn't learn much in jail."

"Yeah?"

"Let McIntire tell you, okay? I'd rather you heard it from him. He's got all the details."

"Sure. Let's go. Anchorage, I assume?"

Ben nodded. "Afterwards, we might as well stop in the lab and see if Timmons learned anything from what the team turned in on your house and that place in the trees behind the dog lot."

Heading for Jensen's truck, they met Phil Becker coming in.

"Hey, where you off to?"

"Moule's parole officer in Anchorage."

"Got anything for me to do while you're gone?"

"Yes, actually. I struck out on Collins. Stilton—you know, the one with the kids—didn't know a thing. DMV has nothing. See what you can come up with in tracking her down, would you, Phil? I'm not giving up on that one. She's got a nasty attitude—could be a real grudge-holder."

"Absolutely. I'll get right on it. File on your desk?"

"Yes. There were some character witnesses in that case. You might see if you can contact any of them."

"Right."

John McIntire looked about the way Jensen expected. His carrot-red hair was combed neatly back from receding temples as freckled as the rest of his face and arms. Eyes as blue as a Celtic sea met Alex's with a welcoming grin as he rose from behind his desk to offer a hand to each of the two troopers. Two creases of concern reasserted themselves between his eyebrows as he sat back down, after offering them chairs and coffee from a pot that filled the small room with a rich irresistible aroma.

"My primary indulgence," he told them, pouring three generous mugs full and taking his own back to the desk, which was covered with files and papers. "You want to know about J.B. Moule, right?"

"Right," Caswell agreed. "Just tell us what you started to tell me on the phone, please, John."

"Yes, well . . ." He glanced down at an open file and frowned more deeply as he studied it. "James Robert 'J.B.' Moule. You already know his trial history, so I'll skip that. You were involved in that arrest, Sergeant Jensen?"

"Yes. The assault took place in a Palmer trailer court—a disagreement over a six-pack of beer that Moule started to walk away with after an afternoon of drinking. The guy who rented the mobile home—shack, really—objected and was attacked. He was the friend of a supposed buddy of Moule's—also a part of the drinking party—who called us and the ambulance. They were all drunk, and Moule has a record of violence, especially when he drinks."

"That seems to be the pattern—and from his attitude, I don't think it'll be long until he's back inside."

"Nothing changed?"

"Worse, if anything, but he's not as dumb as he used to be. He learns quickly—just the wrong things. Time inside just made him colder, more cautious—and slick. He's walking a very narrow line and, so far, getting away with it, but only because he's being very careful and very clever.

"He reports to me regularly, does exactly what he's supposed to do—spent some time in a halfway house when he got out and made no specific trouble there—you know, best behavior? But he's the type who says just what you want to hear—sneers at you while he mouths all the right words. To be honest, not many of them bother me, but he makes my skin crawl. Has the eyes of a predator—watches you the way a cat watches a mouse, waiting to see if you're going to drop your guard and give him an opening to pounce and gobble you up, or anyone who gets in his way. I'd love to put him back inside, but he gives away nothing we can use. And he knows it."

"What's he doing for work? Where's he living?" Jensen asked.

"Well, it's hard to imagine, but he's living with his father—another piece of the game he's playing, I imagine. His old man probably abused him as a kid—knocked him around, but seems to have the patience of Job now. The rest of the family won't have anything to do with him—wouldn't, even before his conviction—and his sister testified against him. She's left the state with no forwarding address. Can't say I blame her, single mother with two small kids to think about. But his dad just won't give up, and it can't be easy—calls me every so often for advice, and I haven't much to give him. I think J.B. is staying with him for the time being just to keep us off his back—make it look good on the surface.

"He's been working construction all summer—got out last spring. Couple of arguments with co-workers, according to his boss, but nothing we could pin down. After one incident, the other man involved in the disagreement was seriously injured in an accident on his way home from work—something to do with the brakes—but no one could prove Moule had anything to do with it."

"Brakes?" Jensen straightened in his chair and cast a narrow-eyed look at Caswell.

"Yeah. They went out, he couldn't stop and wound up in an intersection where a van plowed into his side of the car. Paramedics resuscitated him twice on the way to the hospital, and he made it. He's on permanent disability—lost his left arm."

"Were the brakes tampered with?"

"Not so anyone could positively tell, and there wasn't even a prayer of incriminating Moule—lot of suspicion, no evidence."

"Anything else?"

"Not since he got out."

"But there was that nasty incident on the inside," Caswell spoke up. "The other thing I wanted you to hear. Go ahead, John."

"Moule did his time in Seward at Spring Creek. He was part of one of those small gangs of prison bullies; no surprise, given his temper and inclinations. There was a kid, not quite twenty years old, doing a deuce for auto theft—wasn't a bad kid, just decided to run away from home, but made the mistake of 'borrowing' a neighbor's car to do it. They caught him at the border, heading for Canada and the Lower Forty-eight. Somehow, though nobody could prove it, at Spring Creek he got sideways of Moule and company. Next thing, he was found bleeding in the shop, with a couple of dents in his head."

"And nothing to implicate Moule?"

"That's what I mean when I say *slick*. Everyone knew he was responsible, but there wasn't one solid thing to stick him with; no less than a dozen other guys had been there at the same time, and of course no one was talking—not a word. Some cons even make other cons cautious. They had to let it go—a vicious, calculated assault and he got away with it. Makes me want to puke. Also makes me very careful how I deal with him. I got a wife and three kids—one in college."

"And the boy he assaulted?"

"Brain-damaged. They're maybe going to teach him to count—after he learns to talk—but he never will."

A silence fell over the room, into which McIntire dropped small sounds as he refilled their coffee mugs. After a long minute, Alex shifted in his chair.

"We'll need his residence and work addresses. I think this one we follow up on now. Keep your fingers crossed, John, and maybe we can get you enough to get rid of Moule for a long, long time."

"I won't ask what, but I guess you know about how much that would hurt my feelings."

"Give us information on the kid he hurt, too," Caswell said.

"Michael Wynne. He doesn't even remember who he is."

"That's okay. Just putting a finger in every dike."

"His family's pretty bitter—with good reason, I think. Tried to sue, but got nowhere with it. Take it easy on them, okay?"

"I think that if they understand we're on their side, it'll be all right. Might even give them a little something positive, if we can get him."

"Yeah, you're probably right."

"Well, here's Tweedle-Dee and Tweedle-Dum. I kinda thought you two might come rolling in sometime soon."

Hearing his name mentioned, Assistant Coroner John Timmons had whipped his wheelchair around a corner in the crime lab and was grinning at Jensen and Caswell, who had just asked for him.

"Hey, you're the one who does the rolling, remember? We just plod along."

"Sure . . . sure, Alex. How's Jessie doing? You got her well stashed?"

"You better believe it. Nobody knows where—and nobody will."

"Good . . . good."

Alex knew Timmons meant it, but he seemed slightly distracted.

"Listen. I've got a couple things for you, but neither amounts to much. Nothing you can use to establish a suspect, but maybe to identify somebody you've got an eye on. Come on back."

They followed him into the heart of the lab, past people busily working on cases: an artist working with a witness on a computer sketch for identification, a patient technician putting together shards of window glass that were laid out on a table top like a giant jigsaw puzzle, and, as they passed the door, the muffled sound of a shot from an adjoining room, where a tank of water stopped a bullet for use in matching others collected from some crime.

Timmons, as an assistant coroner, was primarily concerned with autopsies and the bodies of victims of violent crime. But his interests did not confine themselves to that field alone. He was a tinkerer and, whenever possible, tended to watch and learn from other experts in the lab and elsewhere. Through the years he had picked up a host of talents that reached into many areas of criminal investigation. Coupled with infinite patience, his knowledge helped to wring useful facts from the details of many cases.

"The dirt on those traps you brought in?" he reminded them. "Well, I kept at it, and there's one thing I think you should know. The basic soil matches, and I'm all but positive that it came from the valley."

By *the valley,* he meant the Matanuska Valley, northeast of Anchorage, that held the towns of Palmer and Wasilla and the community of Knik.

"But it also has chemical traces of conifer wood ash. Now, the Miller's Reach fire burned half of everything out there last year and put that kind of wood ash into the soil for miles around, but the concentration was heaviest in just a few places in the area, where more of it drifted and fell. Knik Road is one of them."

"So it shows what we already know—that it was in the dog lot?"

"Yes, but that doesn't help much. We know it was there. There's another thing—well, several things, but one that may count, since you won't find it on Knik Road—cement dust."

"Cement dust."

"Yes. Seems an unusual thing to find on an animal trap, because it wouldn't ordinarily be found where one would be used. Must have come from where it was kept or transported."

"Doesn't tell us much—could be anywhere."

"True. Didn't I just say it wouldn't net you a new suspect? But if you find one who lives around cement of some kind . . ."

"Right. I see. You said you had a couple of things?"

"Here."

Timmons waved a hand at a nearby table, indicating several numbered plaster casts which Jensen recognized as the boot prints that had been found in the brush at the back of the dog lot at the cabin.

"Now, I've tried my best to duplicate the odd pressure that made this print. This is the original, by the way," he said as he handed one to Alex. "These other four are my own attempts—in the order I made them, with the same type boots."

The four all looked remarkably similar. Caswell shook his head and turned to Timmons.

"Okay, I give. Let us in on it, John."

"Look carefully. The only two that come close to matching that pressure are the third and fourth ones. Do you see why?"

Jensen took a long look and made a guess at the slight difference he saw.

"They all appear to have had the weight distributed, like the search team said, to the inside, as if the person who wore them was knock-kneed. But the original and those other two look deeper in the middle of the print."

"You've got it. Ever see a foot shaped to make a deeper impression in the middle?"

"No. That's where the arch holds it away from the ground."

"Exactly. The only way I could get the third one was to have a much smaller person wear the boot, so the ball of their foot was positioned in the middle. But, being much smaller, the foot tended to slide around in the boot if they walked, making prints with inconsistent pressure.

"To make the fourth—the one that worked—I had a person with a foot too big for the boot put it on, but it would only go on partway, so they were walking almost on their toes—at least on the ball of the foot. The heel of the foot would not touch the bottom of the boot at all; only the heel and toe of the boot itself were making a print as they came in contact with the ground, but the ball of the person's extended foot put pressure in the middle of the print, creating that odd, deeper spot."

Jensen nodded slowly, still intent on examining the results of the experiment.

"Good work, John," he said finally. "The way your mind works is amazing. But what does it mean?"

Caswell cleared his throat and frowned as he reluctantly gave Alex one possible, if unwelcome, answer to his question.

"You were wondering if there could be more than one person involved. If there is, one of them has feet bigger than the boots that made that print."

19

Caswell followed Jensen from the lab and paused as Alex stopped in the parking lot, thinking hard.

"You know, that cement dust on the traps could fit right in with Moule's construction job. I'd like to know exactly where he's working and if it has anything to do with concrete."

"Good thought. Should we take a run to the address McIntire gave us?"

"I think it's more than in order. I want to see that construction site, talk to the foreman, and get a look at Moule."

The construction site in south Anchorage was loaded with cement. It seemed to Alex that the condominium that was nearing completion a few blocks from the shopping district at the intersection of Dimond Boulevard and the Old Seward Highway was being built of nothing but concrete. He was already collecting a few samples for Timmons when a heavyset man in a yellow hard hat walked out of a portable office and across the yard to investigate the presence of the two strangers poking around his site.

"Help you with something?" he asked, tucking the thumbs of his beefy hands into his belt, a frown of curiosity and confrontation beetling his heavy brows.

Jensen presented identification, introduced himself and Caswell, and learned in exchange that he was speaking to the foreman of the project, Al Peters.

"We're working a case that may have something to do with this site," he explained. "You have a J. B. Moule working here?"

The frown deepened. Peters sighed, glanced down past his beer belly to the toes of his scarred, cement-splashed leather boots, then back up at the trooper, and sucked his front teeth.

"Yeah—against my better judgment—but he didn't show for work this morning, so I can always hope that he's quit. What's he done now?"

"I understand from his parole officer that you've had trouble with his aggressive behavior."

"*You* could call it trouble. I'd probably use stronger language. Couldn't prove anything—not enough to fire him. He's a real piece of work, a real bone-deep mean bastard. Most of my crew leaves him strictly alone—walks wide circles around him."

"Tell us about it."

The essentials of the description of Moule's confrontations with his co-workers matched what John McIntire had told them earlier, except that Peters labeled them fights, not arguments.

"I almost handed him his walking papers after the second one—when Vern's brakes—or lack of them—almost got him killed. He was a good man, worked for me eight years. We all figure Moule was responsible—just can't say how. Unfortunately, even firing him wouldn't be the last of it. He all but promised he'd retaliate if we didn't leave him alone, and that we wouldn't like whatever he had in mind. I don't go around asking for violence—or sabotage. Long as he does his job this year, I'll put up with his attitude. Season's just about over, anyway and I don't want to fight with the authorities."

"He miss any work?"

"Fair amount. Comes and goes. Works just enough to keep his parole officer off his case, if not happy."

"Can you give me specific dates?"

"Sure. Come on into the office and I'll show you his record."

They walked together across to the portable office and up steps built of raw lumber. Inside were three desks, one clearly belonging to the foreman and the one nearest it empty except for a pile of blueprints. From the third, a thin woman with a tired-looking face glanced up as they entered. Peters waved a casual hand in her direction—"One of our bookkeepers"—then gave her a moment's attention. "Feeling better, Judy?"

"Yeah, I'm okay. Maalox and something to eat took care of it."

"Good." He turned back to the troopers.

"Well, here's the time sheets." He handed Jensen a book that included the summer's work schedule for each man, and Alex flipped through the pages, paying particular attention to the last two weeks.

J. B. Moule had missed a considerable amount of work—at least half his work hours in the preceding week. The Tuesday Jessie's brakes had failed, wrecking the truck, he had worked all day, but Wednesday he hadn't showed up till just before one o'clock. Whenever the tampering had been done, Alex thought it unlikely it would have been during the day, while she was watching the dog lot. Thursday, the day Jim Bradford's goat had been injured, Moule hadn't come to work at all. Friday he was also absent. The other harassment—the rock through the window, the vandalizing of the Knik cabin, the traps in the dog lot—had all been done at night or on the weekend. All Moule's work record proved was that he could have had the opportunity for most of the trouble.

"If he was angry at someone, do you think he might harass someone else—someone connected or related to his real target?" Jensen asked Peters.

"Ah, so that's the way the wind blows. It's an interesting question that I won't ask you to explain." He paused, considering, then nodded. "I wouldn't put much of anything past him. He'd do whatever he figured would be most effective, cause the most damage and pain, whatever."

"Ever notice what kind of boots he wears?"

"Can't say I have. Work boots, pretty much like the rest."

They talked for a few minutes more, but gained little. Peters was as uneasy about Moule as McIntire had been—as little inclined to go out of his way to take risks with J.B.'s temper.

"Wouldn't hurt to keep our visit to yourself," Jensen suggested as they were leaving.

"Hey, I'm not about to let it get back to him that I was talking to the cops."

"Please have a word with your bookkeeper, too."

"Judy? Sure. She doesn't know Moule—only comes into the office a couple of days a week. She and her husband handle our books, but they do most of the work at home. She's okay; but I'll speak to her."

"Thanks."

"Moule doesn't exactly inspire warm, fuzzy feelings, does he?" Caswell commented as they drove across town to the home address McIntire had provided for Moule.

"Nope. This feels like a bad one, and all the pieces fit so far. Seems a little odd, though, that he wouldn't do better at covering his tracks."

The Mountain View address turned out to be a duplex that not only needed paint badly, but had a piece of plywood replacing the broken part of a front window. A tired-looking green Chevrolet sedan sat close to the building in the driveway, with room behind it for another vehicle. One rear tire was flat, the axle held off the ground with a concrete block. The front fender on the driver's side was a mismatched tan replacement.

"Must not be here," Cas said. "That can't be what he uses to get back and forth to work."

They could easily hear commentary from a radio or television through the thin walls of the apartment.

"Somebody's home," Alex said. "Must be hard to heat this place in the winter."

On the step next door, a youngster of ten or eleven, in a stained jacket with a ripped pocket, sat idly spinning the wheel of an overturned bicycle and watched them walk up to his neighbor's front door.

"Hi, there." Caswell nodded in his direction.

"He ain't home," the kid said, giving the wheel another spin.

"Who 'ain't'?"

"J.B. ain't—not since Saturday. Just his old man. You the cops?"

Caswell didn't answer the question, but gave Alex a knowing glance and lowered his voice. "Pick it up young, don't they?"

Jensen shrugged and shook his head in response, rapped on the door, and stepped back to wait.

It was soon opened a crack to reveal a discouraged and weary expression on the face of a graying man in his late forties. A yellowing bruise discolored his left cheekbone.

"Yeah?"

"Mr. Moule?"

"Yeah."

"Could we talk to you for a few minutes, please?"

"What about?"

"It's about your son, J.B."

The line of his lips thinned and his shoulders drooped as he swung back the door to allow them access to a small living room. Turning his back, he walked away from the door, leaving it open, and switched off the television news he had been watching.

"Sit, if you want," he said, waving a hand at a sagging sofa. Jensen did and was immediately sorry, as a broken spring prodded his thigh. Caswell, noting his wince, perched on the arm in self-defense, a twinkle of amusement in his eyes that he didn't allow to reach his mouth.

"What's the kid done now?" Moule's father asked, seating himself on a wobbly dinette chair, and lighting a cigarette with a kitchen match.

Kid? Jensen mentally questioned. It had been a long time since J. B. Moule could qualify in that category.

"Your son lives here with you, right, Mr. Moule?"

"Yeah, since he got out of jail. At least he usually shows up sometime every couple of days."

"He didn't show up for work today. You have any idea where we might locate him?"

"Nope. Doesn't tell me where he's going, or when. Left . . . ah . . . this morning sometime. I don't know when—early, I guess. Don't know when he'll be home. Sometime pretty late, I guess, or maybe tomorrow."

He was lying, and not well.

"Don't, Mr. Moule. The kid next door says differently. How long has it really been since you last saw your boy?"

The father looked at them in haggard silence for a minute, saying nothing, clearly knowing that his attempt to cover for his son was not working. Unconsciously he wrung his hands in his lap, twisting his fingers together in demoralized frustration. Turning his head, he stared blankly at the dead television screen as he gave up and told them what seemed to be the truth.

"Saturday."

"What time?"

"About noon."

"Say anything at all about where he was going or when he would be back?"

"No. Like I told you, he doesn't . . ."

His voice faded and he lifted a hand to rub at the bruise on his face.

"He's giving you a pretty bad time, isn't he, Mr. Moule?" Caswell asked suddenly in a quiet voice. "He give you that bruise, too?"

"No." The answer came too quickly, making the truth apparent to the troopers.

"You don't have to let it be that way," Ben told him sympathetically. "You know it's against his parole. If you want it to stop, we can do something about it—with your help."

"No," he said sharply, shaking his head. "It was just the once . . . really. He's not such a bad boy. Just . . ."

Yeah, thought Alex sadly. Few of them ever are, at least to their parents—just misguided.

"Mr. Moule," he asked, "does J.B. have his own room in this house?"

A nod.

"Could we take a look at it, with your permission, please?"

The elder Moule got to his feet, holding one elbow tight to his ribs, hinting at hurts he was too proud or ashamed to mention. Without a word, he led them to a short hallway and pointed to a closed door at the end.

"I better tell you," he said, hanging his head, looking down at a worn spot in the carpet. "You may find a gun in there."

He turned and headed back to the small living room, where they heard the sound of television switched back on.

But the first thing they found was not a weapon. Lying on the floor at the foot of the unmade bed was a pair of work boots covered with dry cement. Carefully turning one over to examine its sole, Jensen held it up for Caswell's inspection.

"This look familiar?" he asked.

There was no mistaking it. The pattern of the tread matched the prints they had found in the woods near the Knik cabin—and the casts Timmons had examined in the crime lab.

They had searched the room far enough to find a shotgun

in the back of the closet when the front door slammed open hard enough to rebound off the living room wall, and the loud roar of a voice angrily shouting stopped them.

"Goddammit, you fuckin' old fool. Where the hell are they? You stupid idiot, let the law in here without a warrant?"

As J.B. came crashing and stomping down the hall to the door of his room, Jensen did not hesitate, but quickly drew the .357 Magnum he usually wore on duty in town. The sight of it momentarily halted the flow of invective the younger Moule was spouting, as well as his approach. He hesitated, glowering, in the doorway, clearly furious at their presence and his father's part in it.

He was wider, stronger looking than Alex remembered from the trial, and he noticed again that Moule's head appeared small compared to the rest of him. As if it belonged to a child, it seemed to sit almost directly on his shoulders without benefit of a neck, emphasized by an upper body so well muscled that it seemed to strain the seams of his gray flannel-lined jacket. He had obviously taken advantage of bodybuilding equipment in prison. His eyes, nose, and mouth were oddly spaced, close together in the middle of his face below a broad forehead, which was accentuated by a receding hairline that bared the front half of his skull, except for a fringe over his ears.

"What the hell you think you're doing? You got a warrant? If not, get the fuck out of my house."

"We have your father's permission, so stop right there, J.B., and don't make any moves or you'll regret them. Lean over, put your hands on the wall, and spread your legs. You know the drill."

"Fuck you. You got nothing. You can't just fuckin'—"

"*Do it*," Alex barked at him, remembering Moule's threats during and after the trial, as well as his reportedly vicious temper and attitude. "If you don't do it now, I'll assume you're resisting arrest and add threatening an officer to the list. You're still on parole, Moule. Don't try it."

It had been a long time since he had seen such total, all-consuming rage on anyone's face. For a long moment, Moule swayed in the door, clenching and unclenching his fists, seeming to exude heat, using every ounce of his shrewdness and cunning to assess the balance of the situation and his chances of upsetting it. As Alex returned his glare, weapon ready, and gave him not an inch of opportunity, he finally turned and stiffly assumed the position the trooper had demanded, still alert and ready to cause trouble.

Taking no chances, Caswell quickly handcuffed and searched him, turning up a handgun and lifting a large, exceedingly sharp hunting knife from a scabbard on his belt.

"Sit down, Moule. I want you on the floor and away from the wall."

He complied resentfully and sat awkwardly while Jensen read him his rights, and, still carefully guarding his prisoner, turned to the next steps in the arrest.

"Will you go call for some backup and the investigation team, Cas? I want them to take this room apart—and whatever vehicle he's driving. And bring me a large evidence bag for these boots, okay? We'll take them on over to John.

"I think your arrogance has finally caught up with you, Moule. The weapons alone are parole violation enough to put you back inside. That and some new charges should keep you there for a long, long time. And you must know there are a lot of people who won't be the least bit sorry—starting with me."

"New charges? What new charges? You got nothin' on me."

"Don't count on it. We'll talk when we get you to Cook Inlet Pretrial."

J.B.'s father, who had remained in the living room, was visibly shaken as he watched his son—still tossing curses in his direction—removed to the back of the patrol car that had quickly appeared. But he said nothing, and Jensen thought that, along with the distress in the man's eyes as he silently watched the arrest take place, he detected a shred of relief.

20

At six o'clock Monday morning, Jessie awakened to a world gone berserk.

Fastening aside the blankets that covered the front windows, she looked out into nature's chaos. The storm had increased to major proportions, battering the island with rain that pounded from heavy, dark clouds, barely visible through roiling mist and wind-driven salt spray. Huge waves assaulted the beach, crashing upon rock and driftwood, hurling foam into the air. Though it had turned and was on the ebb, the tide was high enough to make her appreciate two enormous logs, half sunk into the sand between the beach and the house, that deflected most of the waves and prevented them from washing closer. Everything outdoors was so wet it was impossible to tell which was seawater and which was rain.

She made a dash to the outhouse and came back streaming water that had blown through every possible opening in the slicker she had worn. Changed into jeans and a sweatshirt, she hung her partially soaked sweats by the new fire and grinned ruefully at Tank, who had also been out and now lay steaming, as close to the heat as he could comfortably tolerate.

"Not much reason to wash my face this morning, is there, guy? Couldn't get much wetter."

Nevertheless, she heated water and luxuriated in its warmth, while coffee brewed. Whatever was happening with the weather, it felt good to be clean.

A gust of wind, heavy with ocean spray, hit and drenched the front windows with a crash, startling her and making her wonder momentarily if they would hold or shatter. Then she remembered that they had endured for many years, and was awed at the resilience of glass.

The beach house had never been intended as solid shelter against inclement weather. Constructed primarily of uninsulated planks, it was rife with tiny cracks that allowed heat to be snatched away. The most comfortable spot to be found was next to the woodstove in the fire pit, where she could hear the wind howl resentfully down the chimney pipe, a giant bellows encouraging the flames. Settling by it, with a sweater around her shoulders and a mug of coffee between her hands, she watched the turmoil and commotion of the gale that swept around her drafty refuge.

Intensely powerful, almost menacing, the results of the storm were also extremely beautiful, especially the waters of the cove. Each deep wave that threw itself furiously upon the beach inspired a low rumble that was more vibration than sound as the stones, large and small, growled and shifted under the water's weight. From each incoming crest, spray was whipped by the wind into spume that flew out horizontally like smoke. Jessie could understand why this extreme churning reminded others of galloping horses with manes streaming in the current of their forceful passing, the thunder of their hooves in the pounding of the breakers. But to her, the wild surf seemed more closely related to the swift running of ravenous gray wolves through an Arctic blizzard of fiercely flying snow.

The rhythm of the sea was fascinating and strangely hypnotic. Jessie watched for over an hour, refilling her coffee and making toast, replacing the sweater with a wool shirt that she pulled on over her sweatshirt when she grew cool. She added more wood to the fire periodically, but always returned to her observation.

At eight, she tried to call Alex and swore when the fury of the storm resulted in nothing but static on the line. Assuming he would check and realize that the absence of a call was the fault of the weather in the bay, she was not terribly concerned, but would have felt more satisfied had she been able to reach him. She wanted to relate her encounter with Rudy the night before and assure him that she had successfully solved the mystery of the island's intruder, let him know that the older man was no threat.

At nine, she went out again twice into the driving rain: once to refill a two-gallon water container from the stream near the back door, and a second time to retrieve eggs and sausage from the cooler behind the house. She returned only damp around the edges, having donned waterproof pants, slicker, boots, and a sou'wester hat in anticipation. These, however, dripped pools onto the floor by the door when she hung them up to dry. She took the food to the counter by the propane stove, where she grated potatoes for browning, cut fat slices from another of the loaves she had baked the week before, made a second pot of coffee, and set out a skillet ready for use when Rudy appeared.

But Rudy did not appear. By ten o'clock, she was growing concerned. By eleven, convinced something was wrong, she considered the options and decided on a trip across the meadow that had once been a lagoon, to see if the weather had somehow caused the A-frame to collapse, trapping him in the rubble.

As Jessie got back into her rain gear and rubber boots,

Tank remained unmoving in his place beside the warm stove, giving her a look that told her he was not excited by the idea of another trip outdoors.

"Come on," she told him with a grin, checking that her Smith and Wesson .44 was on her hip, and slipping the box of ammunition into her pocket. She debated, then decided not to carry along the cell phone, since it was impossible to use at the moment and would undoubtedly remain so until the storm abated. Leaning the shotgun against the bench near the stove, she leaned over to give the husky a pat or two of encouragement.

"Come on, guy. You won't melt. We've had lots worse, and colder, on the Iditarod."

Reluctantly, he got to his feet, stretched, and started to pad slowly across the room. Halfway to the door, he stopped suddenly, listening intently to something she couldn't hear.

Oh, good, she thought, it's Rudy . . . finally.

As she reached to unbar the rebar slides she had installed, the husky stopped her with a growl that reverberated deep in his chest, rising until the warning of it tensed his muzzle, exposed his teeth, and raised his hackles, along with her anxiety. Bracing his feet, he lowered his head and stared past her at the wooden door, as if he could see through it and what he saw on the other side aroused animosity.

"What the hell . . . ?"

A pounding rattled the door on its hinges, leaving her no time to think.

"Who is it? Rudy? Is that you?"

A moment of silence. Then his voice.

"Yes . . . it's me, Jessie. But don't—"

An odd sort of thud interrupted what he had been about to say.

He's hurt, Jessie thought. That damn A-frame's tumbled down, or he's fallen and hurt himself somehow.

Tank still growled menacingly.

"Stop it, Tank. It's Rudy. Be quiet."

She worked the slides, one of which hung up for a second or two before it slipped from the hole she had drilled in the frame. Pressing the latch, she pushed the door to let Rudy come in, and gasped as it was snatched away from her and swung wide.

In the opening Rudy stood, white-faced, wearing the slicker she had loaned him, a smear of blood on one side of his face, injured and, from his expression, frightened and sorry as well. It was obvious that he had been given no choice in persuading her to open the door and the blood told her he'd been hit. Behind him, holding a long, sharp knife in a fist that rested on Rudy's shoulder near his throat was another man—a stranger that Jessie knew, as surely as if he had introduced himself, was her stalker.

She was suddenly cold all over and aware that her heart was thudding like a hammer in her chest as fear made her instinctively step away from the door. How the hell had he found her? How could he have known? Who was he? Oh, God—what did he want? What would he do now?

He was of average height, but taller and larger than Rudy's small frame. She could not see his face, for he wore a dark green ski mask that revealed only his eyes. But it was the eyes that caught and held Jessie's attention—sharp, intelligent, resentful eyes of no particular color—gray-brown-greenish. Full of anger, determination, and something else she couldn't quite identify . . . hesitation? They narrowed at the sight of her, but a flicker of satisfaction gleamed in them briefly.

"Hello, Jessie," he said in a mild mid-range voice, with no accent, no specific inflection, almost a monotone. "Yes, I think we'll come in, thank you. Take care of the dog, or I will—and you already know I have no love for dogs."

He nodded as Tank snarled and rumbled hostility. The dog stood his ground, but was confused by the sight of Rudy. Backing farther into the room, Jessie caught his collar in one hand and admonished him to silence with a single sharp word, never taking her eyes from the men. They stepped into the house and the man in the mask pulled the door shut behind them.

Once inside, he shoved Rudy forward into the kitchen space and out of his way. Jessie considered the .44 under her coat, but, reaching into a pocket, he took out a handgun as he unzipped the green rain slicker he wore and lifted a black sweatshirt, sliding the knife into a sheath that hung on the belt to a pair of loose fitting jeans.

Rudy turned to face him and backed up against the stove. "I'm sorry, Jessie. I—"

"Shut it, old man." The flat tone was cold, but Jessie thought it also contained a hint of nervousness. "I don't need you now that I'm in, so you'll be better off if you keep quiet, right?"

Rudy fell silent, staring miserably at the floor, after a glance of apology at Jessie.

Sou'wester in one hand, Tank's collar in the other, she, too, froze, waiting to see what would come next.

It was very quiet, except for the howl of the wind around the house and the crashing of the stormy surf on the beach. The man in the mask stood without moving or speaking, watching her thoughtfully.

"Well," he said in a minute or two, "no questions. You seem to know who I am."

Then she was angry as well as afraid, but very cautious. Who was this arrogant bastard? There was nothing about him that she recognized, though she could see little.

"You're the shit who's been harassing me," she spat out. "You hurt my dog and wrecked my truck, almost killed us. What do you want? What did I ever do to you?"

Behind the dark green mask, he made a strange, half-choking, half-chuckling sound.

"Easy, Jessie. There's no hurry—no hurry at all. We're going to spend quite a lot of time together, you and I. Maybe I'll even keep the old man around, if he behaves—and if you do. There's nothing else you need to know at this point."

She ventured a glance at Rudy and saw that he was looking at her with eyes that had lost their humility and were full of something else. He blinked rapidly and very slightly twitched his head toward the back of the house.

Quickly she returned her gaze to the masked man.

What was Rudy trying to tell her?

The stalker reached once more into his slicker pocket and took out a roll of duct tape.

"Just so we can all relax and stop watching each other so carefully, I think you should sit down. Now—where?"

As he looked over the furniture in the room, assessing each chair and bench, Jessie glanced again at Rudy.

In a flash, she knew what he was going to do, for as the stalker looked away, Rudy had reached to the stove behind him and taken firm hold of the coffee pot that was still on a low flame.

Oh, Rudy, no . . . it's too big a risk, she thought, and almost spoke, but bit back the words and kept silent, afraid the gun would be turned on her friend.

"I think that one will do nicely."

Having settled on the captain's chair near the front windows, the man in the mask began to turn back.

"Now, Jessie, I want you to—"

Rudy hurled the pot directly into the masked face, hitting the man's forehead with a thump, splashing hot liquid into his eyes and soaking the mask and coat front.

"Run, Jessie. Go. Go."

His thin shout combined with a howl of pain from the stalker.

She spun and sprinted toward the back of the house, snatched at the shotgun as she passed it, but missed and knocked it to the floor, where she was forced to leave it. She could hear Tank scrambling beside her and the sound of Rudy's following steps—through the curtain into the storage room, past the bunks, to the rear door. Fearful of not having time to unbar it, she was both relieved and chagrined to find she had neglected to refasten it after carrying in the water from the stream. Well, somebody loves me, she thought as she took advantage of her error. Throwing the door open, she leaped through it into the storm, trying to decide in an instant which direction to flee.

There was really no choice. At high tide, the storm made the beach an impossibility, and she could not go east around the house on either side without being seen and caught if the stalker came out the other door, so she ran up the hill toward the shed that housed the library and shop. A crash from behind made her risk a quick look back.

Rudy was struggling to get up from where he had fallen on the step at the back door of the beach house. He saw her hesitate.

"Don't stop," he called. "Run. I'm okay."

He wasn't, and Jessie knew it—had seen him testing a knee that must have slammed painfully into the ground. But he was right—what good would it do if they both were caught? She was already ten yards away and aware that the stalker would follow almost immediately. What if he shot Rudy? But, she knew, there wasn't time for anything but escape, if she could manage it. Reasoning out a plan of action would come later.

She chose—and ran on up the hill, past the back of the shed, and into the trees and brush beyond it. Going over the crest, she heard a wordless yell behind her. Her heart sank at the sound of a shot fired, but a thud hitting the trunk of a nearby tree told her Rudy had not been the target. Then she knew she had dropped out of sight, going down the steeper western side of the hill, slipping and sliding into a thicket of devil's club as she stumbled, fell, and rolled almost to the bottom. Going to ground within the dense clump of the thorny stalks tangled with ragged berry runners, she lay still, trying to silence her gasping breath, knowing he would listen for the sounds of her passage and presence, and use them, if possible, to track her down. Thrashing through the brush would only advertise her path of escape—as she had followed Rudy's the night before. But the storm would cover most of any small sound she made from this hiding place, as effectively as it would keep her from hearing the direction from which her pursuer would come.

As Tank, on his belly, crawled in beside her she wrapped an arm around him to hold him down and gripped his muzzle with her other hand to keep him still.

Very low, he growled.

"No," she breathed in his ear. "Quiet, Tank."

He was. Good dog. He was in danger, too, and seemed to know it.

She waited, listening with all her might for whatever would come next.

Dammit—dammit. I could die here. What went wrong? Where are you, Alex, when I need you? Knight in shining airplane, indeed. But—not your fault. How could any of us know he would find me so easily? How *did* he find me?

Did Alex even know yet who this monstrous evil was, or that the stalker was no longer lurking in Knik? How could he? With a sinking feeling, she remembered that the cell phone was not in her pocket. She had left it on the table in the beach house. Now, even if the storm cleared or calmed enough for her to call, there was no way to contact him—or anyone else, for that matter.

21

Jensen stepped out of the interrogation room, where he had spent the last two hours with Moule, Caswell, and an APD officer who had operated a video camera, taping the session. Lifting both hands to his temples, he ran his fingers back through his hair, held his head for a second, and huffed in frustration.

J. B. Moule, contemptuous and recalcitrant, had told them almost nothing—practically daring them to prove they had anything with which to charge him. He had refused the offer of an attorney, but also refused to give them any information, except that he had been nowhere near Knik in the last month. Knowing he was already in serious trouble for parole violations, he had belligerently kept his mouth shut, glaring in anger at anyone and everyone.

"We'll have to wait for word from John at the lab on the boots," Alex told Cas. "Let him sit in lockup for the night. We'll try again when there's something more to hold over him.

How about we find something to eat. I'm as empty as last year's bird's nest."

"Linda called and said to bring you home for some of that goulash you're so fond of."

"Hey, I'm for that. Let's go."

As they drove away from Anchorage in Jensen's truck, Caswell called to check on the weather in Kachemak Bay, which was, if anything, worse than it had been in the morning.

"Well, no news may be good news," he said, hanging up the cellular phone. "If she needed to, she could always use the radio at Millie's."

"Check with the office in Homer just to be sure, will you?"

Cas complied, but Jessie had not communicated by radio, either.

"She's okay, Alex. It'll clear tomorrow and you can get through, or she can. Maybe later tonight, even."

"Makes me nervous."

"We've got the perp, and she'll be glad to hear it when you finally talk to her."

They reached the Caswells' house to find Phil Becker waiting eagerly to fill them in on what he had learned about Mary Louise Collins. He had been assisting Linda in the kitchen— draining macaroni, mixing salad, opening beer for the two of them.

"Better get on the outside of one of these," he told the other two troopers, uncapping a second pair of Heinekens as they came into the warm room, which smelled deliciously of bacon, onions, and cheese. "Beer goes bad if you leave it in the refrigerator too long. I barely rescued this one before it spoiled."

Linda smiled at his foolery.

"He even set the table, Ben. Got the forks on the correct side, too," she teased her husband.

"Use 'em right-handed—ought to go on the right side of the plate," he responded, grinning. "Practical—reasonable, don't you think?" he asked Alex.

"Absolutely. No question about it." Jensen accepted the beer Becker handed him and raised it to his lips as he turned to Linda. "Need any more help?" he asked, and took a long swallow.

"Nope, we're all set. Why don't you guys go out on the deck. It's been warm out there all afternoon. I'll call you in about half an hour, when dinner's ready."

"Trying to get us out from underfoot, huh?"

"You bet. Too much law in one civilized kitchen."

Laughing, she shooed them toward the back door.

The three troopers followed her advice and found comfortable chairs on the deck, facing the backyard and, beyond it, the picturesque mountains of the Chugach Mountains that lay to the south of Eagle River. The sun was about to go down behind the western peaks in a blaze of color, but until it did, the quiet space was, as she had indicated, warm for September.

Almost before they were settled, Becker began to talk.

"Mary Louise Collins," he informed them, "is still in Palmer."

"What a shame for Palmer," Cas commented. "She can't be much of a concerned citizen, or up to anything good."

"You're probably right, though she's at least working steadily and has established a permanent address in a trailer park on the east side. But the company she keeps fits right in with what we know about her already."

"Why? Who's she seeing?" Jensen asked.

"Well, I tracked her to the pub were she works—that pit called Aces Wild—and spoke with the owner, an extremely stupid sort who looks and acts like he got the shit kicked out of him once too often."

"That's a biker bar we know personally."

"Right. She's the night bartender—been there over six months. The owner, a questionable alcoholic named Purdy—

who's probably his own best, or worst, customer—says, and I quote, 'She may be a bitch on wheels, but she keeps the S.O.B.s in line.' I'd say keeping things cool would be a valuable ability, considering the regulars in that hole. Evidently she doesn't take guff from anyone, and looking the way she does, I'd be willing to bet she gets handed plenty."

"Why? What's she look like?" Caswell questioned, the only one of the three who had not seen Collins.

As Jensen grinned and nodded, Becker drew an hourglass shape in the air, "Great pair of . . ."

"—Ears?" Linda Caswell finished, giving him a grin, along with an all-innocence, wickedly wide-eyed glance, as she stepped out onto the deck with a bowl of chips in her good hand. "I'll just assume that's what you were going to say."

Leaving the chips, she vanished back into the house, as he sputtered till his ears turned red and the other two men burst into guffaws at his expense.

"If you're going to say something you don't want her to overhear, never turn your back on a door Linda might come through," Cas advised, when he could catch his breath.

"Collins *is* pretty spectacular in that particular department," Becker confirmed.

"She's that, all right," Alex agreed, "but powerful, too—broad shoulders and strong arms. She could easily have killed that old woman five years ago, and she's probably in better shape now than she was at nineteen."

"She's living with a guy who works Aces as a bouncer," Becker told them. "Tough, leather freak—biker—former professional wrestler from the East Coast somewhere, tattoos and all. Purdy says he's bonkers over her, would do anything to keep her and keep her happy. She evidently leads him around by the balls. Interesting, since—and here's the bomb—he's missed work for over a week and she won't say where he's gone. *On business* was all Purdy could get out of her, even when he threatened to fire—would you believe—*Spike?* Spike Jones."

"You *are* kidding, right?"

"Nope. Can't be what he was born with, but that's what he calls himself. Thought I might go back tonight and put a little pressure on Mary Lou, see what I could find out about him. Whatcha think?"

Jensen frowned thoughtfully, remembering Collins's vitriolic last words as she left the court five years earlier. Her furious statement echoed again in his mind: "Someday I may decide to make you sorry—or dead. And you'll never know when or where it's coming from."

She was definitely not the type to shrug off old hatreds.

He shifted uneasily in his chair, emptied his beer in one long swallow, and looked up at Caswell, who was also frowning.

"It's not as clear, that's for sure," Alex said. "But we'd better check it out before we assume Moule's our man, and before we interrogate him again in the morning."

Cas nodded, chewing at his upper lip.

"You got Moule?" Becker questioned in surprise. "Hey, fill me in."

They did, and used the briefing to review the facts of the afternoon's arrest. Becker listened in fascination till they finished, then asked, "John's working on the boots?"

"Yeah," Jensen told him. "I think maybe I'll see what he thinks before we check out Collins at the Aces."

"We're all going?"

"Looks like we'd better."

As he headed for the phone, Linda called them to the table, so he made the call short, reaching Timmons at home, where he abandoned his own dinner to share what he had learned in the lab before leaving for the day.

"It's the same pair of boots, all right. Couple of nicks and scratches match up perfectly."

"No doubt?"

"None. But if they fit, I can't quite see how he made the prints with that odd pressure point."

"Trying to make it look like someone else wore them?"

"Maybe. Or someone else *did* wear them."

"Who?"

"How could I know? That's your department, friend. I just draw the pictures. You have to decide what they mean."

Shaking his head, Alex hurried to join the other three for dinner, where for at least half an hour, he forgot the boots and focused on enjoying his meal.

The Aces Wild occupied the ground floor of a square, nondescript two-story building that had been built near the railroad tracks in the center of Palmer when the town was young. Age had not improved its unattractive appearance, nor did the collection of motorcycles parked in front. The walls were predominantly a dirty yellow-brown that had flaked away around corners, doors, and windows to reveal a colorful history of the varied decorative inspirations of its past owners, none of which had lasted long. Once a retail store of some kind, it had originally had large plate-glass windows on either side of the front door. Plywood had been used to cover them, and then coated with the same ugly paint that insulted the walls.

As the three troopers approached, the door swung open and two men sauntered through it. The beefier of the two was dressed in black jeans, heavy boots, and a leather vest over a grungy T-shirt with the sleeves ripped off to expose his well-muscled and tattooed arms, one of which was wrapped around the shoulders of his companion, an anorexic youth in a studded leather jacket with hands crammed into the pockets. He did not appear pleased with his present company, but hunched his shoulders and allowed himself to be dragged along by the larger man, pale, greasy hair hanging lifelessly from under a filthy orange bandanna that encircled his head.

"You're late," the biker groused. "You'd better have my goddamn stuff."

"Aw-w, Mike—come on. It was a fat weekend. Gimme a break, okay?"

The biker looked up, caught sight of the three men walking toward them, scowled, and studied them through narrowed eyes before yanking the youth off in the opposite direction, a derogatory "Pork" floating back, just loud enough to be heard.

"Don't bother," Jensen told Becker, who had taken a step in their direction, his attention attracted by what appeared to be a drug deal in progress. "It's not going to happen while we're here."

He opened the door and they walked into the controlled chaos of egotistical male one-upsmanship. Somewhere in the crowd of mostly men and a few scattered women a jukebox was blaring heavy metal music. Two pool tables were in use at the front of the room, with several quarters lining the rail of each, challenges for the winners of games in progress. Another noisy bunch was gathered to watch and make rude comments as a tall man with a drink in one hand used the other to skillfully toss darts at a board on the side wall.

"Gotcha now, Shorts. He's wailin'."

"Damn fuckin' wizard on the triples."

The board was situated so that anyone heading for, or coming from, the restrooms—creatively labeled HOGS and SOWS—must pass directly through the line of fire.

A television set above the U-shaped bar in the rear was tuned to the Monday Night Football game, watched by most of the drinkers that filled the tall stools around it, though Jensen wondered how they could hear the commentary over their vociferous efforts to encourage whichever team they favored, combined with the rest of the noise in the place.

Unable to make himself heard to Caswell and Becker above the din, he jerked his head in a direction away from the hazardous game of darts and led the way around the bar to an open space, where a pair of distracted barmaids in jeans and tight, low-necked T-shirts were busily coming and going with trays of mixed drinks and pitchers of beer. When the space was momentarily unoccupied, he stepped up and leaned across, put his elbows on the bar, and waited to catch the eye of the dark-haired woman who was working hard in the well to keep a steady supply of liquor flowing into glasses, fill pitchers, and pluck the tops from beer bottles.

"Hey," a frustrated whine at his elbow. "Move it and wait your turn. You're in my way."

Looking down at the young woman with a tray who faced him, he smiled vaguely, as if he didn't understand, then turned back to watch Collins, and waited.

"Doncha hear so good? You're in the . . ."

Mary Lou Collins swung around to see what was causing the problem and her eyes met Jensen's. Like a video that had been paused, catching a performer in mid-action, she froze, staring at him with immediate recognition. A look of irritation and dislike swept across her face, replacing the harried smile she had been giving someone at the bar the moment before. Glancing at Becker and Caswell behind him, she took two strides that brought her to a point directly opposite him, face to face, and curled a lip.

"Well, well. My old pal, Jensen. What the hell are you doing in my bar, cop?"

"I want a word with you, Mary Lou."

"Just like that? You got anything says I have to talk to you?"

"That's not the way it works, and you know it. You can give me a few minutes here, in *your* office, or we run on down to *mine*. Your choice."

"Fuckin' bastard. What do you want, anyhow?"

"Watch your mouth. I'll tell you what I want when you come outside with us."

Resentful and angry, she first attempted to stare him down. He watched her mind work shrewdly behind the wrath in her eyes, as she reached the conclusion that it wouldn't be worth the effort to refuse—that only humiliation in front of the very people she worked hard to manipulate lay in that direction.

Even angry, she was, indeed, an exceptionally attractive woman. Her thick, dark hair hung below her waist in waves, commanding attention. The expression on her face, however, was anything but engaging.

Spinning around, she beckoned imperiously to an older man, who, on his knees, was refilling the cooler with bottles of Budweiser from a carton on the floor, and barked an order.

"Fill in for me, Buck. I'll be back in a couple."

A fat-faced rowdy on the barstool beside Jensen suddenly nudged him with a shoulder and looked up in distaste.

"You want I should get rid of this guy for you, Mary Lou?"

She didn't take her eyes off Jensen.

"No, thanks, Rick. I can handle it."

Raising the hinged section of the bar that doubled as setup space for the barmaids, she slipped through the opening and stalked toward a door in the rear.

The troopers followed close behind her into the alley that ran behind the building, where she whirled and confronted them again, angrily.

"All right. Now . . . *what*?"

"How's it going, Mary Lou?" Jensen asked her quietly.

"None of *your* fuckin' damn business how it's going. What do you want?"

"Well, I understand you've got a friend who's gone missing for a few days."

"What're you talking about?"

"*Spike* is what I'm talking about. Where is he, Mary Lou?"

Stubbornness filled her narrowed eyes as she half smiled without humor and cocked her head to one side.

"Who?"

Alex shook his head. "Don't bother. We know you're sharing living space with Jones and that your roommate's been missing for a week or more. Where is he?"

"How should I know?"

Taking a cigarette from a package she had brought with her from the bar, she lit it with a match from a book tucked under its cellophane and blew smoke laconically in his direction. Then she tossed her luxurious dark hair back over her shoulders and glanced at Becker, who was following her part of the conversation with interest.

"Hi, honey."

Embarrassed, he took a step back, which provoked a sardonic smile as she returned her attention to Jensen.

"You know," he told her.

"Prove it. He was gone when I got home from here a week ago Friday. Haven't seen him since. Why? You got some special reason to be looking for him?"

There was a stillness and a strange, attentive satisfaction in her expression that alerted Jensen and worried him.

"Reason enough. Give it up, Mary Lou. What else?"

She allowed her animosity to show again, glared at him in defiance, tossed the cigarette to the dirt, and ground it out with a vicious twist of her foot. A tattooed line of blue and red flowers encircled her slender ankle.

"You got nothing, pig. I don't know where he is, and wouldn't tell you if I had him stashed behind the bar—which I don't. Now I'm going back to work. Any problem with that?"

Turning contemptuously, she wrenched open the door and disappeared, with a flounce of her dark hair, back into the Aces.

Jensen shook his head in resignation and disgust as Caswell moved to follow her.

"Let her go. She knows exactly where Jones is, but we're not going to get a thing out of her. I think we'd better get a fast trace going on her boyfriend. I don't like the feel of this."

22

Jessie lay silently in the thorny thicket of devil's club and salmonberry runners, listening intently. The rustle and moan of the wind in the trees and the crash of the surf were all she could hear, but she knew that somewhere in the fury of sound and motion the stalker would be searching for her, focused on recapturing her, not willing to lose his prey. Where the hell was he?

She tensed at an unexpected sharp screech, but it was only the inanimate protest of one tree trunk rubbing against another somewhere on the hill above. Had she left evidence of her fall down the slope, marks on the ground? Would he see and recognize them, and track her to this hiding place? She waited, holding Tank close, hand on his muzzle. He squirmed, attempting to free himself.

"No. Stay," she whispered, and the wriggling stopped. Thank God it wasn't one of the Darryls, who would have assumed she was playing a game and continued to struggle against her.

The rain rat-a-tat-tatted in large drops on her rain gear, a sound that, from inside, seemed loud as a drumroll—a give-away—but she hoped it would not be any louder to someone else than the rest of the storm's cacophony against leaves or the metal roof of the shed on the hill. There was nothing else to hear. Water collected, overbalanced, and poured off one the broad leaves of the devil's club onto her head, but she dared not move away from it or put on the sou'wester, without losing her already limited ability to hear. Water ran down her face and dripped off her chin.

Suddenly there was a thrashing in the brush on the hill. Peering carefully through a small opening between the leaves, she caught a glimpse of a dark figure standing perhaps twenty feet above, looking carefully across the meadow that lay beyond her to the west. Deep in Tank's chest, under her arm, she felt a vibration, the beginning of a hostile growl.

"Sh-h-h," she hissed in his ear, and the growl subsided.

Her hair. Could he possibly spot her light hair in the thick foliage?

Careful not to shake the foliage, with one hand she slowly pulled the dark sou'wester onto her head over her dripping hair, then laid her face down on her arm, against the wet sleeve of her waterproof coat, to conceal its pale color, and waited, barely breathing. Nothing happened. For a long, tense period of perhaps five minutes she waited, frozen, before venturing a quick look. The figure was not visible where she had seen it, but where had he gone?

There was no way to tell. She lay back down, holding Tank, who tucked his nose inside her coat. Either the bastard was still looking and would find her, or he had given up and gone back to Rudy. She hated to think of the kind old man as a captive of this brutal, malicious stranger. There was nothing more she could do either way, so she *did* nothing, *moved* nothing, *thought* of nothing—remained as still as a part of the hill-side and made her mind a blank, became a pair of ears and a heart hammering in her throat and chest, and waited—for a very long time.

A trickle of rain running down the hill pooled against the dam of her coat sleeve and spilled cold water onto her wrist, its small additional discomfort bringing Jessie back to life. Peering up cautiously through the brush, she saw no one. Nothing moved. Would he have waited this long in such weather? She hoped not, but he had exhibited exceptional patience before.

Tank shifted against her, still alert. Slowly, vigilantly, she reached up to move one of the large, flat leaves aside for a better look. Nothing. The hillside above was empty, but what if he was hiding, too, and still waiting—watching for her to come out? She would have to chance it—couldn't stay where she was.

With infinite care, she rose slowly, cautiously parting the broad leaves for an even better look. Nothing. She got to her feet, wincing at the chilled ache of her body. Intentionally or not, this guy was causing her some serious physical pain. There was no sign of anyone on the ridge above her. Turning slowly in a circle, she examined everything in sight. No one. Now to get away, as far as possible, as quickly and surreptitiously as she could.

The back of one cold hand felt on fire, pincushioned with needlelike thorns from the devil's club through which she had fallen. A knee and one elbow—pounded against something in her tumble down the hill—protested with pain as she flexed them. Wiping the rain from her face, she noticed blood on her benumbed hand and discovered a deep scratch on one cheek. The tape on the bridge of her nose seemed intact, but her two injured fingers throbbed more than the rest of her and she hoped they had not been rebroken.

What should she do? Where should she go? The most important thing was to make sure she was not caught off guard again and taken prisoner by this person, whoever he was. He? Was it a he? The voice had been mid-range and sounded like a man, hadn't it? But not so terribly low that it couldn't have been a woman, she thought. Well, she would assume it was a man until she found out. But now she had to find a place to hole up where he would not find her, where she could not be surprised. Where?

The A-frame was clearly out of the question. He had almost certainly caught up with Rudy there, or on his way to the beach house for breakfast. And what about Rudy? Had he been caught? Was there anything she could do to gain his release? Not now. Not before she settled herself in some protected spot where she could think clearly and plan. Perhaps then she could find out how and where he was, assess the situation, and formulate some effective strategy to rescue him.

Jessie did not stand still as she contemplated her predicament, but made her way out of the thicket of thorns as fast as she could and, drifting quietly north, slipped into the denser woodland away from the shed and beach house, taking Tank with her. It immediately grew darker as trees closed in on all sides, but there was some small shelter from the rain that continued to fall in torrents. With care, warily observing everything around them, they progressed up and beyond the hillside and into the wilder part of the forest. The going was somewhat easier in the shelter of the trees, where there was less brush and the miserable, aptly-named devil's club.

She paused in a small open space to pick out as many of the thorns in her hand as she could, though some had broken off, leaving sharp bits beneath the skin that would soon begin to fester painfully. At the same time she examined her elbow and knee and found no breaks in the skin. She could ignore them for now, since there were more important things to claim her attention and, tender or not, they seemed to work adequately. Their discomfort and the growing pain in her broken fingers reminded her that all the pain pills the doctor had prescribed, along with her own bottle of Advil, were still in the beach house, unreachable. Too bad, but she'd have traded them all for the cell phone.

A crash and a thump ahead startled her and brought her

to her knees on the damp spruce needles that covered the earth and helped to muffle the sounds of her passage. She froze, acid terror rising in her throat. A dead limb, soaked with water, had fallen from a tree, striking a rotten stump on its way to the ground. Taking a deep breath to calm herself, Jessie consciously thrust her fears from her mind and went on up the hill, evaluating her alternatives, feeling more confident now that she was away from the beach house and its open ground.

In all likelihood, she was more familiar with Niqa, its layout and resources, than her stalker. She had been there often, walked most of the habitable areas and some of the wilderness that surrounded them. This would give her an edge. What else could she think of that would add to her advantage?

She wished again for the cell phone and shotgun she had left in her hurried escape from the beach house. Both were now in the hands of the stalker, but perhaps he would think the shotgun was her only weapon, not realizing she also had the handgun. He was no fool, however, so she doubted he would assume anything. She did not like the idea that he had two guns—the shotgun and the one of his own that she had seen before she ran. There was also the knife he had held at Rudy's throat. Damn. Poor Rudy. She could do him no immediate good, so she purposely shifted her thoughts away from the old man. Later, when it was possible, she had to think of something.

In the buildings at the other cove, as well as Millie's beach house, there were all kinds of things that could help her. Food was one thing she must have to keep up her strength, especially outdoors in this kind of weather. She realized that, having missed breakfast in her wait for Rudy, she was hungry, and thirsty as well.

Stopping for a moment, she tipped her head back and let rain fall into her open mouth, but this was unsatisfactorily slow. Looking around, she spotted a tiny pool caught in the half-fold of a devil's club leaf. Delicately, she tipped the leaf and let the single swallow of water run into her mouth. Several more were sufficient for the moment, but she knew she should find something that would hold enough water to carry with her from one of the creeks.

Tank sat down and watched this odd procedure with a cocked head that made Jessie smile.

"You're going to be hungry, too, buddy," she said softly, "though you, at least, got a good breakfast."

There would be food—and, probably, medicine—in the storage of the kitchens and pantries of the houses on the other cove, if she could reach it without being caught. The beach house was probably out of the question, but the others might provide. She reached into her jacket pocket for the keys, but found only a wadded tissue along with the box of ammunition she had put in earlier. Well, a win—and a loss. A search through the rest of her pockets yielded nothing more, and with a sinking feeling she remembered laying the keys on the chest by the bed the night before, where she could easily find them. Damn! Well, windows could be broken if necessary. There were other ways to gain entry to what she would need, but they would be less efficient and more obvious to anyone looking.

When she estimated that she was perhaps a quarter of a mile from the beach house, she started toward the other side of the island, having decided to move to the area above the second cove, find a place to hide, and wait for darkness. Her knowledge of the island would be a larger advantage in the dark, when she might not be seen or shot at from a distance. Hungry or not, she would wait for it.

Tucking her hand with its injured fingers inside her coat, she tried to protect and warm it, hoping it would ease the pain. Instead, the throbbing increased as the chill receded, until she gritted her teeth and took it out again to let the cold rain anesthetize it. What had the fall done? Had she broken the fingers again? Removing the tape and splints in the shelter of her coat so they wouldn't get wet, she examined the site of the break in each finger. They seemed fine, with no additional swelling. Then she felt each joint and found that the ring finger—the one that throbbed most—was dislocated in the knuckle nearest her palm. Dammit. What now?

With the knowledge of similar accidents she had witnessed in other dog sled drivers, she knew it should, and could, be put back in place. But would it hurt less if it was relocated? She knew the process was painful, but had never done it, or had it done, herself. Frowning, she thought it over. How hard could it be? Either she could do it or she would find out quickly that it was impossible. It hurt a lot anyway and was, she decided, worth a try.

Gripping the finger just above the dislocation and below the break, so she could hold on without causing further injury, with a quick, firm motion she pulled hard on it.

Fierce, stabbing pain knifed immediately through her finger, hand, and arm, sharp enough to make her gasp, cry out, and almost let go, but she kept up the tension, sucking air in through her teeth as the agony continued. Tank whined softly at her feet at the sounds she was making, knowing something was wrong. She ignored him, focusing completely on what she was doing—and its result.

Suddenly, with a small audible pop, the bone and cartilage slipped back into place and the intense pain was less—not gone, but transformed into the ache and hurt of distress instead of its former torture. Moaning in both anguish and relief, she cradled her hand against her stomach, gulping great lungfuls of damp air, and waited for the discomfort to fade.

There—that hadn't been so bad, now, had it? Yes, dammit, it had, she thought. Worse than bad, but . . . Her last groan turned to what was almost a chuckle, as, amused at herself and still holding her arm against her body, she went on through the woods, forcing her concentration back to the problem of retaining her independent strength and freedom.

A few hundred feet farther east, she stepped across a tiny creek, but, moving on, she suddenly stopped and broke a medium-sized branch from the willow that grew beside it. Peeling the bark from some of the smaller twigs, she broke it up and put it in her mouth, recalling that this part of the willow supposedly contained a natural painkiller that might ease what was left of her aches and pains. If she had been able to boil water, she could have steeped the leaves. She hiked on, chewing the rather bitter mass that she was glad to find also seemed to make her feel a little less hungry, though she thought longingly of the sausage she had meant to cook that morning, and the thick slices of homemade bread she had sliced for toasting.

Tank stayed close beside her as they crossed the island, and she was grateful for his company. The pit of her stomach had tightened into its familiar week-old knot. Breathing deeply to retain her calm, Jessie refused to think about it, knowing she would need all her wits, skills, and best response time if she was to keep from falling into the hands of this horrible person. Better to keep thinking of what could be done than to fall into a *what if* mentality.

Without help from Alex and Cas, she had only herself and Tank to depend on. That would somehow have to be enough—she would have to *make* it so.

Where was the stalker now? What was he doing—planning? Would he anticipate her moves? Could he? Of course. He could easily anticipate her priorities—escape, safety, food, water, shelter. It was almost pathetically simple and he would guess that she would try to avail herself of as many of these as possible.

He doesn't need to spend time searching the island for me, she thought. All he has to do is wait long enough and I'll have to make a try at the supplies in one of the houses. So, she decided, I should make that try as soon as possible, before he's settled in, ready and waiting.

It would be frustrating, for, though he could not be on both sides of the island at the same time, she had no way of knowing where he would be at any given time. She almost wished she had gone back to take a look, had some idea what he was doing and, therefore, his plan of action. For all she knew, he could be waiting for her wherever she attempted to supply herself. But he could not watch all the buildings all the time, unless . . . What if Alex had been right? What if there were more than one stalker?

23

"He swears someone stole his boots."

"Sure they did."

"Says he can prove it."

"How?"

"A week ago last Thursday he didn't go straight home after work. Changed his work boots for a pair of tennis shoes and stopped by a bar, leaving the boots in his truck. He didn't lock it—says he never does. The next day, when he looked for the boots to wear to work, they were missing."

"Right. How does that prove they were stolen at the bar? They could as easily have disappeared in his own driveway, if, as you say, he didn't notice they were missing until Friday. Or maybe they weren't stolen or missing at all."

Tuesday, the day following his arrest, J. B. Moule had continued to refuse to answer questions and insisted on having an attorney present. An appointed one had showed up close to noon and spent over an hour with his client. Now he was attempting to convince Jensen that Moule had played no part in Jessie's harassment.

Jensen was a hard, if not impossible, sell. But the young public defender, much in need of a haircut, while standing firm and addressing the homicide sergeant earnestly, was giving it his best try.

"He says his father and the boy next door will confirm that the boots were missing during the time he says they were. He made a fuss—was mad about it. He has a temper, you know."

"I'm well acquainted with his temper. Because of it, his father would say anything J.B. wanted. I'd listen to the kid next door, but Moule probably has him intimidated as well. Anyway, if they *were* stolen, how'd he get them back?"

"Found them in his truck after work on Monday."

"Right. You expect us to believe that? Someone borrowed them on Thursday, developed a guilty conscience over the weekend, and returned them on Monday."

Jensen allowed his sarcasm to show in a loss of patience, then decided to let the defender see a little of what he was up against.

"Look. The boots belong to Moule, and the lab says that they match the prints we found in the trees beyond the dog lot at Jessie Arnold's Knik cabin. He had the opportunity and his past threats toward me give him motive to harass Arnold. With John Timmons on the stand to demonstrate that his boots match the casts of those prints, no jury is going to believe those boots were stolen. Besides that, there's a dozen parole violations we're working on. He's going back inside, whether or not he's charged with harassment and attempted murder."

However, when Cas met with Alex later at the crime lab, he had as many reservations as Moule had violations.

"The boots could have been stolen, Alex, and he's got alibis for some of the stuff we've uncovered. I'm not completely convinced we've got the right man here. There's no real link between him and the traps. He's not a trapper and neither is anyone in his family, according to his father."

"Well, maybe there's a lot he doesn't know—doesn't want to know—about his misguided son."

"What about those computer-generated notes?"

"There'll be an answer to that one, just wait and see."

"You're not usually so stubborn, Alex. What is it?"

"I just don't want to see this bastard slide out from under . . ."

He was interrupted as the door opened to admit Becker, who had been working on the problem of Mary Lou Collins and her missing boyfriend.

"I think I've got a line on a guy who may know where to find Jones," he announced, pulling out a chair and perching on the edge of it with enthusiasm.

"Who?"

"Well, I've got a friend, Warren Thatcher—a pilot at Elmendorf—that I snow-machine with in the winter. He's got a Harley he rides when we run out of snow, and he sometimes hangs with a couple of guys who drink at the Aces. Thought I'd give him a call and, sure enough, he knows Jones—doesn't think much of him, but knows him to say hello to. Warren says Jones has a close buddy, a Dennis Falconer, who works as a mechanic in Wasilla and may know where we can track him down."

When Jensen and Becker drove to Wasilla to hunt up the man Phil's friend had mentioned, they found an ancient service station that no longer pumped gas and had been converted into a garage of sorts that was hardly more than a workshop, cluttered with tools and parts, on a side street half a block from the airport. Old junker cars and several motorcycles stood around, the majority of which seemed to be a source of parts for others in various states of repair.

Following the sound of voices, they went through a side door and found two men in greasy coveralls examining the engine of a Harley-Davidson that looked as if it had barely survived some kind of wreck. Jensen wondered if its driver looked as bad.

"Shit, Gus, take a good look at the thing. I still say it's the fuel pump," one of them was telling the other in an annoyed tone.

They turned their heads to see who had come in, then one of the two stood up and came toward them.

"Help you with something?"

One knee didn't bend, and he swung the leg stiffly as he walked. Jensen, also noting that he had a prosthesis with a hook instead of a left hand, guessed that this man's experience with motorcyles was more comprehensive than just their repair.

"We're looking for Dennis Falconer," Jensen told him, displaying his identification. "He work here?"

"Dennis? Whatcha want him for? He's . . ."

A heavy wrench came clanging across the concrete floor toward them and the motorcycle fell over with a crash, as the second man shoved it and took off toward a door on the opposite wall.

Becker was immediately after him, bounding over the fallen machine, covering ground with a speed that allowed him to reach the door only seconds after his target had disappeared through it.

"What the hell?" the crippled mechanic asked, following as quickly as he could move, in a rolling gait that reminded Alex of the awkwardness of a man in a three-legged race.

At the door, Jensen saw that Becker's famous flying tackle had connected and brought down the mechanic he pursued. The two were wrestling in the dirt of a vacant lot, dust flying, as the runner tried desperately to break Becker's hold and get away. Between them, the troopers managed to subdue and handcuff him.

"What the fuck's going on, Dennis?" Gus asked.

"Nothing you need to worry about, Gus," he spat. "Call Teresa. Tell her to get hold of Spike and tell him . . . well, just tell him . . . you know. Okay? And have her get Mary Lou headed my way with some bail money."

"Yeah, sure."

At the mention of Collins's name, Jensen gave Becker a warning glance, and the younger trooper nodded knowingly as he dusted off his clothes and picked up the gray western hat he'd been wearing. It was more than a little crushed from having landed on the bottom of the tussle. A mouse that looked certain to turn pretty colors was rising under Becker's left eye, but Falconer, his nose bleeding down the front of his coveralls, had suffered worse damage.

Jensen was waiting eagerly, when Mary Louise Collins showed up to make bail for her boyfriend's buddy.

"He hasn't been charged with anything—yet," Jensen told her. "But now that you've come to visit my office, you and I are going to have another little chat. I think you'd better give me some specifics on where to find Jones. And don't tell me again that you don't know. We've already been informed that you do."

Collins stared furiously at him from a chair in an interrogation room at the Palmer troopers' office.

"Is that what that idiot Dennis told you? In his dreams I know—the stupid S.O.B. Like I told you last night, I haven't a clue where Spike's gone. Haven't seen him in more than a week."

"And you intend to stick to that story?"

"Yeah, of course. It's true."

"I don't think so, Mary Lou. I *can* hold you for obstructing justice, you know. And I may just do that."

She glared at him through the long, dark lashes of her narrowed eyes.

"I haven't done anything you can hold me for. You can't arrest me for *not* knowing something."

A knock on the door preceded Becker, with a satisfied look on his face.

"A minute, Alex?"

Outside in the hallway, he eagerly spilled what he was practically bursting to tell.

"Hey, you're going to love this one. We printed Falconer when we brought him in?"

"Yeah?"

"Remember those two motorcycles stolen in Palmer last month?"

"Yeah."

"Well, guess whose prints match some of the ones we lifted off the pieces of them that we found at the dump?"

"Oh, yeah? Well—it's a small world, isn't it?"

"They also match some we took off another one that was stolen, stripped, and left in a vacant lot in Anchorage a little over a week ago."

"Chop shop?"

"That'd be my guess. Should we send someone to take a long, close look at that place where he works?"

"Un-huh—and wherever he lives. Tell Ed to lock him up and start the paperwork. I'll be down in a few minutes and we'll see what he'll give up when he knows what we've got on him. You said *some*—on the prints. That mean there were more you didn't identify?"

"Yeah, one more person. Think they might belong to Jones?"

"Worth a try. We might get lucky—if we can locate him. You might also check to see if he's got prints on file."

Caswell sat down with Becker in Jensen's office an hour later to discuss what they had so far and what they could do with it, but he wasn't as focused on the stolen motorcycles or as delighted in breaking the case as the younger trooper. They were still holding both Falconer and Collins for questioning, though they wouldn't be able to hold the woman much longer without something with which to charge her. Both she and Falconer had continued to maintain that they knew nothing of Jones's whereabouts, though Dennis Falconer was of the opinion that Collins could reach his friend if she wanted to. Jensen was becoming more inclined to believe the mechanic, who had admitted taking apart the stolen machines for parts but insisted that Jones was responsible for the thefts, and that he knew nothing about them—thought the machines belonged to Jones.

"How should I know they were stolen? He brought 'em in. I tore 'em down. I had no idea they weren't his."

"Yeah, and if my granny had wheels she'd be a . . . motor-cycle," Becker had not been able to resist commenting, earning an incredulous and amused look from Jensen.

"Do you usually strip fairly new machines in perfectly good, running condition?" Alex had asked. "You knew just what you were doing, Dennis. What did you do with the parts?"

"Spike took 'em. And I *don't* know where he is. He said he had some personal business and would be back when he got back—maybe a week, maybe more. He *didn't say* where he was going. Ask Mary Lou."

There was an attitude about Collins's denial that didn't convince the troopers that she was as uninformed as she claimed.

"She's laughing at us," Caswell suggested. "There's a look when she says she doesn't know—a hint of sarcasm, almost a grin—that shows in her eyes."

"I know what you mean," Alex agreed. "I think she knows exactly where he is—*and* what he's up to."

Cas was thoughtfully silent for a time.

"By the way," he asked, "did you check on that former boyfriend of Jessie's?"

"Yes. He's clean. Has all kinds of alibis. I've cut him from the list."

Caswell nodded, then frowned, still thinking.

"Look," he said finally. "Without a doubt we can put Moule away on parole violations, but we're going to have to do more work on the harassment to convince me."

"Why? Take me through it."

"Well, here's the picture, as I see it." He stood up and walked to a blackboard in one corner of the office, on which he began to list the days and events of the previous week.

"The incidents with the traps happened on a Saturday."

He wrote *"Saturday—traps found."*

"One was found early that morning and one later in the day. They were probably set and left on Friday night."

On the board, he put *"Friday—traps set"* above what he had already written.

"A note came that same Saturday in the birthday package that had been tampered with, right?"

He added *"note in package"* to Saturday.

"Two notes had come earlier—one in August."

Alex agreed.

"Nothing happened Sunday. The note arrived at Iditarod Trail Headquarters on Monday."

He wrote, *"Monday—ITC note* and *brake line punctured."*

"Tuesday was the accident with the truck, but the brake line was most likely punctured during the previous night, not in daylight, when the perp might be seen, so put it under Monday."

He wrote, *"Tuesday—truck crash."* Then, *"Wednesday—flowers, note, and pictures."*

"While Jessie was in the hospital, the lilies, pictures of the women in the dog lot, and another note arrived there. Nothing Thursday. Friday we flew Jessie to Kachemak Bay. A lot happened that day. The goat was attacked by dogs and the note left on your neighbor's door. The boot prints were found in the trees behind the dog lot."

On the board he wrote, *"Friday—goat injured & note to*

Bradford," then went back and added *"boot prints made"* to the Monday notation.

"Actually," Alex told him, "Bradford's goat was hurt on Thursday. He came to yell at me on Friday about it."

Caswell moved the note to Thursday.

"At two o'clock Saturday morning, you got a rock through the window with note number five. On Sunday, you went home to find the cabin had been trashed."

He wrote, *"Saturday—rock breaks window; another note"* and *"Sunday—B&E, cabin trashed."*

"That's it, right? Except for the phone calls, I've covered everything?"

Jensen and Becker took a long minute to go over what Caswell had written, then agreed.

"Simplified, but basically that's what happened," Jensen nodded. "What's your point?"

Cas turned once again to the board.

"Let's go back and add the times we know Moule had opportunity—was available to do any of this. From what his boss and parole officer say, I mean.

"If the traps were set on the first Friday night, he could have done it—can't prove where he was. He says he always goes to a local pub on Friday night, but can't verify that particular day.

"Anything done on the weekends or evenings was done at times he was not at work and has no real alibi—including the birthday package note. The notes that were mailed could have been posted at any time a day or two before they were delivered. This includes the ITC note. Dropped in a postbox, they could have waited hours for a postmark and don't prove anything.

"Tuesday he was late to work and—"

Alex interrupted. "That's not right, Cas. His boss said he worked a full day on Tuesday, but didn't come in until just before one o'clock on Wednesday."

"Are you sure? I have Tuesday written down in my notes."

In answer, Jensen took out his own notes and thumbed through them until he found his record of their conversation with Al Peters.

"Yeah, here it is—Wednesday."

"I think maybe we'd better check that one, just to make sure. But for now, I'll take your word for it and make it Wednesday that he was absent from work in the morning. He was also missing all day Thursday and Friday, when a lot of this happened."

"And the break-in happened that following weekend," Jensen added.

"Right. Now—I thought there was a way he could have worked it out somehow. But if he missed the afternoon's work on Wednesday, as you've got written, then there's a problem. John McIntire says Moule was in his office on Wednesday morning. If he met with McIntire at eleven-thirty and left at twelve-fifteen—as John has in his notes—and went to work just after one, he couldn't have brought the flowers, pictures, and note to the hospital during the noon hour. There just wasn't time to make a stop and arrive at work when his time card says he clocked in."

"Could have paid someone to deliver them."

"Maybe, but the receptionist says it wasn't a florist's delivery—just someone who walked in, gave it to her, and said it was for Jessie Arnold. Another thing to check?"

"Right."

Cas suddenly stopped his explanation and frowned, thinking hard.

"What?" Jensen asked.

Hesitantly, he began to think aloud, a process he usually avoided, preferring to complete his analysis mentally before attempting to express it. As he defined his idea, words came faster.

"Well, the pictures . . . those pictures of Linda and Jessie in the dog lot . . ."

"Yeah. The ones he took while they were watering the dogs."

"That happened on Tuesday, right? Just before the accident?"

"Yes. They were out there when Billy Steward showed up. That's how he happened to be in the truck when they crashed."

"And you just said that Moule worked a full day on Tuesday. Yes?"

"Yes, so . . ."

Cas, words coming quickly now, interrupted him. "So if he was working in Anchorage, then he couldn't have taken those pictures in Knik."

Stunned, Jensen thought it over.

"You're right. He couldn't. But . . ."

It was Becker's turn to interrupt. "They found some camera stuff in his room when they searched it."

"They did? Why didn't I know that?"

"Didn't know it was important. Still don't. It was in the back of a closet—camera, film and some negatives. It's at the lab."

Jensen grabbed and dialed the phone.

"John? Understand they found some negatives and a camera in Moule's room and brought them to you. . . . Yeah. . . . They are? Damn! That ties it up. Thanks for getting right on it."

He turned back to the two waiting troopers with a grin.

"Those negatives are the roll of film he took, including those for the pictures he brought to the hospital. We win!"

"All *right*," Becker enthused.

Jensen turned to Caswell, who nodded, but was wearing a tense expression that conflicted with his agreement.

"Looks like it, but there's something else that concerns me."

Jensen and Becker waited.

"It fits, but don't you think it seems to fit a little too well?

Up until now, Moule had managed to keep from leaving evidence that would convict him of a lot of things—that kid McIntire says he almost killed and left brain-damaged in prison, the guy he fought with at work whose truck brakes went out, and who knows how much more. Doesn't this evidence make him look pretty sloppy? Would he leave the camera and film in his room? Why would he suddenly stop covering his tracks—well, tracks are part of what he left, aren't they?"

"Maybe he just got cocky," Becker suggested.

"Maybe, but it seems out of character, doesn't it?"

"Are you saying that Moule's being set up?" Alex asked.

"I'm just saying it seems a little too convenient."

"But, who . . ."

"Don't know. Anyone and anything's possible—even that he got cocky, after his success with the other incidents I mentioned. But if he was being set up, there's another thing to consider."

"Yes?"

"The last thing on this list—the break-in at the Knik cabin—happened on Sunday. Yes?"

They nodded.

"Okay—what's happened since? It seemed to have been escalating, but this is Tuesday and we haven't heard anything at all from our stalker since sometime Sunday. It's like everything stopped when he broke in and found that Jessie wasn't there. Why?"

"He's stopped, knowing his notes and stuff won't reach her?" Becker ventured.

"Possibly."

"Or," Jensen said, slowly and reluctantly, apprehension showing plainly on his face, "you could be right—it isn't Moule—and whoever it is may not be here at all."

He followed this thought up, logically, with another.

"Jones isn't here. Collins knows something that's amusing her—and I don't like the feeling of her smug satisfaction.

Could they be working this together—set up Moule to take the fall . . . and have somehow figured out where Jessie is, Cas? Dammit. And I can't even reach her, with that storm in Kachemak Bay screwing up the phone."

"Hey," Caswell cautioned. "Hold on a minute. Don't jump to conclusions just because it's Jessie and rattles you. We still don't know for sure that Moule isn't the one we want, even if I'm beginning to think there's something going on here that we're not seeing. If he is, we've got him contained."

"But if he's not?"

"Then we still don't know that it's Jones, either. I want to know where he is. So it's time we made a concerted effort to get it out of Collins, or find someone else who knows. I also want to know more about Moule's stolen boots, for another thing, and whether it was Tuesday or Wednesday that he missed work. We can ask Al Peters to check that. There was something else we were going to check. What was it? Oh, yeah—who actually delivered the flowers? Let's get that receptionist to take a look at Moule and see if she can identify him."

24

Hours after it was full dark, after midnight, Jessie slipped like a shadow from the protection of the trees onto the bluff above the eastern cove and moved toward the house of Millie's daughter. For a long time she had been sitting on a log, camouflaged by a clump of brush, watching for any movement or light. Though she couldn't see the buildings below the bluff, everything else had remained still as the darkness increased, deepened, and settled into the early morning hours. The wind had decreased a little, but it still rained steadily, and she was damp through, chilled, and miserable. Still she refused to give in to it and go back to the small amount of cover she had found earlier.

Sometime that afternoon, she had stumbled across a place deep in the forest, where a huge tree had fallen in some prior storm and formed a hollow beneath its tangled root base that was just large enough to shelter herself and Tank if she curled into a ball, knees to chest. As they huddled together, it had kept them dry and a little warmer, and enough devil's club grew around it to form a curtain of concealment. She had waited out the daylight there, even slept for a few minutes intermittently, knowing she was all but invisible, her dark green rain gear blending with the natural forest colors. Twice she had heard someone or something moving through the brush not far away, but lay still as the sound faded away. Animal or human, it had not stumbled upon their hiding place.

It had continued to rain and the ground under her had been cold. She wished she had dressed more warmly, had another sweater or two under the slicker and leggings under her jeans. Her feet were cold in the rubber boots with only one pair of socks. Still, Tank, resting against her, was warm, though his coat was damp and nothing dried much in the humid air. Moist cold, she had decided, was worse than the dry cold she was used to during the winter. Even if the temperature was below zero, if it was dry she could always keep warm by adding layers of insulation between herself and the air—down clothing, sleeping bags. Damp cold crept in and permeated everything she wore, drawing the less-than-comfortable temperature in with it.

After it grew dark, she had moved down the hill and selected the observation point near the narrow trail that crossed the island, where she could see most of the house and the area around it. The lower building that contained the shop, apartment, and sauna was obscured by the bluff, but she could examine most of the space beyond it, including the cove's rocky beach, without being seen. She hid herself as well as she could, Tank beside her on the ground, and watched, taking her time to be as sure as possible that the enemy was not present. She would have only one try at making an attempt at the supplies in one of the houses and did not want to fail at what could make the difference between freedom and capture.

She also scanned the cove for any sign of a boat.

During her time in the hollow it had occurred to her that given the fact that the stalker could not walk on water, he must have had some way to reach the island. He had to have come in a boat, probably alone, and he had to have left it somewhere. If she could locate it, she could escape Niqa and head somewhere else—anywhere. Even in the rough surf, Tutka Bay should be reachable, and there were full-time residents and telephones on that mainland. She could get help—to contact Alex and, perhaps, rescue Rudy. At worst, if she could reach only one of the nearby islands, at least it would not be this one, where she was trapped with an obsessed maniac—but that would leave Rudy, unless she could somehow free him and take him with her.

There was no boat to be seen, so it must be hidden. After she attempted her planned break-in, she would have to make a serious search. It *had* to be there, and she told herself she *would* find it.

When she had waited, seeing, hearing nothing suspicious, she crept silently down the trail, passing tall brown grasses that swished together damply, mixed with salmonberry bushes that waved runners in the wind like reaching fingers that clawed at her coat sleeves. Listening intently, taking one cautious step after another, Jessie used almost ten minutes to reach a low muddy spot before the tiny bridge, perhaps fifty feet away from the back of Millie's daughter's house. She could hardly see in the dark, wished she had a flashlight, but knew it would have given her away anyway.

About to step into the edge of the grass to avoid the mud, she stopped, as Tank growled low in his throat. What? Was there someone? She froze, waiting, listening. There was no sound.

The husky surprised her then. Moving close to her, he took her left hand in his mouth, gently but firmly, and applied pressure to tug her back, away from the trickling creek with its miniature bridge.

Jessie, totally astonished, trusted him and allowed herself to be led. He had never done such a thing before, but he was evidently aware of something she had missed. She was his

human and where he didn't want to go, he clearly didn't want
her to go, either. Ten feet from the creek, he released her hand
and sat down in the trail, looking up, first at her, then at the
bridge, conspicuously satisfied with his action and no longer
concerned. So, she reasoned, it was not *someone,* but rather
something.

She laid a hand on his head, rubbed his ears, and whispered, "Good dog, Tank. What is it, good dog? Stay. You
stay."

He licked her wrist.

Then she went back. Cautiously, she searched the trail,
poking into shadows with a stick, parting the tall grass on either
side, until she found what had disturbed him. Cleverly hidden
in the grass, exactly where she would have stepped to avoid
the mud of the swampy spot, was a trap like the ones that had
been left in her kennel in Knik. Jaws open, sharp iron teeth
upward, it lay in ambush, waiting for her careless weight to
spring it, tearing flesh and tendons, perhaps breaking a bone,
as it had Nicky's.

She stared at it, repulsed and shaken. So he had not been
content simply to wait for her to attempt a raid on the supplies.
What other booby traps might he have left her, assuming she
would come eventually? This one told her he was confident
and willing to cause injury to assure himself of her capture.
Who the hell was this person, and what did he want? It frightened and confused her.

Tank suddenly growled behind her, and she turned, just in
time to see a dark figure rise out of grass in the dark beyond
him and loom toward her—tall and with a strangely shaped
head.

Tense with anticipation, almost without thought, Jessie
whirled and was in instant motion. With one long leap she
cleared the muddy spot, touched down momentarily in the
middle of the small bridge, and leaped again. Her momentum
carried her far enough beyond the bridge so that if a second
trap had been secreted on the opposite bank of the creek, she

would clear it. Then she was running flat out toward the black rectangle of the house that belonged to Millie's daughter. It remained dark, but she knew her way around it—had walked it only days before. She called for Tank as she ran and heard his paws on the wooden bridge as he bounded after her without barking, praying he would also avoid the trap. Over the sound of her own breath and pounding feet, she tried to listen—to know if the dark figure was in pursuit.

As she rounded the corner of the building, Tank now running close beside her, she heard a sharp, familiar crack, and the great crash and thump of someone falling, behind her at the creek. Immediately there was a howl of pain, cut off in mid-lament, that was replaced with what sounded like muffled curses.

A sense of satisfaction swept through her as she realized that whoever had loomed at her out of the dark must have stepped in his own trap. But was it the stalker himself, or did he have a partner? She had no way of knowing and had no intention of going back to find out. Unsympathetic, she ran on, slowing only slightly to take more care in the dark, concerned that she might trip and fall, making herself vulnerable again.

Reaching the long flight of stairs leading down from the bluff to the shop and sauna building below, she paused to listen—ahead of her, as well as behind. The night was silent again, except for the patter of rain still falling on the foliage around her.

Slowly, one tread at a time, she descended the weathered steps, right hand on the rail, as quietly as she could in a pair of rubber boots and rain gear that whispered and crackled as it folded around her knees with each step. She could hear the surf on the rocks of the crescent beach of the east cove as the tide flooded in, and smell the sea in the wind.

Without further incident, she reached the bottom of the stairs and once again stopped to look and listen. What she needed now was to get into the apartment over the shop, collect what she could find in the way of food, medical supplies, and anything else that would be of assistance under the circumstances, and then get out—fast—before she was caught.

She thought of the lock on which she had used a key on her previous visit. Without that key, how could she get in? She walked slowly to the large double doors of the shop. If they weren't locked, she might be able to find a tool that would allow her to separate the hardware that held the lock on the door. Miraculously, one side of the door was open when she turned the catch that held it. Slipping inside, she paused for Tank to follow before pulling it closed. The space around her was pitch-black.

Completely blind, she was compelled to feel her way, with hands and feet, across the large open space that held a multitude of random hazards on its dirt floor to trip or bewilder her—boat motors, coils of rope, boxes of parts, a table, lumber, things with jagged edges and odd shapes she couldn't identify. She barked a shin on a metal pipe, scraped the back of one hand against something rough, and was frustrated at the slowness of her passage through the threatening, invisible obstacle course.

From other, daylight trips to the island, Jessie vaguely remembered a workbench along the north wall and finally reached it without doing herself serious injury or knocking anything over to create a revealing disturbance. With infinite care for things that could fall and smash, or sharpnesses that could slice her reaching fingers, she began to search the bench for something that would help her break the lock. She identified nails, wrenches, a box of some kind of bolts, cans of paint, several large saw blades with knifelike teeth that made her stomach lurch, a machete, the chain for a saw with its wicked piercing edges. Was everything sharp? When her hand grazed a scythe, she felt it bite the side of one finger. Jerking it away, she sucked at the tiny unseen welling of blood, and its metallic taste made her feel a little ill. Hesitant now, she forced herself to reach beyond it and was rewarded when her hand fell on the handle of what turned out to be a large, heavy claw hammer. Perfect. As closely as possible, she retraced her path through the maze of unseen objects to the door, avoiding the length of pipe that had bruised her shin, and, sighing in relief, slid through the door, opening it just enough to let herself and Tank out into the rain again.

All was quiet. She leaned against the shop door and waited, her senses alert. When they warned her of nothing unusual, she moved, cautiously and deliberately, around the building to the foot of the steps that led up to the apartment, then stopped, knowing she would box herself in with this venture. Just go, she told herself, and began to climb quietly. It seemed a hundred steps to the landing, but eventually she stood outside the door and, with her good hand, took hold of the lock to feel for the best spot to apply pressure with the claw of the hammer.

It swung from the hasp and twisted in her hand—unlocked.

Shocked into holding her breath, she struggled to remember—and was certain that she had locked it when she left. Examining it with her fingers, she understood. The lock had been cut open, with a hacksaw or some other kind of shear.

She stood completely still, unable to move for a moment or two. Was this another trap? It would be reasonable for the stalker to leave the door unlocked and, expecting her to make a try for the supplies inside—wait there to take her unaware. Was he on the other side of the door, greedy for her to open it and walk into his trap? Should she go quickly back down the stairs and disappear without the supplies she needed? Fade into the forest and be safe?

She almost did that. But, half turned away from the threat, she suddenly knew that it was only fear—a paranoia of her own creation. She had no way of knowing what lay beyond the closed door unless she opened it.

Then, to her chagrin, she realized what was wrong with the picture. The lock hung in its hasp, holding the door closed. There was no way to put it there from the inside. She had come close to letting herself be frightened away for nothing.

But there was another door to the right of where she stood. This one opened directly into the apartment's kitchen and had another exterior lock. If it had not been opened to let someone in there could be no one waiting.

Jessie moved along the landing to this second door and felt for the lock. It was there, secured. Drawing a deep breath, she went back, steadied her hands, and lifted the damaged lock from its hasp. Opening the door, she went in, and could tell immediately she was alone—the place was cold and silent.

The alarm she had experienced did not entirely vanish, however. She felt more than a little claustrophobic, and knew that what she wanted most was to get back outside and away. Adrenaline heightening her senses, she decided to take a risk in favor of speed. Finding a box of kitchen matches on the woodstove, she struck one, shielding it between her hands, and looked around. A candle stood in its holder on the table. She lit it and blew out the match.

Hurriedly tugging the case from a pillow, she took it to use as a bag and, as quickly as she could, began to put useful things into it. From the pantry in the kitchen, she dumped in several cans of whatever was on the front of the shelves— soup, green beans, tomato sauce, peaches. A box of crackers followed, and a jar of jam—sugar energy. Shoving aside a plastic container of rice she couldn't cook, she found a small canned ham.

Tank would also be hungry. She snatched three cans of beef stew and several envelopes of powdered milk.

The pain in her right hand had settled down to a dull ache and her head ached, too, from hunger. Turning to the medicine cabinet above a washbasin, she took Band-Aids, gauze, adhesive tape, a bottle of Tylenol—from which she shook three and gulped them down without water—alcohol swabs, and a wide elastic bandage, leaving behind scissors and a thermometer. Nearby was a towel that she grabbed, along with someone's toothbrush, toothpaste, and a bar of soap. Thinking for a moment, she threw in the box of matches and three candles, wrenched from their holders. She found a small flashlight with weak batteries, had no time to search for replacements, but took it anyway. From a kitchen drawer, she collected a can opener, a spoon, and a paring knife. She filled a plastic bottle with water at the kitchen sink.

The pillowcase was growing heavy. What else did she need? Going back into the other room, she glanced around quickly. The light of her candle caught the yellow color of a thick length of nylon cord, which she tossed in. Anything else? No. What she had collected would take care of most of her needs for the moment. It was time to get out.

As she blew out the small flame and swung around toward the door, a can in the pillowcase hit the cast-iron stove with a loud metallic clank. Damn, she thought. That could be heard even from outside, if there was anyone listening. She took one step and, as if she had created trouble with that thought, there was a thump from somewhere deep in the building. She froze, heart jumping in her chest.

Then she could hear someone moving—the footsteps of someone taking no time to be quiet, hurrying on a wooden floor, and knew instantly where the sound was coming from.

Oh, God, she thought, there's someone in the sauna.

This time, she knew, it would not be Rudy.

25

"No, sir. He doesn't look anything like the man who brought the flowers for Miss Arnold. That man was taller and had a thinner face. He wore dark glasses, so I couldn't see his eyes. But he was polite—only stayed a minute. No, this isn't him."

The receptionist from the hospital shook her head decidedly as she refused to identify J. B. Moule as the person who had brought the lilies, pictures, and note after Jessie's accident.

"Thanks, Mrs. Porter," Jensen sighed, with a sinking feeling. "We appreciate your coming in so early this morning to take a look. Do you think you'd recognize the man you saw if we do find him?"

"Oh, yes, I know I would. I thought at the time that he looked very much like my nephew, Brian. You just call me when you catch him, young man. And I'm sorry this isn't the one."

She patted Alex's hand in motherly apology and went purposefully out the door.

"Well, so much for that theory," he told Caswell. "I guess I was running on overtime on Moule."

"We still got him off the street," Cas assured him. "Things aren't all bad. Peters won't be disappointed. I'd still like to ask him whether it was Tuesday or Wednesday, though. Making that sort of mistake bothers me."

"We could stop by, since we should go into the lab anyway," Jensen suggested. "There's a lot we need to know. How did those negatives get into his closet? I don't understand how he made those boot prints if he didn't have something to do with this. Do you suppose he's telling the truth and someone really did steal his boots and did the rest of this to set him up? I want to talk to Timmons. He's almost never wrong. And we have no answer to how and where the computer-printed notes were done. The computer, at least, hasn't showed up in Moule's possession, but it has to be somewhere."

"I know it doesn't happen very often, but stranger things have happened than Timmons being wrong. Let's go check out the time cards with Peters first, or it's going to eat at me."

At nine o'clock, they found Al Peters on the second story of his almost finished building, supervising the installation of windows—something besides concrete, for a change.

"You find Moule?" he asked, before they could tell him why they had come back.

"Yeah," Jensen assured him. "You'll be glad to know he won't be back to work this season—maybe not for the next few, if you're lucky."

"Hey, nobody's gonna complain, believe me." Peters grinned at the carpenter with whom he was working. "Hear that, Bud? Moule finally got himself put away again."

"Fuckin' *fine*" was the carpenter's only comment, as he spit on the ground and walked away, but Jensen thought it

probably exemplified the feelings of most of Moule's co-
workers.

"Hey, so what can I do for you guys?" Peters asked. "You
didn't come all the way out here just to tell me you got enough
to put him back inside, did you?"

"Nope. We need you to check again on that day you said
he came to work late. Each of us wrote down a different day,
and we need to check an alibi against one of them." Caswell
grinned at him, sheepishly ashamed of what he perceived as a
senseless, unprofessional error.

"No problem. Let's go down and I'll make you a copy of
his time card. Then you'll have it . . . uh . . . like official."

They left the building and crossed to the mobile home that
Peters used as an office. Inside he quickly found the time card
and made a copy.

"Wednesday," Cas confirmed. "It *was* Wednesday. Sorry,
Alex. Don't know what I was thinking."

"You should be more perfect than the rest of us?" Jensen
kidded.

As he was about to thank the contractor for the extra trouble, the telephone rang and Peters picked it up.

"Oh, yeah, Judy. I've got the stuff ready. You coming
in? . . . Oh, really. . . . Well, yeah. I guess I could drop it
off. . . . No, that'd be okay. . . . Oh, he did? When was that?"

He frowned and scratched the back of his neck with his
free hand.

"He say what Moule was doing? No. . . . Well, he won't
be back. Got himself arrested again. . . . Yeah. Okay, see you
in a while."

He hung up, grimacing.

"Couldn't happen to a nicer fellow. Damn, that man does
get up my nose."

"Moule? What'd he do now?" Jensen asked.

"That was Judy Wynne. You remember—she was here
when you came in before. She and her husband, Ross, keep
the books for us."

Jensen nodded. "Thin-faced woman."

"Yeah. Supposed to come in today to pick up the time cards for last week, but can't leave home because Ross's gone off someplace. They've got a crippled kid. You know . . . mental? One of them has to be there all the time with him.

"Anyway, Ross asked her to tell me that he doesn't appreciate Moule coming into the office and using the computer when he's here trying to work. Weird. Can't think what Moule could have been up to."

Caswell gave Jensen a wide-eyed look, in recognition of the warning bells that were suddenly ringing in both their minds, before he asked quietly, "What computer?"

Peters caught the tone of his voice and narrowed his eyes. "Something else?"

"Maybe. What kind of computer?"

"Here." He pulled the cover off a Macintosh that stood on the desk Judy Wynne had been using when they saw her at the office. Next to it stood a laser printer.

"And Moule printed something out on this?" Cas asked.

"That's what Ross told Judy. Brought in a disk and didn't even ask—just told Ross to move across the room, booted it up, and printed something out. Then he shut it down and left."

"When was this?"

"A week ago Saturday, about nine in the morning, according to Judy. Ross said he was surprised that any of the workers were here, let alone Moule."

Jensen had been doing some rapid calculations in his head.

"That was the day the note appeared in the birthday present. Have we missed something here, Cas?"

Caswell, on the other hand, was looking skeptical.

"Doesn't make sense. Why would he make such an overt move? Almost as if he wanted a witness. Was anyone else here when Moule supposedly printed out that . . . whatever it was?"

"No, just Ross."

"So there's only his word it ever happened. There's something really screwed up here, Alex."

"Anything I can help with?" Peters offered.

"I'd like to talk with Mrs. Wynne," Jensen told him. "Better yet, I'd like to talk to Ross Wynne. He's the one who says he saw Moule use this computer."

"Well, I gotta make a run out to take her the time cards. Why don't you come along and I'll introduce you. She said Ross wasn't home, but at least you can talk to her and find out when he'll be back."

The Wynnes lived in a duplex several blocks south of International Airport Road and west of Arctic Boulevard, an area of older tract houses and multiple-family dwellings. It needed paint, as did the ten-year-old compact car in their driveway with a crack in the windshield that, encouraged by cold weather, had transected it from side to side, a condition with which many Alaskan residents were familiar. One small ding, the minute winter blew in, would immediately spread to the frame. Jensen sometimes thought the state's vehicles were all held together with safety glass and duct tape, and was amused to notice a piece of that silvery tape holding a damaged taillight to the body of the car.

Judy Wynne was small, with dark hair and watchful eyes that seemed to fill the upper half of her face. She was so much thinner than she should have been that she reminded Alex of pictures he had seen of concentration camp victims. She looked worn and tired, and there was something in the resignation with which she answered their knock that made him feel that she had seen more than her share of pain and its results. But as she opened the door, her back was straight and she held her chin up, ready to confront whatever the world brought her. She was slightly confused that Peters had come with company, especially when he introduced them as troopers and asked if they could talk with her.

"What about?" she asked, an anxious look replacing the

polite smile with which she had greeted her boss. Then, before
he could answer, she burst out, "He's done something bad,
hasn't he?"

"Who?" Peters asked.

"Ross. Ross's done something."

"Ahhh . . . no, Judy. These men just wanted to ask you
about . . ."

"Could we come in, Mrs. Wynne?" Jensen asked. "It would
be better if we could sit down and explain."

She gave him a long, insightful look that spoke volumes of
how she was interpreting his request, then invited them in with
a nod and led them into a small living room. Other than a
battered sofa, two straight chairs, and an ancient coffee table,
it was almost empty. A television set occupied one corner,
tuned to a children's show, the sound turned down to a barely
audible murmur. In front of it, a young man in his early twent-
ies sat in a wheelchair, staring slack-faced at the garish, colorful
cartoons that were an ironic contrast to the stark room. He
didn't even glance up to see who had come in.

Jensen halted at the sight of him, causing the other three
to turn questioning looks at him.

"Wynne," he said. "I know that name from . . . John
McIntire. And this . . . ?" He directed his question to Judy
and raised a hand toward the young man. "This would be . . ."

"This is Michael—my son. *Michael*," she said quietly, as if
emphasizing his name made him real.

Her eyes, holding Jensen's, were as honest as clear water,
the expression in them still.

"He was hurt," she said, and the eternal grief of mothers
who lose children rippled that still pool, though Alex could tell
she had no tears left to shed for this particular agony—or none
that she would let a stranger see. For a second or two, time
stopped in that small house, for him and for her, as they looked
at each other and spoke without words.

I have lost enough, she told him. *Don't make me lose any
more.*

And he replied, *I wish I didn't have to, but I have no choice.*

Taking a deep breath to steady herself, she turned, walked to one of the straight chairs, carefully, as if she might lose her balance, and sat with her hands in her lap, waiting.

Peters looked at Jensen. "You want me to make myself scarce?"

"No. If it's all right with Mrs. Wynne, I'd like you to stay. We might need your help."

She nodded. "It's all right."

Caswell walked across to a window and stood, his back to the room, looking out into the backyard. Jensen and Peters sat on the sofa. Michael had not moved or acknowledged their presence.

Alex took a deep breath and spoke gently.

"Your husband isn't at home. Is that right, Mrs. Wynne?"

She nodded.

"When will he be back?"

"I don't know."

"How long has he been gone?"

She didn't speak immediately, and Alex identified a wariness in the way her eyes narrowed, and she pinched her lips together as if she would rather not answer him.

"He left on Sunday afternoon . . . late."

"And he didn't say when he'd be back?"

"He said he had something to take care of, and that he'd be back as soon as he could."

"Where was he going?"

She hesitated.

There was a lot he was asking her that had nothing to do with the formal questions, and they both knew it. It was clear that she wanted to answer what he asked her, no more. But there was more. He watched as she turned her head to look at the young man—the boy, really—in the wheelchair, and made the choice, because of him, to tell this trooper what she knew— or suspected. He didn't imagine her husband had told her much.

"Mrs. Wynne?"

She looked back at him and, if possible, sat up even straighter in her chair as she spoke in a soft monotone.

"For the last two weeks he's told me he was working on a special project in Palmer. He's been gone out there a lot. He said it was just a one-time job that would be over soon and he wouldn't have to go back. He said he was cleaning up someone else's sloppy work and putting the books in order. When he left Sunday, he said he had to go down the Kenai Peninsula to finish up part of it and would be back sometime midweek."

"Why did you wait till today to tell Mr. Peters what your husband told you to say about J. B. Moule using the computer at the job site?"

"It seemed an unnecessary complaint. We need this job. It's the best one we have."

"Do you know where and how to reach your husband? If there was an emergency . . . "

"No. He hasn't called—didn't leave me a number."

Something shifted in her eyes and Alex could see that she was deeply concerned and vulnerable in her suspicions.

"Is that usual?"

"No. He always leaves me one, in case . . ." She glanced at her son in explanation. "I never know when . . . Michael . . . sometimes has seizures."

As if this confession had shattered something essential, her expression slowly crumpled into an aspect of appalling anguish, but there were still no tears. She brought her hands up and for a long moment covered her face. When she took them away, she was once again in control, but there was no pride left in her posture. It was her responsibility to ransom what could be salvaged for her son, so she couldn't afford pride— but there was an honorable kind of dignity on her face.

"Ross . . . isn't really a vengeful man, Sergeant. He's just a broken one. He loved . . . was so proud of Michael. We couldn't have other children, so he invested everything—his whole life—in Michael. It cost him too much, when his

only . . . only son was . . . destroyed . . . this way. It might
have been better if . . ." She stopped, couldn't finish the
thought—but he understood.

"And because Moule was the cause of that destruction and
got away with it, your husband couldn't let it go."

"No. But he . . . couldn't help it. It tore him apart."

Alex nodded and for the moment didn't ask her any more
questions. It wasn't necessary. The details could wait.

He knew that Ross Wynne had told his wife a lie about
Moule's use of the computer, why he had, and where they
would find him. What he didn't know was how Wynne had
found out where Jessie was—and he could only pray they
weren't too late.

26

Jessie desperately looked around for a way to escape as she listened to the sounds of whoever was hurrying around the building in her direction. A window opened onto the roof of the single-story sauna, but there was no way to conceal herself and she would still have to find a way to the ground. Could she wait to see which of the two doors the stalker entered and slip out the other to the stairway? No. They were too close together and she would easily be caught, if she tried. All she could do was put as much space between him and herself as possible.

Frantic, she went back into the kitchen, checking everywhere for a possible third escape route. On the west side of the room was a door that was never used. It opened into mid-air high above the shop doors where the builder had intended to add another flight of stairs leading down, but had changed plans after the door was installed. It was secured by sliding bolts but Jessie could not remember it ever being opened. It might be nailed shut to keep anyone from accidentally falling from it to the ground below.

Crossing to examine it, she jerked back the lower bolt, stiff from lack of use. The upper one was not so easy. It moved, but stuck halfway, still holding the door shut. Grabbing a skillet from the counter, she used the edge to hit it once, hard. It snapped open. Not nailed, the door to nowhere flew open at her shove, but its hinges let out a squeal of protest.

The sound of feet pounding on the lower stairs added impetus to her movements. Tossing the pillowcase away from the building, with its collection of supplies, she quickly lowered herself to hang by her hands from the doorway and dropped the ten feet to the ground, rolling to her feet, unhurt. Looking up, she could just make out her husky staring down at her and knew he would never jump so far, even with encouragement. There was only one alternative.

"Here, Tank. Come on, boy. Come here."

He did what she expected, turned back into the apartment. The door by the stairs crashed open and she could hear the sound of steps, as the person from the sauna entered the farthest room.

"Where are you? Hey—mutt. Dammit. What the hell?"

Grabbing the pillowcase, she dashed to the corner of the shop in time to hear her dog coming fast down the steps. He bounded up to her and they both ran west, away from the building, into the cover of some brush, heading toward the beach.

Whoever was in the apartment would have to come back down the stairs before he could follow. She had an encouraging thought. If the person, in supreme confidence, had been using the sauna for its intended purpose, he had likely undressed to do so and would have to put something on before pursuing her out into the dark and rain. She just might have a head start.

Several other ideas followed. There must be two people involved, both looking for her. If the one on the hill had been caught by the trap, then this must be another, for the footsteps she had heard had not sounded like those of an injured man. If this was the man who had taken Rudy hostage—and it had certainly sounded like his voice and attitude—then where *was* Rudy? Could he have been imprisoned in the beach house on the other cove? Could she possibly reach and rescue him before her pursuer caught up with her? It was worth a try, she decided, and altered her course up the hill to the trail she had not yet used—the one that ran along the cliff, high above the beach.

It was more uneven than the trail through the upper forest, full of the large roots of trees, and hollows that made her stumble and lose her balance. Wet branches slapped at her, tore at her hair, impeding her progress. Reaching into the pillowcase for the flashlight as she continued to flounder along the trail, she pulled out a sticky hand. The jar of jam had broken when she threw the bag from the second-story door of the apartment. It now coated most of the items she had collected and had scattered broken glass into the mixture of canned food and supplies.

Dammit.

She thought she could not bring herself to put her fingers back into the bag to sort through those razor edges in the dark. Pausing, and taking one deep breath before she could think more about it, she gingerly reached in and soon located the box of matches. In the glow of one hand-cupped match, avoiding the shards of glass, she found the flashlight, wiped it off on the pillowcase, and turned it on. It put out just enough light to give her an impression of the trail, as she went rapidly on toward the west cove, and lasted for perhaps ten minutes, until she reached the most difficult spot where the cliff, continuously caving off over the years, had created a rock fall, partially consuming the path. There the light finally died, leaving her in the dark again.

Halting until she could gain a little night vision, she heard the waves crashing on the rocks as the returning tide groped its way back up the beach. It had not yet reached the foot of the cliff. The wind had come up again and was howling through the trees, showering her and Tank with almost as much water as fell from the sky. The storm was back to batter Niqa Island and the rest of Kachemak Bay. It would be a horrible night to spend outdoors.

As soon as she could differentiate between the shapes of the trees around her, Jessie continued, though more slowly and carefully. Successfully maneuvering around the top of the rock fall, she gained a little speed and finally came out on the hill above the east end of the cove. There was a wooden stairway, but she was already well beyond it and didn't want to waste time going back. Millie's house stood halfway around the cove's curve, so, knowing she would make better time on the beach than in the trees above it, she clambered down the bank to make her way along the highest, sandy section.

In the open, the storm struck her with strong gusts of wind-blown rain and spray from the wild sea. It was just light enough to see the foam of giant waves crashing on the rocks, and she could smell the pungent scent of salt water that filled the air. About halfway to Millie's, Tank suddenly stopped, then dashed forward, as a large, dark shape left the water and moved swiftly over the rocks, coming up the beach. Before he could intercept it, it vanished into the brush beyond a pile of logs.

An otter, Jessie realized, relaxing a little from an instant moment of panic and resuming her hurried hike. It was not one of the sea otters—strong swimmers that floated in beds of kelp, raising their young at sea, subsisting on clams, urchins, clams, and fish—but a large land otter that couldn't be bothered by a storm, familiar with and at home in water, but spending most of its time ashore. She remembered that one had killed and gobbled up most of a flock of geese Millie had raised on the island one summer, and was relieved to see Tank come trotting back to join her, obviously feeling he had routed the intruder.

The house was totally dark and silent when she reached the beach in front of it. Hesitating, she wondered about a trap or ambush of some kind. Stashing the pillowcase near a log where she could find it easily, she moved carefully around to the back door. It was open. She went in. The fire was out and had been for some time, for the large, dark room was cold as well as vacant. A quick search through the rest assured her it was empty.

Where was Rudy? Where had the bastard taken him?

Disappointed, Jessie felt a frustrated concern for her piano-playing friend, whose brave action had allowed her to escape. Could he have also been in the sauna and shop building? Had she crossed the island *away* from him in her rescue attempt? It didn't seem likely that the stalker would take him along for a hot steam, encumber himself with guarding the older man. Where would he secure his prisoner? Or—her stomach lurched—would he have decided holding him was unnecessary and . . . He had helped her get away, after all. As she thought about it, she looked around, hoping to locate the shotgun, but it was missing.

Then she remembered the radio. Could she use it to call Alex or the Homer authorities? The cell phone hadn't worked, but would this stronger, battery-powered equipment allow her to contact someone?

Crossing the room, she hunted through the items on a shelf above the radio and found a flashlight. Good. This would go with her when she left—as would the extra batteries she found with it. Turning to the radio, her shoulders sagged in disappointment and frustration. It was there, but smashed beyond use. The stalker had made sure she had no way to summon help from the outside world. As she turned angrily away, the light picked up fragments of something shiny on the floor. He had also broken the cell phone, crushing it into bits of plastic and wires.

As she switched off the light and dropped it in her pocket, there was a thud and the sound of someone running down the trail behind the house, barely discernible over the roar of the storm. It hadn't taken him long to race across the island and catch up with her. Almost cetainly he had seen her light. Could she escape before he circled the house to intercept her?

Moving swiftly out the back door, she dashed around to the beach, retrieved her makeshift bag of supplies with a grab, and raced back in the direction she had come, Tank at her heels. At the hill that led up to the trail above the beach, she paused and looked back, listening for sound that could be heard over the howling of the wind. Tank whined, and through the fog of flying spray she made out a figure coming along the sand, following the depressions her feet had left.

The stalker was closer than she would have believed he could be, and coming fast. As she whirled, something thumped the log beside her, sending small splinters of wood flying. A shot. He had shot at her.

She groped for her own .44, but thought better of it. A duel on open ground would not be wise; he hadn't missed by much. Dodging around logs, she ran toward the hillside, but a short distance farther along the beach was the flight of steps that would be faster and easier to climb—if she could reach it in time.

She couldn't. As she hurdled onto the second step, another bullet hit the handrail a foot from her hand and a third thudded into a step above her. Leaping from the stairs, she looked around wildly for an alternative.

Where the sand and rocks of the beach ended there was a prominence of dark stone, too high and sheer to climb, that jutted out toward the open waters of the cove. Around it, on the other side, east of the cove and the threat of her stalker, was the long rocky section that lay below the cliff and was only exposed at low tide. When the tide was in, it lapped the cliff, a few feet deep, leaving nowhere to go and stranding anyone careless enough to be caught between the coves. With the force of the storm, she could anticipate that the waves would do more than lap. They would come crashing in against the cliffs like battering rams. Though the tide was coming in, it was her only chance.

As she hesitated, another bullet chipped fragments from the rock, which flew through the air to sting her face and left hand. If he was shooting at her, he was a remarkably bad shot. But, with a sinking feeling, she realized that he wasn't trying to hit her.

Unless she refused to move, his intention was to drive her around the rock to the dangerously narrowing area below the cliffs, where she would have nowhere to go as the tide came in. He wanted to *drown* her. It would seem an accident, when and if anyone found her body—the result of bad judgment in attempting to cross between the coves in a place she should have known was unsafe, especially with the storm driving waves in far above their normal high tide level. Still, what could she do? If she refused, and forced him, he probably *would* shoot her and make sure her body was washed out to sea.

She chose the cliffs. There, at least, she might have some kind of chance. Staying where she was meant certain capture, or death if he shifted his aim. Grabbing Tank by the collar, she hurried around the rock, flattened herself against its far side, drew the .44, and waited to see if he would follow. He did not.

After a few minutes she ventured a look around the rock and, rewarded with another rock-chipping bullet, realized that she was visible against the pale waves breaking dimly behind her. But she had seen the brief hot flash of his gun and knew where he was. Among the logs of driftwood, high on the beach, he had settled to wait—either for high tide, which would undoubtedly sweep her into the sea, or until she grew desperate enough to try to make it back onto safe ground and make herself a target for his gun. Neither choice was in her favor.

Who the hell *are* you? she wanted to shout at him. What do you *want* from me?

As she leaned into the protection of the rock, the first waves began to splash over rocks that had fallen from above and lay scattered among the sand. The smaller stones growled as they shifted uneasily in their beds, and swirling froth drew uneven lines of foam that the wind caught and tossed away. Spray flew like a waterfall to drip from Jessie's waterproof coat, hit and pricked her face like icy needles.

Slipping the handgun back into the holster at her waist, she turned and, lugging the pillowcase with its borrowed supplies, started in the only direction left to her—east along the slender corridor between the water and the cliffs. Then, suddenly, she was furious. No one deserved such malevolent, spiteful, hateful manipulation.

By God, he hasn't got me beat in this yet—and he won't, she thought. She simply couldn't let him. There had to be a way to get herself out of the danger in which she now found herself. If she couldn't contact anyone for help, then she would simply have to help herself.

Lighter, sandy spaces between the rocks began to disappear, until she was clambering through the dark over piles of stone that were treacherously slippery with heaps of tide-swept kelp that covered large barnacles sharp enough to slice shoe leather, let alone rubber boots. Soon she could feel cold water seeping in through the damaged soles to soak her feet.

Behind her, Tank whined, and she realized that the pads of his feet were even less well protected than hers. She picked him up and, stumbling, carried him until she reached a small, isolated space of sand and pebbles. There she put him down and carefully examined each of his paws with her fingers. Except for one fairly shallow cut that oozed a little onto her hand, they seemed all right.

Suddenly she felt completely exhausted and discouraged. The adrenaline rush that had sustained her from the trap on the hill through her near encounter with the gunman at the cove had ebbed and left her feeling weak and depressed.

I'm hungry, she thought. Carrying this food and starving. Dumb. I'm not thinking straight.

"Come on, guy. We'll find a drier place and eat some of this stuff I'm dragging around."

As she walked away from the thrashing surf and wind, she

saw that she had reached the place where the cliff had caved off into the steep slide of huge rocks, tumbled like giant blocks. It had created a deep cut in the vertical wall that extended at least thirty feet before it was blocked by fallen rubble. Still it would provide a partial shelter from the wind and rain.

Finding another small, open sandy spot, she sat down cross-legged, back against a rock, opened the pillowcase, and dumped its contents out in front of her. Cautiously locating Millie's flashlight, she made a tent of her rain coat by pulling it over her head, and switched the light on. Avoiding the pieces of the broken jam jar, she separated her limited collection from the shattered glass and most of the jam. The items were sticky, but could now be scrubbed off in the sand and rain with little danger of cutting her fingers. She buried the glass shards deep in the sand and set a rock on top of them.

Opening one of the cans of stew, she stirred in a package of dry milk with the spoon and poured it out on a flat rock for Tank, who began to wolf it down. The taste of it on the spoon almost inspired her to open another, but, deciding she should save it for him, she set the other two aside and open a can of tomato soup instead. It was concentrated, but she gulped it down with a handful of crackers and drank some water from the bottle she had filled. Almost immediately she felt stronger.

, When she got back to her feet, she discovered that the incoming tide had halved the available space below the cliff and in some places was even washing against it. Any question of either returning to the cove where the stalker waited or going on to the east cove had been effectively canceled. The narrow passage was filled with perilous waters, trapping them where they were. It would take some time for water to fill the area in the cut below the rock fall, but sooner or later it would reach the sand on which she stood. The only escape was to somehow climb up the rock fall itself, a thing she would hesitate to attempt even in daylight.

Jessie realized that, in the back of her mind, she had known all along that this could finally be the only alternative open to her. It would not be easy, especially in the dark, and might not be possible at all. Her concerns were three: that she would not be able to make it to the top, that she might not be able to make it with Tank, and that the stalker would anticipate her effort and be waiting there.

All she could do was try. Repacking the supplies, she managed to fasten the pillowcase securely to the back of her belt, encouraged Tank, who in spite of the bad weather was inclined to settle in for a nap, and, determining a likely direction, scrambled over the first rocks at the foot of the steep cut, toward the fall itself.

27

The bottom of the rock fall was not slippery with kelp, nor did it have barnacles covering its stones, like those on the beach, where the salt water regularly washed twice a day. Out of the reach of most high tides, the cracked and broken pieces of fallen rock remained naked of sealife. They were wet, however, and Jessie found them treacherous because the dark hid their uneven, sometimes water-slick surfaces. Several shifted or fell under her feet, forcing her to move slowly and with great caution.

Tank was not pleased to be following her through this new puzzle, but came hesitantly along behind her, and seemed to have an easier time of it. He can see better, she thought, remembering times when he, in harness, could tell what was ahead of them in the snow more accurately than she could and would make detours around obstacles in the trail.

Carefully, she clambered over rocks and boulders until she finally arrived at the primary section of the fall that filled the end of the cut. Off and on, through this first effort, she had used the flashlight, filled with the new batteries she had found in the beach house. Now she dropped it back into her pocket; she would need both hands for the steep rise she was about to attempt.

"Well," she told Tank, "here we go. Come on, fella. If I can do this, maybe you can, too."

This part of the slide was an enormous heap of rocks, large and small, and between them were piles of dirt that had also caved off. The dirt was half clay and the rain had turned it to a slime that was treacherously slick. Jessie soon decided that she would not recommend rubber boots, slightly too large for her feet, as a choice of climbing gear. Their shallow tread provided little traction and the flexible soles slipped easily, making it difficult to retain her footing. She was tempted to take them off and climb in her stockinged feet, but decided to wait and see if this became absolutely necessary.

By the time she reached the top of the acute slope of rubble, she had fallen several times, slipped back a step for every two she took, and was covered in muddy clay. Tank was little better off as the gooey stuff oozed between his toes and clung to the hair on his feet in cakes. More than once Jessie paused to clean it off as best she could.

What remained of the face of the cliff rose perhaps thirty feet above them, but the dark made its configuration almost invisible. It would have to be climbed mostly by feel, rather than sight, and was a task Tank could not handle without assistance. From the pillowcase, she took the length of yellow nylon rope, knelt beside him, and tied one end around his chest and shoulders in a makeshift harness that would not constrict his breathing or crush his ribs. It was a trick she had learned in sled dog racing and she hoped it would serve in this instance as well.

"Stay," she told him, and, tying the other end of the rope to her belt, turned to the cliff.

He whined as she moved away, but did as he was told, trusting her command.

Knowing she could go up, but that retracing her steps would be impossible, made the next few minutes seemed like hours. They were some of the worst Jessie could remember. There were few handholds on the face of the crumbling surface of the steepness and those she found she searched out blindly and with difficulty, able to use only the thumb and first two fingers of her right hand, because of the splints that enclosed the other two fingers. Lack of secure support for her feet in the ill-fitting boots often forced her to draw herself up with her arms and shoulders, hoping there would be something to relieve the painful pressure before the strain grew too intense. She was thankful for the hours she had spent in weight training, getting her body in shape to endure the rigors of distance sled dog racing.

Once, a protrusion she had tested and thought safe gave way, leaving her to dangle dangerously by her left hand, frantically hunting until she located a narrow ridge for one toe that saved her from falling back to the rocks. Sucking in air and relief, she was glad she could not see what lay under her, for, as the distance grew between herself and the mass of rubble below she knew that a single false move could send her plummeting to disaster.

A little more than halfway up the precipice, she found a narrow, foot-wide ledge and paused to rest. The rope that connected her to Tank had only a little play left in it and would not reach to the top. She would have to lift him up to this ledge, then climb the rest of the way and repeat the process.

When the burning had left her trembling arms, she looked down and quietly called to him.

"Okay, guy. Good dog. I'll pull you up. Come, good puppy. Here you come."

Bracing herself, she pulled the rope till she could feel his free weight on the other end. He yipped once as the rope tightened and pinched somewhere, and wriggled a little, but was used to being lifted and moved by his harness, sometimes hauled out of holes on the Iditarod and other winter trails, and so did not struggle.

"Stay, Tank. It's okay. Good boy."

Slowly, with great care, hand over hand, Jessie raised her lead dog gradually through the air, trying not to pound him against the hard wall, as the force of the wind caused him to swing slightly. She could feel it thrumming the line in an increasing frequency as she collected the length of the rope until he stood beside her on the slim projection.

"Good dog," she told him, scratching his ears in appreciation of his trust. Would she have let someone pull her up such a questionable distance? Not likely, she thought, and not often.

"Stay, now. Stay still."

Again he obeyed, and she hated to leave him, knowing he could easily fall from such a narrow space if he moved, but was comforted that the rope to his harness was still firmly attached to her belt.

Once again she began to climb.

The last and steepest section was even more difficult, for there were spaces that were nothing but clay—not a stone to hold or step onto. Almost at the top, with several feet left to negotiate, Jessie realized that she had had climbed her way into a seemingly impossible situation. With one foot on a small outcropping of rock and a hand clinging to another, she searched every inch of the steep face. Nothing. She could hardly breathe with the strain. Then, as she took her hand away from the rock, it brushed against a root that the collapsing soil above had exposed and left hanging. The tree, she hoped, was still firmly planted in the ground, for this root must serve as a line—it was her only option.

Heart pounding, she transferred her weight a little at a time, till she was hanging from the root. Moving one hand and then the other, favoring the right, she began to raise herself up, finding small resting places for her boots on the surface of the cliff to give her precarious balance. With less than a foot to go, she found a stone on which to place the toe of one boot, then discovered another, heavier root, which she tested and grasped. One hand on each root put her in a better position— made the job a little easier. Still, her arms shook with the effort and her shoulders burned as if hot wires had replaced the muscles. Only a foot more . . . six inches.

Without warning, the larger root that she had thought most secure, suddenly broke away. The force of its parting wrenched Jessie from her support on the wall and sent her swinging like a pendulum across it. Grasping the other root with both hands, she desperately struggled to pull herself up its length to the top. If she fell, she would not only land on the hard, jagged rocks below, but her descent would jerk Tank from the ledge to drop after her.

Her injured hand slipped, the broken fingers aching with the punishment, and there was a second of eternity when she *knew* she was not going to make it.

"Give me your hand," a voice said, calmly and firmly, from the top of the cliff. "Reach up and give me your hand."

Startled, Jessie came very close to panicking and letting go, then realized it and redoubled her grip. She stopped breathing and looked up, but could not see well enough to distinguish the identity of the head and shoulders that leaned over the edge. It was only a shape, a figure in the dark, but she had no doubt who it was. He had figured it out and waited for her— found her—helpless.

Damn . . . damn . . . dammit.

She could not go back down. There was nothing to do but what he suggested.

"Don't think about it. Just reach up."

Letting go with one hand, she did.

"Careful, I've got two broken fingers."

She felt the solid grip of a strong person as he grasped her wrist and lifted her steadily upward until she was lying on her belly on the lip of the wall, gasping a combination of relief, fear, and anger.

Out of the frying pan, she thought, and rolled over, away from him and the drop, feeling the hard lump of supplies in the pillowcase under her back. Sitting up, she stared silently at his dim shape in the dark, waiting for what would come next— feeling her pulse pound in her throat.

"Better pull up your dog," the voice in the dark reminded her.

"Why? So you can shoot him?" Jessie's words were clipped with fury and fear.

"So we can get out of here before whoever is hunting you shows up."

She frowned, confused, and looked again at the figure she could barely make out in the blackness. The head was oddly shaped, and she realized that he was wearing something—a hat of some kind that came down over the upper part of his face. Doubt filled her mind. Was this the same person she had encountered with Rudy in the beach house?

"What . . . who the hell are *you*?"

From the sound of his voice, she thought he was grinning.

"I'm the guy you suckered into stepping on that trap by the creek earlier this morning."

"But . . ."

"Listen, Miss Arnold. My name's Gill—Terry Gill. And let's just say I'm a friend of a friend, okay?"

"What fri . . . ?"

"I'll explain it all later, okay? Right now I'd like to get your dog up here and move our base of operations before we have to deal with the guy who's after you."

Jessie hesitated a moment longer. Was this person who he said he was, or could he be in league with her stalker—*be* her stalker? Did it matter? Did she have a choice? Uncertainty pulled her in conflicting directions. Whoever the man was, Tank was still down below on the ledge and would have to be rescued.

Reaching both hands behind her under the slicker, she untied the rope connecting her to Tank and handed it to him. As he took it, she eased her handgun from its holster and leveled it at his body.

"You pull him up, Mr. Gill," she told him. "I'll just make sure you do. Then we can go somewhere else and straighten this out. And while we're at it, what's that thing on your head?"

"It's an infrared night scope," he told her, ignoring the gun and beginning to pull on the rope. "Lets me see very well in the dark."

Carefully but hurriedly, hand over hand, he raised Tank from his perch on the narrow ledge, up the rest of the cliff and over the lip. As he was set down on solid ground, the dog began to growl at his benefactor.

"Stop it, Tank. It's okay," Jessie told him, hoping she was right but taking no chances. "Now take that rope off him and let's go."

Gill removed the temporary harness and stood up. From the ground behind him, he retrieved a rifle with another scope attached.

"You want to carry this, too?" he asked, holding it toward Jessie. "Look, we've got a problem here and really should get going."

It was a disarming move, encouraging her to trust him, but was it calculated to do exactly that?

She shook her head. "No. You carry it, but you lead."

They started toward the east beach on the path along which she had earlier fled.

"Now," she said, "who are you, what are you doing here, and why?"

"Okay. I'm with a pararescue unit. Your buddy Jensen called and said he was worried about you being out here alone with no protection. He asked if I could come and hang out, just in case, so I did. That's it. I've been here since . . . ah . . . Sunday—no, Saturday."

"So . . ." Jessie said, temper rising, "you were assigned to baby-sit me without my knowing it. Alex knew I wouldn't agree to it, so he just went ahead anyway and told me nothing. Dammit. I really resent that."

"Hey," Gill objected, "relax. He's just worried about you. It's okay."

"You think so? He knew how I'd feel about it," she replied in a tense voice. "I told him I didn't want anyone else."

Though Gill had rescued her from an almost certain fall from the cliff, Jessie found she was incensed at Alex's deception. There were few things she valued more than her independence, but one of them was honesty. She had trusted him to honor her wishes—left Knik and come to Niqa on the conditions she had set out. It hurt and infuriated her to have that trust disappointed. She knew that he didn't always tell her everything, but had always counted on him to speak the truth in what he *did* tell her. She felt betrayed and misled.

She swallowed hard and decided to leave it alone for the moment. There was too much going on to waste time on anger. Later, when this was over, she would confront him about it, straighten it out. She deserved an explanation, at least, and he would have to know how his deception had made her feel.

Looking ahead of them, she realized that she could discern the trunks of trees and some of their foliage. A thin hint of morning light had begun to steal in among the green of the forest.

"Where're we going?" she asked Gill, who she could now see was dressed in an ill-fitting camouflage uniform and poncho that kept the rain from soaking him. He had removed the night scope from his head and carried it in one hand, the rifle in the other. He looked like a military man, and that fact, at least, was encouraging. Tank was keeping close to her, bringing up the rear in their marching order.

"There's a spot on the east end of the island, away from the rest of the buildings in the trees—an old shed that was used for some kind of animal."

"Goats," she told him. "It was used for goats several years

ago. They used to have several. Made cheese from some of the milk. One little one used to play tag with the cat."

"Could be kind of nice, living out here."

"Yes, I think so. They had other animals, too—rabbits, a turkey, a pig named Sir Francis Bacon."

She heard him chuckle. "Well, I've got supplies there and we'll need some of them."

Jessie noticed he seemed to be limping slightly, favoring his right foot.

"It was you who sprang the trap by the bridge? I thought . . ."

"Yeah." He grinned. "I could tell what you thought. Didn't mean to scare you into running like you did—and you run pretty good, by the way. I stepped on the darn trap and it got my foot, but the boot sole took most of it. The teeth sliced through the top and did a little damage—not too bad—couple of stitches' worth. I got it taped."

"Why didn't you speak up—say something?"

"Would you have listened?"

She thought about it as they continued to move along the trail that followed the line of the cliff, and knew that she wouldn't have paid any attention. Finding the hidden trap had heightened her sense of threat and she would have been off across the bridge at the slightest hint of his presence no matter what he might have said. She was still not completely comfortable with this supposed friend of Alex's, but was growing to believe he was telling her the truth.

As she considered, she realized that the rain had almost stopped, though the wind was still blowing hard and she could hear the surf pounding the rocks below. In the thickness of brush and trees somewhere above them on the hillside, a stick cracked and something rustled the bushes.

Instantly Gill was alert, dropping to a crouch.

"Get down," he hissed, facing the direction of the sound, rifle aimed and ready.

A large, dark shape moved toward them, finally stepping into an open space.

Jessie grabbed Tank's collar, halting his lunge before it happened. "No," she said sharply, and he gave up with a disappointed whine.

"The moose," she breathed, grinning. "I'd forgotten that there's one on Niqua. Somehow she swam across from the mainland years ago and has been here ever since. Every so often, somebody sees her. I never have until now."

As they watched, the huge animal moved casually away and vanished like an apparition into the forest.

"Come on," Gill told her, getting back to his feet. "It's getting light. Let's get going."

28

"Where the heck were you all yesterday afternoon?" Gill asked Jessie as they neared the east cove end of the trail by the cliffs. "I looked everywhere for you. What's his name was looking, too."

"I found a place under a fallen tree back up the hill," she told him. "Crawled in and waited for dark. I thought I heard someone a couple of times, but you—or he—went away when I didn't move."

"Pretty good spot, evidently. I didn't see you."

They came around a curve that passed beneath another huge fallen tree. It had come down years before and obviously been too large to remove, so the trail had been established under it.

Jessie, now quite confident that Gill was who he said he was, tucked her .44 back into its holster and hurried a step or two to catch up with him as he bent forward to pass under the obstacle. Without warning he froze and she almost ran into him.

"Don't move," he warned her in the same quiet tone he had used earlier. "Stand very still for a second."

She watched him carefully as he examined something on the other side of the tree trunk.

"Now step back a couple of steps," he told her, "just enough to let me move out from under this thing."

She complied and he eased back until he could stand upright again.

"What is it?" she asked, unable to see anything threatening.

"It's a nasty deadfall," he informed her. "This old log makes it invisible from here. You can't see that there's another log just past it, carefully balanced, ready to fall. All you have to do is brush against a specific branch and the last thing you'd notice would be that second log falling on you. Good trick, huh?"

"How did you know?" Jessie asked, eyes wide.

"I'm supposed to know." He grinned. "It's my job and I'm good at it."

She and Tank followed as he moved up the hill and gestured to show her where to safely walk around the trap. He was more than competent. He had spotted the trap she would never have seen, and suddenly, Jessie was very glad for his company and expertise. If she had missed this trap on her way over, it must have been created since that time.

But where was the stalker? She had seen nothing, heard nothing of him since he had shot at her on the west beach. She wished Gill had shown up then with his rifle. Two of them could have pinned the stalker down and forced him to surrender. Well—that was then, and it hadn't happened. Thankfully, he'd been there, at least, to drag her off the cliff, when she certainly would have fallen.

They continued along the trail till they came to the bluff above the second cove.

As they came out on the clear ground near Millie's daughter's house, Jessie halted, peering down to the rocks of the beach below them. It was full daylight now, and she could see clearly.

"Terry . . ."

He turned to see her face, alerted by the concern in her tone.

"There's something down there, high on the rocks, next to the water. The tide's turned and left something. Do you see?"

She felt a little light-headed, could feel her heart thudding against her breastbone, and it was suddenly hard to get enough air into her lungs. The something was blue . . . and tan . . . and the dark green of a slicker that she knew she herself had taken from one of the hooks by the door of Millie's beach house.

"Oh, God, Terry . . . it's Rudy. He's hurt. We've got to go down and help."

She darted off, Tank beside her, and half ran, half slid down the bluff, not taking the time to cross to the long stairway. Then she was racing across the open field, over the sandy rise, and onto the beach toward her piano-playing friend.

Startled, it took Gill a moment to follow, then he loped after her and caught up as she dropped to her knees beside the still form that lay on its back, where the sea had gently laid it and retreated, twisted in the slicker and tangled in a strand or two of kelp. The gray-green eyes were slightly open, but no longer shone like the waters of the bay. They were dull and lifeless, though the expression on his face was relaxed and peaceful.

For a long minute, Jessie looked and wept softly, knowing there was nothing, now or ever, she could do for him.

"This is the old guy that played the piano?" Gill asked.

"Yes. You heard him?"

"I was on the hill behind the house. Saw you chase him down. He was no threat."

She shook her head. "Rudy Nunamaker was a good person. Just a sweet, harmless man with a kind of old-fashioned charm. He liked Debussy . . . and apricot brandy in his tea."

Gill nodded, but shrugged a little impatiently.

"He was an old man. Let's get him up off the beach. It's pretty clear he drowned somehow."

He wrapped the body in the slicker that hung from it, and Jessie helped him carry Rudy into the tall grass on the other side of the rise and lay him carefully down against a driftwood log.

"He had a boat," she said. "Maybe he tried to go home."

"Home?"

"He had a little place in Jakolof Bay. Only came here a couple of times a year."

"Somebody miss him?"

"Someone might, I guess—people around here watch out for each other—but not soon. He said he'd lived alone for a long time." Though she had known Rudy only a short time, she was dejected, saddened by his death.

She looked up at Gill's face and was a little surprised by the uneasy expression in his eyes. She hadn't been able to see him in the dark, during her rescue from the cliff. Now she assessed his worried, dirty face, and long-fingered hands.

"What happened to your face?" she asked, suddenly, noticing a redness and cut over one eye.

"Hit by a branch," he told her. "Yours?"

She had forgotten about her black eyes and how she must look.

"Wrecked my truck," she told him.

He nodded and turned away. "Oh, well . . . come on," he encouraged, "let's get going." Leaving Rudy, he led her toward the building that housed the shop, sauna, and upstairs apartment.

"I thought we were going to the goat shed."

"Changed my mind. We'll go up here, where we can look out around us. Make sure no one creeps up without our seeing them. I'll go down to the goat shed later."

It sounded like a good idea—warmer and drier—and Jessie had to smile a little. Ironically, she would be returning the items she had so hurriedly tossed into the pillowcase to where they belonged.

Gill trotted up the stairs to the apartment, his boots clattering loudly on the steps. She followed, wondering how he could be so sure there was no one waiting for them inside, remembering her own apprehension and hesitation as she had listened at the door earlier. Well, if there was someone, he would be in front to take care of it. If nothing else, she could run again.

The rooms were as empty as before. The door that opened into the air above the shop was still swinging on its hinges, leading nowhere. Tank wandered over to it and stood looking out into the gloomy morning.

Gill pulled it shut, but didn't bother to close the sliding bolts. Crossing straight to the window that overlooked the cove, he carefully examined the area. Satisfied, he leaned his rifle against the wall by the door and pulled the poncho off over his head, sat down on the edge of a straight chair, and nodded at Jessie.

"Get some of that wet stuff off. Make yourself comfortable. We may be here awhile. Don't know about you, but I'm hungry. Think you could find us something to eat while I stand guard?"

Remembering the supplies on the kitchen shelves, she thought she could, but making herself "comfortable," as he put it, appealed even more than food. Setting down the pillowcase bag, she pulled off her muddy boots, and waterproof jacket and pants, removed and wrung out her socks. Unbuckling her belt, she took the holstered .44 from it, but, not content with being completely separated from her firearm, laid it on the kitchen table, near where she would be cooking.

"Could we build a fire?" she asked. "I'd really like to get warm—and dry."

"Sure, why not?"

He took kindling and paper from a handy pile on the floor and laid it in the cast-iron stove.

"Got a match?"

Jessie found the box she had put in the pillowcase and, while he worked at getting the blaze going, also took out the canned ham to use in improvising a breakfast. Locating a can of coffee, she filled a pot with water and set it to perk on a stove much like the one at Millie's beach house. That done, she lit the oven and began to combine the ingredients for biscuits, gathered from the storage pantry. The idea of something hot to eat made her aware of her own healthy appetite, and the tension that she could still feel as a stiffness in her back and shoulders. Her injured fingers had all but stopped aching, but glancing in a mirror she saw that the area around her eyes was now an ugly yellow, along with the darker bruises.

While she worked, Gill moved back and forth between the two rooms, unable or unwilling to settle, keeping watch from the windows. Jessie could hear his even steps on the wooden floor and was reminded of her own discomfort upon moving into the beach house—how she had worried about light and smoke giving away her presence. She thought of the smoke from the woodstove now rising in its chimney to be whipped away in the wind, practically invisible, but carrying a smell that could provide information to the stalker. Did he know that Terry Gill existed? If he came looking, would he expect her to be alone?

As she slid the biscuits into the oven and took out a skillet for frying ham, Gill walked over to stand near the stove.

"How's it going?" he asked.

Tank moved closer to Jessie as she turned to answer and suddenly growled again.

"Hey. What's wrong with you? Stop that," she admonished, and looked up, intending to apologize for the impolite behavior of her dog, but was startled into silence.

Gill had frozen at the sound and stood staring at Tank with a lip curled in an expression of extreme distaste. Aware of her astonishment, he took a deep breath and raised a hand to hide his mouth for a moment. For that moment, all she could see were his eyes, suspicious and wary, looking straight into hers.

The nightmare realization that she had been deceived was instantaneous. Jessie recognized those eyes—knew she had looked into them before, from behind a mask, across the room in Millie's beach house, facing a handgun. Rudy had stood there, as well, miserably aware of his status as accomplice to the threat, before he took a chance, threw the pot of hot coffee directly into those eyes, allowing her to escape. Rudy, who was now cold and wet, shrouded in the slicker she had loaned him, and would never go home to his little place at the end of Jakolof Bay.

Suddenly she knew what had made her uneasy as she listened to Gill pacing a few minutes ago. His steps were even. What had happened to the limp he had exhibited earlier? Since climbing the stairs, he had shown no sign of it, and he had gone up those stairs with a clatter, uncaring at the noise, not favoring his supposed injury. He wouldn't care, would he, if he knew there was no one to hear it or to notice even a thread of smoke from the chimney? He had known the place was empty. And what kind of survivalist didn't have a match to build a fire?

Other clues flooded into her mind.

". . . Sunday—no, Saturday," he had said. The stalker had showed up on Sunday. Was his correction a slip of the tongue, his change of words an attempt to keep her from connecting the two in her mind?

Had he seen the deadfall on the trail, as he had claimed, or known its location because he had placed it there? Had he left it rigged for his own protection—to catch someone else? Had it been there at all, or was he only telling her so, in order to gain her trust in his abilities as a pararescue expert? She remembered his grip on her wrist at the cliff. Though strong, his long-fingered hand had seemed too soft for the rugged outdoor work of pararescue—survival techniques, emergency medicine, parachuting into remote locations.

"He was an old man," he had said about Rudy, and she had dismissed this apparent lack of feeling as impatience with the situation. Perhaps Rudy had had assistance in his drowning.

She stared at him, rigid with the fear that was rising like a sickness in her chest. He stood directly between her and the .44 that she had so carefully left on the kitchen table. She noticed that his camouflage uniform didn't fit, seemed made for a larger man. Was there a real Terry Gill? If there was, what had happened to *him*, that this stranger now had his clothes? She thought again of Rudy, and didn't like the possible answer her thoughts suggested.

The wary look in his eyes changed and became certainty. Taking a step backward, he picked up her .44 from the table and held it casually aimed in her direction.

Tank growled again, louder now.

"Well," he said, with a sardonic half smile, and his whole attitude changed, along with his voice. She recognized the tone he had used in the beach house. "I guess we've gone about as far with this charade as we can. I suggest you keep the dog away from me, Jessie. I'm not fond of dogs—nor they of me, as you can see."

Reaching down, she took firm hold of Tank's collar and hushed him with a word.

"He knows you're afraid of him."

"Does he know you're afraid of me?"

"Probably."

"Good," he said. "Don't forget that. We're back to where we started, aren't we? Minus the old man, of course. No one to create a diversion this time, right, Jessie?"

"Did you kill Rudy for that?" She needed to know.

"As a matter of fact, I didn't have to. He took his boat into the cove in the worst of the storm. I saw him capsize from the hill. He couldn't make it to shore. He was headed this direction, though—probably hoping to find you."

She stared at him, white-faced, a great shard of grief twisting in her throat for Rudy and his courage, joined by the fear that made her breathless, and her anger.

"He wouldn't have tried that if it hadn't been for you."

"No, Jessie. He wouldn't have tried if it hadn't been for *you*," he said evenly, and, in the same flat tone. "Watch that ham, it's going to burn. You finish cooking breakfast, while I decide what to do with you."

He leaned against the wall beside the door and trained the gun in her direction. She looked at him for a long moment, then turned to automatically flip the ham in the frying pan, while trying to concentrate beyond her anxiety.

He would not be so easy to surprise this time. He was alert, tense, and ready for trouble. Knowing that he wouldn't hesitate to shoot Tank, she made the dog lie down on the floor by her feet. He was not happy, but did as he was told and stayed there quietly. As long as Gill did nothing to threaten her, Tank would obey, but his eyes followed the man's every move.

"Is there really a Terry Gill?" she asked him.

"There was. He wasn't expecting the trap I set for you. Lost his rifle in the fall and didn't know I was there until too late."

"How did you know Ah . . . Jensen sent him?"

"Who else?"

"So you killed him, too, and took his clothes."

"No, Jessie," he chided her, almost gently. "I haven't killed anyone. He won't be showing up anytime soon, but he's alive. He just doesn't interest me."

His expression changed from one of watchfulness to a grimace of anger and hate. "There's only one person I want to see die," he said through clenched teeth.

"Why me? Just tell me that. What did I ever do to you? I don't even know you."

He shook his head. "Ah, Jessie. You're just the means to an end. Haven't you figured that out yet? I wonder how long it will take your friend Jensen."

29

Jensen *had* figured out most of what was going on and was on his way, but it was taking longer than he liked.

"How soon can we get to Homer?" he asked Caswell, who was driving his truck east on Tudor Road toward the crime lab as fast as traffic would allow.

He had tried again to reach Jessie on Niqa, but there was still nothing but static on the line, and Caswell had seldom seen him so frustrated.

"As soon as I can get my plane and take us there," he answered, glancing at his watch. "It's ten-thirty. It'll take me over an hour from here to be airborne. I can come back and pick you up, but if you come with me to Wasilla, we can fly directly without the Anchorage detour."

"I'll come with you, but I need to stop at the lab first to pick up the gear in my truck."

"Gotta warn you, we may not be able to make it. I won't be able to land in that unprotected cove in the kind of weather they've been reporting. It's blowing like a son of a bitch."

"Can you get us to Homer?"

"I think so. There's a sheltered lagoon near town that may be a little rough, but I can have a shot at it. Worst case, we go back to Soldotna and drive the rest of the way down."

"I'll risk it."

"You know, he may not have been able to make it to Niqa, either. It can get pretty isolated in a real blow."

Jensen's jaw was stubbornly rigid, and what he spit out was half sarcasm and more tension.

"He's been down there since Saturday. He just might have been able to find a way out there in that amount of time, don't you think? So we'll have to do the same, but a lot faster. There'll be some kind of boat—Coast Guard, something—that can make it. I'm not leaving her out there alone—not if Wynne's there, too, and there's a hell of a chance he is. I think we should count on it. Now I wish we'd sent someone out there, whether she liked it or not. I'm too damned easy, Ben, and she's too damn independent for her own good."

Cas hesitated, but said nothing, and turned his attention to what he would need to ready his plane.

Caswell's estimate was right on the money. An hour and a half later, they were halfway to Homer, bouncing around the sky, knocking Jensen's knees and elbows on interior parts of the plane. The weather was lousy on the Kenai Peninsula, but the storm had centered on Kachemak Bay. According to the Weather Service, it was about to blow itself out, was now only half as fierce as it had been for the preceding twenty-four hours. They should be able to land at the lagoon near Homer, though it might be a bit dicey, but a flight to the rocky beach of Niqa Island was still out of the question and would remain so for at least another day.

As they hit an air pocket and dropped sickeningly, Jensen hit his head on the window frame.

"Ouch, dammit. Couldn't you fly something a more reasonable size?"

Cas grinned, but kept his concentration locked onto maintaining the progress of the small plane.

"Did I tell you I found out how Wynne figured out where Jessie was?"

"No. How?"

The grin had vanished and Cas looked a little embarrassed.

"As I filed a flight plan for this trip to Homer, I realized that I did the same thing for the flight last Thursday. Didn't even think, just filed it like always. My fault."

"What's wrong with that? I thought you had to file one and it was private information."

"Well . . . if you do the books for the right people, and if you have a friend who owes you a favor . . .

"I made a phone call, just to check. The clerk I talked to stuttered and stammered some before he admitted that he'd copied the plan for his 'friend.' Of course, he didn't have any idea why Wynne wanted it. Sorry, Alex. I should have either not filed one, or filed one for a different destination."

"Hey, don't worry about it. We can't catch everything."

Jensen settled gloomily into his seat.

"Wynne did a good job of setting up Moule, didn't he? Getting himself hired on to do the books for Peters so he'd be close to Moule was inspired. What a twisted plan. Pinning a completely different crime on him to get even would have been genius if he had pulled it off."

"He might have, if he'd left well enough alone—hadn't added that unnecessary tale about Moule using the computer for his wife to tell Peters. Even then, if we hadn't just happened to be there when she told him, we might never have figured it out."

"Close. It was close. Judy Wynne's an interesting person, isn't she? Telling us what she suspected was hard for her.

Having that happen to a kid . . . well. Moule's an animal—
better locked up. I can almost sympathize with Wynne, but
he'll have the wrong guy in his face if he's hurt Jessie."

"Wynne has no way of knowing we've arrested Moule. It
may make a difference to him, if you're right."

The plane lurched to the left as a gust of wind shoved it
across part of the sky. The lakes of the peninsula below were
gunmetal gray under the heavy cloud cover.

Caswell was glad to have Alex talking about the case. It
eased the stress a little. Cas was sure he was unaware that he
had been almost imperceptibly rocking in his seat, as if he
could encourage the plane to a greater speed with his body.

As if he had tuned in to his friend's thought, Alex frowned
and complained, for the fourth time, "Taking a long time,
isn't it?"

"We're going against the wind. Slows us down some, but
not too much. There's Anchor Point. We're almost there."

Jensen nodded glumly, clenching his fists, frustrated with
nothing positive to do. He did not want to think. He wanted
to be there, do whatever needed to be done. Jessie was irre-
placeable. He was trying not to consider how alarmed he was
for her—how terrified of losing her. That was true, he admitted, he was frightened for himself—afraid Wynne would hurt
her—kill her—to force him to exact punishment on Moule.
The man had no way of knowing that they already knew Moule
was not the responsible party; he would still be acting under
the impression that his plan was working. So *was* this what
Wynne wanted—planned? That Alex should suffer this kind
of dread and blame it on Moule? He had to admit that the
fear that filled his mind and made him conscious of his own
ragged breathing was very effective in creating an overwhelm-
ing desire to lay hands on the source of the threat—and soon.

For another moment he considered what Jessie might be
feeling—then drove it from his mind. She could be helpless,
hurt . . . anything. It did no good to imagine what he couldn't
know—and not knowing was the worst of all. He made himself

concentrate on the streets of Homer that were beginning to pass under their wings.

A few minutes later they dropped out of the sky and onto the waters of the lagoon, skipping twice as the wind tried its best to toss them back into the air, and taxied to shore, where they tied the plane down securely.

"Remember that flight into Nome, when it was blowing so hard?" Alex asked, recalling a storm that had once chased them from landing strip to landing strip during the Iditarod until Caswell was finally able to set cautiously down at the only possible airstrip.

"Yeah. That was another rough landing."

"Not your fault. Most people couldn't have made it at all—me included. My lunch was in my throat and Becker lost his, as I recall. Now, damnation, where's the car that's supposed to meet us?"

It seemed to Jensen that they would never find a boat to take them across Kachemak Bay to Niqa Island. The Coast Guard cutter was unavailable—gone to Seldovia to rescue a fishing boat caught out in the tempest and threatening to sink. Everyone else had hunkered down in the harbor, boats of various sizes and configurations tossing like corks at their moorings, waiting out the storm. None of them wanted to chance the condition of the bay.

It took the Homer trooper who had picked them up at the lagoon the better part of an hour to find someone willing to risk taking a boat to Niqa.

"This is Ted Carver," the Homer trooper told them. "He says he'll take you across in his water taxi."

"That thing?" Caswell questioned, dubiously examining the medium-sized craft the trooper had indicated, which was rocking hard against its fenders at the dock. "I think I'd rather take my plane. This thing doesn't look like it'll float very long."

"It's really quite seaworthy," Carver told him, in his optimistic way. "I've been out in worse weather and it was just fine. You'll get bounced around, but we'll make it. You going out to see Jessie Arnold? You friends of hers?"

Goddammit, Alex thought in disgust. Is there anyone in the area who *doesn't* know Jessie's on Niqa? How did this guy find out? Worse, who's he told? In his hurry he didn't bother to ask.

Carter, in his yellow waterproof suit, began to work with the lines at the bow and stern of his craft. Turning to the two still standing on the dock, he pushed his glasses up his nose and grinned.

"Come aboard and we'll get going. The bay isn't as rough as it was last night and earlier this morning. You're in some kind of rush, huh?"

Well, Caswell decided, stepping into the boat, he looks sturdy enough to keep it on course, at least.

Ignoring the stream of questions, Jensen also climbed in and took a seat next to Caswell in the partial shelter of the cabin that was open to the rear. Carter cast off and started his engine.

It was a long and extremely unpleasant ride. If the waters of the bay were not as tumultuous as they had been earlier, it was not apparent to either of Carter's passengers. Twice Caswell was sure they were going to roll over, but the buoyant craft somehow managed to right itself to continue its battle with the waves. He resolved that he would rather be in his plane in a hurricane than bouncing around where he currently found himself. Trouble in the air, and a person had a chance to reach the ground safely. Turn-turtle on this violent turbulence of water and wind, and he knew he would quickly drown. It was hard to be not in control, and he couldn't wait to get back on solid ground, as they were tossed and thrown from one side of the boat to the other, grasping at anything handy to keep themselves upright and out of the waves that regularly hurled themselves aboard, soaking everything, including their pants and boots. The skipper had handed them waterproof slickers and life vests, which they prudently donned, but from the waist down they were drenched by the time the battered water taxi drew even with Niqa Island and Carter turned to yell back at them over his shoulder.

"Where do you want put ashore? Millie's?"

Jensen nodded. It was where he had left Jessie—and where he expected to find or start looking for her.

"You'll have to wade in," Carter informed them. "I can't take the boat any closer or it'll get hammered on the rocks."

They lowered themselves into the surf from the back of the boat and were instantly half frozen. Struggling over the hidden unevenness of the stones on the bottom, they all but crawled out on the shore, then turned to wave their thanks as Carter swung his boat around to make the run to Tutka Bay.

"I'm not going back across till it calms down some more," he had said as they disembarked—a comment that left Caswell wondering just how close they had been to actual disaster.

"Remind me not to ride with that guy again," he told Alex. "He's totally nuts."

Jensen wasn't listening. After quickly emptying the water from his boots, he was covering ground toward the house, which stood dark and silent at the top of the beach—no smoke from the chimney, no light inside. Neither Jessie nor anyone else had come out to see who had arrived in a boat they couldn't possibly have missed. Nothing moved but a jay that flew away from a bench on the deck and into the trees as the two men went up the ramp and around to the side door.

It refused to open at Jensen's attempt. Something was holding it solidly closed from the other side.

"Jessie," he shouted, pounding on the door with his fist. "Are you in there?"

He remembered the day he had come home to find her

barricaded in the Knik cabin, but here no one came to open the door.

"Dammit. Something's really wrong here."

Hurrying around the building, they found the back door hanging open, swinging gently in the wind. Inside, the house was cold and damp, with an abandoned feeling—as if no one had moved through it for some time.

"Where the hell is she?" Alex, growing more concerned at her absence, allowed his irritation to show.

"Maybe she's gone across to the other cove," Caswell suggested, "found a more secure place to wait out the storm."

"She'd have left a note. Look—all the supplies she brought are still here. She'd have taken some of it, wouldn't she?" he said, and stumbled over pieces of something that rattled on the floor near the kitchen. He picked them up with growing anxiety.

"This *was* the cell phone," he observed in agitation, and gestured toward a shelf. "Millie's radio's been smashed, too."

Caswell had been examining the front door, curious as to what had kept it from opening.

"Look at this, Alex. Jessie's rigged a couple of pretty clever bolts on this door. Something must have scared her."

"What's scaring me is that I know he's here. No question. He's been in here. She wouldn't have smashed up her only communications equipment. We'd better hike on over to the other cove—fast."

30

The man who called himself Gill ate a leisurely breakfast after he made sure that Jessie and Tank were no threat.

"Who are you? Who are you after? Will you just tell me what you want?"

He refused to answer any more of her questions, focused instead on his own plans.

Tearing off a long piece of duct tape from a roll he had found in a storage cabinet, he made Jessie use it to muzzle Tank.

"Here. Tape his legs, too." He handed her more of the sticky silver tape, and reluctantly she did as she was told, afraid he would kill the dog he disliked if she refused to comply.

He made her sit in a chair at the table.

"You can eat, then I'll make sure you can't get away again."

"I'm not hungry," she told him angrily.

He merely shrugged. "You'll be sorry later, but it's up to you. Here, put on your outdoor clothes. When I'm through eating, we'll get out of here."

Taping her wrists and elbows securely, he then sat down to the food she had cooked and now wished she had poisoned.

"Bastard," she hissed, and he got up and slapped a strip of tape over her mouth before returning to his meal.

"Ah, Jessie," he said between sips of coffee when he had eaten his fill. "You just don't get it, do you?"

She glared at him in silence and shook her head.

"You're the motivation. Because of what's happening to you, he'll finally get what's coming to him. It's nothing personal. I admire you—haven't particularly enjoyed harassing you. But it's the only way to make him pay for what he did. Understand?"

Oh, God, Jessie thought, it's Alex. He's after Alex—not me. When Alex can't reach me, he'll come looking for me, and this monster will be waiting for him, but he won't know.

Her stomach lurched and she thought she was going to be sick, but she took a deep breath through her nose, and willed her nausea to subside.

"Don't look so worried, Jessie. It'll all be over soon. I promise."

When he had finished eating, he left the plate on the table and stood up.

"I'm not going to carry you," he told her. "Get up and walk to the door."

Tank struggled in his bonds at her feet. She didn't move, but stood beside him, looking first at her captor, then down at the husky.

He considered.

"All right—but you'll have to carry him."

Tank growled as the fake Gill picked him up and laid him across Jessie's taped arms. It wasn't easy to balance him without the free use of her arms, but she clutched him to her chest and managed, terrified he would be shot if she couldn't.

Carrying the roll of duct tape, her handgun, and his own rifle, the stalker opened the door and waved her through it. They went down the steep flight of steps in silence.

When he directed her around the shop and across a flat meadow to the east, she knew they were headed for the goat shed. A small structure half hidden behind two trees, it was made of rough planks that had aged to a natural silvery gray and was almost invisible from the rest of the buildings. Tall grass and a tangle of berry bushes had grown up around it, further concealing its presence.

By the time they reached it, Tank had slipped in Jessie's arms until only her grip around his chest kept her from dropping him. It couldn't be comfortable, but, seeming to realize it was necessary, he had remained quiet and didn't struggle or whine. She was relieved, however, when Gill opened the door, gestured her in and she could lay Tank on the ground.

With no windows, the shed was dark. In the light from the doorway, she could see an open duffel that seemed full of odds and ends of equipment. At a glance, she identified some rope, the handle of what might be a hammer, and another steel trap. As her eyes grew more accustomed to the gloom, she turned her head to the other end of the shed and was shocked to see a bound figure of a man lying on a moldering heap of old straw. He was taped and gagged like herself, wearing the jeans and black sweatshirt she had first seen on the stalker in Millie's beach house. He didn't move, but gave her a look of sympathy.

"Brought you some company, Gill," her captor told him. "Leave the dog and sit over there, Jessie."

She did as she was told, went to sit by the man she had already figured out must be the real pararescue person, and noticed he wore no shoes and that the white sock on his right foot was covered with blood. The trap. *This* was the man she had heard spring the trap by the bridge. No wonder he hadn't avoided it—he hadn't known it was there, hadn't set it.

Now what? Tensely she waited for what Gill's impersonator would do next.

Laying down the guns, he taped Jessie's knees and ankles together, and though she tried to stiffen her legs to keep a little flexibility, he cinched them tight. It hurt and she hated feeling so completely helpless.

"Now," he said, standing over them, "just stay put. Don't give me any trouble and you'll both be okay. I'm not going to hurt you."

The hell you're not, Jessie thought angrily, knowing he would never leave them alive to identify him. She knew she had to get loose somehow, get away to warn Alex before he walked, unknowing, into another of this madman's ambushes.

Tossing aside the tape, he turned to rummage through the duffel and took out a box of ammunition for his rifle. He went through Jessie's pocket and found ammunition for her .44.

As he went to the door, Tank growled and shifted his position. The impostor paused, looking down at the dog thoughtfully, and scowled. He raised the rifle slightly, and Jessie could tell he was considering the satisfaction of killing the dog he hated.

All she could do was fall forward and make an angry sound past the tape on her mouth, but it was enough to draw his attention in her direction. He gave her a contemptuous look.

"Okay, Jessie. I'll leave him—for now."

Going out, he slammed the door behind him, leaving the three of them in what seemed total darkness. For a few seconds, heart in her throat, she could hear him going away. Then there was silence, as the breath of the wind replaced the sounds of his passing with its own rustle in the tall grass.

"Let's check outside before we race off to the other cove," Caswell suggested to Jensen. "There might be something to tell us what went down here, or which direction she went."

"Good idea, but let's make it quick."

They examined the area around the beach house thoroughly, then went to the beach, where the tide was low, the storm abating quickly, and the waters of the cove recovering their usual calm colors. Caswell found what was left of the footprints Jessie and her stalker had made, high up in the sandy part of the beach. Most of them had been at least partially erased by the rain and blowing spray, but he pointed out what remained of the revealing depressions to Jensen.

"Some of these are pretty widely spaced. Looks like someone—more than one someone—went along here in a hurry."

They followed the marks around the curve of the beach, found where one set of them led to a space between the logs, where another set approached and abandoned the stairs, and where the depressions faded out past the tide line toward the rocks that led to the cliffs. With growing alarm, Alex recognized the splintered marks of bullets on the stairs and stones.

"He was shooting at her," he exclaimed.

"It could be the other way 'round," Cas suggested hopefully.

"Let's get over there."

They went up the stairs and were soon half running along the trail at the top of the cliffs. The rain had stopped and in the treetops the wind had exhausted itself from gales to sighs. Looking up, Caswell noticed a small patch of blue sky to the west and was relieved that the storm had blown itself out.

Reaching the top of the cut Jessie had climbed earlier, Jensen paused to take a look at the marks at the edge of the precipice.

"Someone came up here," he said. "And there're the marks of a line. See where it scored the edge? Here . . . and here. Some of Tank's paw prints, too, so either Jessie came up the face of that, or she helped someone else do it. Probably Jessie. Why would she help Wynne?"

Caswell decided that it was time to confess.

"It may not have been Wynne," he told Alex.

"Who else could it have been?"

"Well . . . you remember I told you I knew a guy in the Air National Guard Pararescue?"

"Yes. And?"

"I probably should have told you—but Jessie was so adamant about not having someone watch over her that I didn't want you tangled in it. I asked Terry Gill to come out and make sure she was okay. He's been here since Friday morning, before we flew in. He could have helped her up the cliff."

For a minute, Jensen said nothing, staring at Caswell, absorbing what he'd just been told.

"You mean . . . ? Oh, boy. Is she going to be mad at me."

"No. It's my doing. Let me take the heat."

"That may seem reasonable to you—and me. But do you really think Jessie's going to see it that way? Would Linda?"

Cas shrugged. "Does it matter? She'll get over it. If he's made sure she's safe, isn't that the important thing?"

"Well . . ." The frown on Alex's face deepened. "We don't know that, do we? Where the hell is she—is he? And what's going on with Wynne?"

He started on along the trail, running now, leaping over roots and obstacles, shoving back overhanging branches and brush that Cas had to watch or they snapped back to hit him in the face. Coming around a sharp curve, Jensen slowed for a log that had fallen across the trail in front of him. There was just enough room to duck under, and he had started to do so when Cas called out from behind him.

"Hey, wait up. You've got longer legs than I do."

Already leaning over and on his way under the log, Jensen decided to finish the motion and pause on the other side. He took two long strides, one under the log, one far enough away to turn around. His first stride tripped the wire release for the deadfall, left in place by Gill's impersonator. His second stride carried him barely beyond its trajectory as it crashed into the ground, just missing his head, grazing his left shoulder and arm with its rough bark.

"Jesus!"

He staggered away from the trap, half expecting more destruction in its wake, but nothing else came down around him.

"What the hell was that? Alex? Alex!"

Unable to see, Caswell was shouting from the other side of the log that now made that section of trail impassable. It was not as large as the other, but completely filled the opening Jensen had gone through.

"Alex? Are you okay? Did that thing get you? Dammit—*answer me.*"

"I'm okay. I'm okay. It just missed. Scraped up my arm a little, but I'm not hurt."

Panting, light-headed with adrenaline, he moved back to take a look at the trap he had so closely, and luckily, avoided.

"You better go around this thing. Easier than trying to climb over."

As he spoke, the crack of a shot rang through the quiet woods and a bullet thudded into the log beside him. Throwing himself down, near the logs and behind some brush, he shouted to Caswell, who had started uphill to go around the trap.

"Get down. Someone's got a rifle up there. Down—down."

Cas dove for cover back the way he had come, rolling to a position next to the fallen log.

"Can you see him?"

"No," Jensen answered, more quietly, from the other side of the barrier that now effectively separated the two. "But he could see me, all right—and see that his trick didn't work like he planned."

"Can we flank him? You go east, I'll go west, and we'll get him between us?"

"The brush is too thick. It'd be a bitch getting through, and he'd hear us coming—know exactly where we were."

"Go back? Go down?"

"Maybe . . ."

Another shot from above gave them the answer to that. The shooter had moved enough to see both sides of the log. The bullet buried itself just over Caswell's head. He scrambled back into a patch of devil's club, swearing as its thorns abused his hands and face.

"Ross Wynne?" Jensen shouted. "We're State Troopers Sergeant Jensen and Caswell. We know who you are and why you're here. Give it up before somebody gets hurt."

His answer was another well-placed bullet.

"Goddammit. He's got us pinned," Caswell observed. "What do you suggest?"

"Don't give him a target," Jensen answered. "We'll think of something."

Again he shouted up the hill to where the shooter was hidden.

"Wynne, I know it's not Jessie Arnold you really want. If you've hurt her, I'll make you wish you'd never had anything to do with her, but I don't think you have . . . have you?"

His angry voice broke just a little on the last question.

There was a silent hesitation from above before Wynne called an answer.

"No," he said. "I haven't hurt her."

Alex took a deep breath, realized the hands that had been gripping his Colt .45 semiautomatic were trembling as he eased off on his hold, and admitted to himself the idea that had terrified him most. His greatest fear had been that Wynne would decide he needed to frame Moule for *murder* to be sure he would be sentenced to a severe punishment—and that Jessie would be the victim of his irrational plot. Could he believe what the man said? Was Jessie really unharmed?

"Wynne, we have Moule in custody. You've won—he's going back to jail. Put down the rifle and we'll talk about all this. If you haven't hurt anyone, we can work it out."

Another silence, then, "No. It's not enough. I want him dead."

"We *can* work it out, Ross. He won't get away with it this time. We'll work the case till we find enough to get him for what he did to Michael. Let the law take care of it."

"The law always screws it up," Wynne shouted, in a furious tone. "You focus on protecting his rights. What about ours—mine and Michael's? He's got to die."

"Look, we know that you've been harassing Jessie Arnold to frame Moule. We can understand why, and can work with you on it. You've had a pretty good reason for what you've done. But I can't promise you he'll get a death sentence."

There was a silence so long that Jensen thought maybe Wynne had gone away—escaped into the forest. He raised himself just a little to take a quick look.

"Wynne?"

The response was immediate in another bullet hitting the log.

"I'll tell you what I want," Wynne called down in a cold, determined voice. "I want you to bring him out here so I can kill him myself. Then I'll let Jessie Arnold go—and that *Green Beret* of yours. If you don't bring him, you'll wish you had, because before this's over I'm going to kill someone."

"Oh, shit," said Caswell, who had been following the exchange from the other side of the log. "He's got Gill, too."

"Can you see any way of getting away from here and reaching him without getting one of us shot?"

"Nope. He's picked a perfect vantage point—he can keep us pinned down, we can't see to shoot at him, and for a bookkeeper he's no slouch with that rifle."

31

In the goat shed, both Jessie and Terry Gill were slowly working themselves loose. Although Wynne had been good at using the duct tape to secure them, he had forgotten one important thing—fingers that cannot pull tape from their own arms can, awkwardly, pull it off someone else's.

The two had first managed to remove the tape that covered their mouths and Jessie was now tugging at the tape that held Gill's wrists.

"Just a little more," he told her.

"This part's going to pull off the hair on your arm. It's going to hurt."

"Who cares? Rip it off if you can. We may not have a lot of time here."

She did.

He grunted, but with an increased freedom of motion was able to accomplish more, and they were soon unfettered.

Gill opened the door enough to give them some light, carefully checking to be sure their captor was not near enough to notice, while Jessie knelt by Tank and worried over how to get the tape off his fur. It would not be an easy or painless procedure.

"Look through that duffel," Gill advised. "He's got a lot of stuff in it. You may find a knife or something sharp."

She found a folding hand saw, blade sticky with sap, that had probably been used to construct the deadfall. Using its jagged fold-out blade cautiously, she managed to cut through the tape that held the dog's muzzle closed, then free his legs. Until she could figure out how to get the tape off without removing the hair along with it, she decided to simply leave it.

Tank, however, didn't agree, and immediately went to work to lick and chew it off, with remarkable success. Soon he was left with only two pieces, one under his chin, where he couldn't reach it, and one on a hind leg.

As Tank gnawed at the tape, Gill went through the duffel, with less reward.

"Thought maybe he'd have some first aid in here."

"Your foot looks awful," Jessie told him. "Can you walk on it?"

The gory sock had dried and was stuck to the top of his foot, which was swollen and, as he hobbled, oozed a little fresh blood.

"Something's broken, and that damn trap cut the hell out of it, but we haven't got any medical stuff, so I'll use some of this tape to stabilize it and see," he said, picking up the roll of duct tape Wynne had so confidently tossed down.

"Have you got anything to wear on your feet?"

"Yeah. Bastard took my boots, but I couldn't get this into one of them anyway. He left those."

He indicated a pair of rubber boots, similar to the ones she was wearing. They looked large enough to accommodate the injured foot.

As he used the duct tape to tightly wrap his foot and ankle,

Jessie upended the duffel and went through its contents, looking for some kind of weapon.

"There's not much." She sighed, frustrated. "He's got my shotgun stashed somewhere, but here are a couple of the things we might use." She held up a crowbar and a hand ax.

"Take 'em. O-ouch!" Gill gingerly pulled a boot over his injured foot, swore, and bit his lip at its pressure. "They just might be useful. Take the rest of that tape, too. If we can catch him, I'm going to put it to damn good use." He stood up and tested the foot. It held him, but he limped in pain when he put weight on it, reminding Jessie of the limp the stalker had faked.

"You can lean on me if you need to," Jessie told him. "I have no use for macho men, especially if they're willing to sacrifice practicality for the sake of their holy egos."

Gill grinned and nodded, but was able to move out on his own.

They left the shed and skirted the meadow, staying out of sight of the windows in the apartment above the shop. He glanced at the filthy adhesive tape and splints on her hand.

"Are you all right? Your face looks like you've been through a war, and what's wrong with your fingers?"

"Broken in the truck wreck, then I got a dislocation I had to put back in place. The rest is dirt and bruises—nothing disabling."

"You relocated your own finger? *Gutsy.* Hurt like hell, didn't it? I had one once."

"I wouldn't like to do it again. Come on. Alex and Cas may show up here anytime. We haven't talked since Sunday and if he can't reach me, he'll be here soon, if he's not already."

"I had a radio, but our friend broke it when he found it on me."

"He smashed the radio at the beach house and my cell phone, too," she told him. "How'd he catch you?"

"This foot. Pitched my rifle into the brush when I fell. I couldn't find it, and couldn't move fast enough to avoid him.

He must have heard me looking and waited—ambushed me in the upper trail."

Jessie noticed that, lame or not, Gill was alert and searching everything around them with his eyes. He moved smoothly despite his limp, and with no hesitation, no wasted motion, constantly aware and ready for anything.

"Where do you think he'll go?" she asked.

"Don't know, but we'd better . . ."

The sound of a shot echoed from the woods beyond the bluff—then another—interrupting what he had been about to say.

"Oh, dammit," Jessie said. "Come *on*. He's not shooting at squirrels. They must be here."

She hurried past the shop and took the stairs two at a time to the top of the bluff, Tank—ragged bits of tape still clinging to his muzzle and hind leg—trotting close, and Gill hobbling rapidly after her. Looking back, she realized he couldn't quite keep up with her and waited impatiently.

As they reached the edge of the forest, they heard a third shot.

"Hey, slow down a bit," Gill told her. "Those shots aren't coming from this lower trail. Whoever's shooting is off it, in the brush and higher up. Let's go farther up and come down from above him—see what he's shooting at before we make any kind of move."

It made sense, though it was all Jessie could do to turn away from whatever was happening west of them. She had visions of Alex caught off guard, hurt and bleeding. But Gill was not only right, she realized, he was trained in handling emergencies and knew much more about what he was doing than she did. She found that she trusted his judgment, and wondered how she had ever mistaken the stalker for him. Still, she was reluctant as she followed him up the hill. He had taken the hand ax and clutched it like a tomahawk, leaving her the crowbar, which she hung on her belt as she used both hands to move aside the brush as quietly as she could. Ahead of her, Gill slid through it with very little noise.

Farther up the slope the brush thinned somewhat and they made better time as they moved through it. The wind had dropped, but still blew hard enough to cover the small sound of their passing.

Gill decided they had gone far enough uphill, turned west for a ways, then started slowly back down through the trees. Motioning to Jessie for silence, he carefully led the way over the uneven ground and soon she began to hear shouting from below. The voices were still too far away to make out what was being said, but she thought she recognized Alex's voice and that of the stalker.

As they came along a small rise and around a patch of devil's club leaves, Gill stopped so suddenly she almost ran into him. He turned and pulled her to her knees beside the broad stump of a downed tree.

"He's there," he whispered to her, and pointed directly below them across a small clearing. "Is that your friend Jensen he's yelling at? It's not Caswell's voice."

She nodded.

"Stay here, okay?"

Again she nodded, and watched as he slipped off into the trees to the right. Injured foot or not, he was very good at melting into the landscape, for in just a few seconds she lost sight of him completely. Now, listening carefully, she could hear the words of the exchange.

"Wynne?"

Who was Wynne? Jessie wondered.

Another shot was fired by the stalker.

"I'll tell you what I want," he shouted. "I want you to bring him out here so I can kill him myself. Then I'll let Jessie Arnold go—and that *Green Beret* of yours. If you don't bring him, you'll wish you had, because before this's over I'm going to kill someone."

There was a pause in the conversation. Jessie leaned back

against a log. It rocked slightly. She looked more closely at it and found that it had not fallen by itself—it had been cut with a saw, for the stump nearby was flat on top. The log was not the whole tree, but only a piece about ten feet long and over a foot thick.

Millie's son periodically culled dead trees from the forest to use for firewood. This seemed to be the evidence of such labor, left to dry, perhaps.

She tested it again to see how heavy it was. It weighed a lot, but rocked easily, one end resting on a large stone.

Gill slipped back to kneel next to her on the ground, having completed his reconnaissance.

"He's got Jensen and Caswell pinned down next to a couple of fallen logs on the lower trail," he told her. "They can't move."

"It was a deadfall," she told him. "He made it and left it there. But look." She rocked the log she had discovered. "Could we . . . ?"

"Roll that down the hill—right on top of him? Yes. Good thinking, Jessie. It's only about thirty feet and there are no trees to stop it and hardly any brush between here and there. I was trying to think of a way to cross it without him knowing; now I won't have to. We'll shove it over the edge and it'll be on him before he has a chance to get out of the way."

"Can we get it going fast enough?"

"You bet. And that crowbar will come in handy."

Positioning themselves one on each end of the log, they coordinated their efforts—Jessie using the tool to push what she couldn't lift, Gill throwing all his strength into shoving the log off the rock and over the edge of the slight rise.

The thick log was resistant at first, but after the first turn, it quickly gathered speed. With thumps and thuds, it rolled, slid, and bounced its way across the clearing straight at the stalker.

Hearing it coming, seconds too late, he leaped to his feet, turning to see what was happening behind him, bringing the rifle to his shoulder as he swung around. There was no time for a shot. The log caught him, on a bounce, directly across the thighs and knocked him flat, rifle disappearing into the brush. It continued to roll over his body, mashing him into the ground, and came to rest beyond his still form against a tree. The thrashing and thumping stopped, the forest was still, and for a moment nothing moved.

Gill was in motion first, hobbling down to make sure Wynne was as unconscious as he appeared. Jessie followed swiftly after him, calling out to the troopers below, concerned they would mistake him for their stalker target.

"Alex. It's me—it's Jessie. It's okay—we got him with a log. Are you okay?"

With an excited woof, Tank went bounding on beyond her, eager to greet his friend.

As she passed Gill, with a grin for their success, she heard Alex's answering shout, "Jessie. Thank God," and the sound of him crashing through the brush, coming fast up the hill toward her.

32

Though it was late afternoon, Alex was breaking eggs to scramble and the smell of frying sausage filled the large room of Millie's beach house. Caswell and Gill sat near the large windows, mugs of black coffee steaming in their hands, enjoying each other's company. Jessie was slicing bread for toast at the table by the front door and keeping an eye on the two jays that had flown in, always hopeful of leftovers.

The cove was warm and sun sparkled from its waters. She noticed a sea otter making itself at home in a gently rocking clump of floating bull kelp that had been pulled loose by the storm, hammering the shell of some creature from the deep on a stone brought up from the bottom. Everything outside looked clean and new. Even the mountains that rose beyond Tutka Bay lifted their snowy peaks in sharp contrast against the blue sky like a postcard scene.

Laying slices of bread in a flat pan, she carried it across and slid it under the broiler of the gas stove. Wiping her hands on the clean pair of jeans she had put on after bathing in the creek behind the house, she turned to Alex and slipped under his arm to give him a hug as he broke the last egg.

"Watch it, woman." He grinned, hugging her back and planting a kiss on the top of her head. "You're disrupting my abilities as a chef."

"Tough."

She stepped away and, fending him off with a whisk, checked to make sure the toast wasn't burning.

"Now, please. I want to know who this guy Wynne is and how you figured it out."

"Just good police work, ma'am."

"Not true," Cas called from across the room. "It was nothing but a lucky break—an accident of being in the right place at the right time—concerning a computer. We were still muddling around over two other suspects, when we stumbled over—"

"And I thought you'd come because you hadn't heard from me and were worried."

"Well . . . that, yes. I told and told Alex that I was so very awfully, terribly worried about you . . . but he, of course, was only interested in the case—ulp."

A damp kitchen towel caught him in the mouth, skillfully wadded and thrown by Jensen, his relief at the successful outcome of their pursuit of Wynne apparent in his good humor.

"Who steals my purse steals trash . . ." he quoted, threatening Cas with another towel, "but he that filches from me my good name—"

"Uncle. Uncle," Cas capitulated, both hands protecting his head. "He was beside himself with worry, Jessie. I promise."

She laughed at their antics as she turned over the bread to toast the other side.

"How's your foot?" Alex asked, noticing a grimace as Gill settled it more comfortably on the pillowed stool on which it was propped.

Millie's storage had provided first-aid supplies for Gill's mangled foot and some pain pills that helped the agony of removing the boot, duct tape, and bloody sock. With it cleaned and newly dressed, he would be okay until they got him to a doctor on the mainland.

"It's all right. Believe me, it's so much better than it was while I was gimping around that hillside, there's no comparison. My backbone's rubbing a hole in my stomach, though."

"That we can fix almost immediately." Alex filched a sausage from the pan, let it cool a bit, and tossed it across to Gill, who competently fielded it with one hand.

While they ate their late breakfast, Jessie told her side of what had happened on the island.

"You said Tank was nervous on Saturday night—woke you up several times wandering through the house?" Gill asked, grinning, when she finished.

"Yes, why?"

"Well, it was cold and wet out there in the rain. I rolled under the house and slept part of the night. He probably heard me."

"Sure he did, but you must have been really quiet. I didn't hear anything."

"You're not supposed to; it's what I'm trained to do."

The troopers then explained to Jessie and Gill about Wynne's obsession with Moule, the reasons for it, and how they had happened on the message he had left for Peters that allowed them to break the case.

"Poor man," Jessie commented, when they had finished the tale. "What a horrible thing to have happen to your child. I don't like him and I hate what he did, but I can understand his anger, and I think I'd like Moule even less."

"Moule is a real slime." Cas frowned. "Shouldn't be allowed to associate with anyone—even in prison."

"So Moule is the *one person* Ross Wynne meant that he wanted to see die. I thought he was talking about you." She laid a hand on Alex's arm. "It scared me, badly—especially when I couldn't do a thing to warn you."

"Well, he almost got me with that deadfall—just missed.

He may have what seems like an understandable hatred for Moule, but that doesn't excuse his harassment of you, Jess, or his disregard for and injury of other people."

"He was the reason for Rudy's death," she said sadly. "I really feel bad about that."

There was a moment of silence as they all thought of Rudy, to whom Jessie had led them after the battle at the deadfall.

"Hey, here's the Coast Guard." Gill spotted the distinctive white vessel that had turned into the cove from Tutka Bay and was headed for the beach.

"You sure you don't want to come back to Homer with us?" Cas questioned Alex. "I could fly two trips today, easy, and get you home by dark."

Jensen shook his head. "No, we'll stay here and get Millie's place put back in good order. You go ahead with these guys." He waved a hand at the Coast Guardsmen, lowering a ramp to the beach. "Jessie and I'll be ready for you to pick us up about noon tomorrow."

The tide was coming in, so it was a shorter walk over the rocks. Caswell doubled as a crutch for Gill, who gave Jessie a hug and a smile before limping up the ramp, and made it onto the deck of the boat without getting the dressings on his foot wet.

"You're one strong lady, Jessie Arnold. Hang in there."

"Not so bad yourself, Gill. Take good care. We'll see you soon?"

"Sure. According to Chinese lifesaving tradition, we're sort of responsible for each other now. We got each other loose from all that duct tape before Wynne came back, right?"

Cas stopped for a last word with Alex.

"We've got Moule cold, but you got anything particular in mind for Falconer, Jones, and Collins?"

"Falconer and Jones—when we locate him—are tied in with those stolen motorcycles. He took the parts that Falconer removed from the bikes and I'll bet he's gone *outside* to sell them—probably Seattle. We'll have enough to convict, I think, considering Falconer's probably scared silly enough to give us Jones in exchange for a lesser sentence.

"Collins? Well—like it, or not, there's not much to hold her on. Tell them to kick her loose, but we'll keep a close eye on her."

They turned to watch as two Coast Guard officers carried Wynne on a stretcher down the beach and up the ramp onto the boat. After the log-rolling, they had put him in one of the bunks in the back of the beach house, knowing he could make no escape attempts. One leg was broken, plus several ribs, and he had a concussion that made Jessie's bump on the head from the wreck seem almost insignificant. Alex wondered about Wynne's wife, Judy, and the fresh suffering that was about to be visited upon her. He hoped she was strong enough to care for Michael alone.

As Caswell boarded the boat, Alex stood with an arm around Jessie's shoulders to see the ramp lifted. They watched the vessel grow smaller and vanish around the rocks at the end of the cove. It would stop again at the other beach to take Rudy Nunamaker's body aboard before heading to Homer. Cas would fly Gill from there to an Anchorage hospital for treatment. When the boat had gone, they turned and walked together up the beach and onto the deck of Millie's house.

The jays had cleaned up the scraps of food Jessie had put out for them and flown away, but the raven, late as always, was back and strutting up and down the wooden bench, seemingly disgruntled at the emptiness of the pan. She grinned at its comical attitude.

"Hey, you're too late, Joker. You gotta get here on time, buddy. Nobody's gonna save your share till you get around to it. Jay One and Jay Two are quick."

The bird cocked its head as if to give her stern disapproval from one eye, black and shiny as a glass bead, then took wing and sailed off over the house.

Tank watched it go, then flopped down on the deck in the sun.

Alex knelt beside him and painstakingly worked loose the piece of duct tape that still clung to the hair on the dog's chin. The piece on his leg had disappeared sometime during the capture of Wynne, perhaps when he had run joyfully down the hill to meet his favorite trooper.

When Alex stood up and went to sit on the bench, Tank jumped up, followed, and lay down, resting his muzzle comfortably on the man's thigh. Alex pulled his pipe from his shirt pocket and spoke to Jessie as he lit it with a kitchen match.

"The vet says Nicky is going to be fine. She'll be a bit too lame to pull a sled, but fine otherwise."

"You know, I think I'll give her to Billy Steward. He could breed good racers with her and that big male he's got—Totem."

"Good idea. Billy's doing fine, too, by the way. And, speaking of injuries, how's your hand?"

"Fine, I think. But I want the doc to take a look at it when I get back to town."

She told him about dislocating a finger in her escape from the stalker, and how she put it back in place.

"Jesus, Jessie. That must have been unpleasant, to say the least."

"Hurt like hell. I'm just glad it worked."

She paused, thinking about her escape in the forest and everything that had happened after it.

"How did he find me, Alex?"

He told her about Caswell's flight plan and went on to fill her in on some of the details—Wynne wearing Moule's too-small boots to make the tracks, the photos of her and Linda in the dog lot, the confusion about Collins and her friend Spike.

"It took us longer than it should have. I'm sorry about that, but I should have made . . . well . . . you really should have gone to Idaho."

She looked up at him questioningly, with a slight frown.

He reached out to brush one of her earlobes with a forefinger and changed the subject.

"Did you know you've lost one of your earrings?"

She nodded. "I think it happened when I was climbing the cliff, and I'll never find it in the rock fall."

"Don't worry, it's replaceable. You've more than earned one earring."

He hesitated thoughtfully and turned his head slightly to look down at Tank, now sound asleep in the sun. Glancing back, he studied Jessie for a few seconds before he spoke again.

"In fact—speaking of diamonds—I've been thinking . . ."

Her gentle fingers on his lips stopped him before he could finish what he had been about to say, surprising them both. She shook her head.

"Don't, Alex."

Dropping her hand to her knee, she closed her eyes for a moment and drew a breath as she attempted to analyze a flood of conflicting feelings.

"Please, don't. Not right now."

There was a deep silence, through which he looked at her with concern and confusion.

"Ah . . . you want to talk about it?"

Reluctantly, "I think I'd better try."

"Go."

She hesitated, deliberating.

"I want to say this right. It's important."

"Yeah, it is—very," he said through stiff lips.

There was a vulnerable constraint in his stillness, a wariness around the eyes.

Why, she wondered, do I want to apologize—to give in and let him ask? Why do I always want to make it comfortable? Refusing to let these questions distract her, she sat up straight and concentrated on clarifyinging her thoughts.

"Okay. You know we can't just go back to what we were before all this happened. There's a lot of fear and frustration, and doing things separately—differently—in between then and now. For instance, while you were focused on solving the problem—the case—there were times when I was focused on some other kinds of things that are very important to me."

"You mean about being safe?"

She smiled sadly and shook her head. "No one's ever really safe. We could do better, but it's not that. I haven't had time to work it all out yet, but it's made me wonder about the way I've arranged things in my life. I'm not sure they're the way I'd like to have them."

"I don't understand."

"Well . . . a minute ago you almost said that you should have *made* me go to Idaho, didn't you?"

He nodded apologetically, embarrassed at being caught out.

"Yeah, I know how you feel about taking care of yourself, but sometimes I feel . . ."

"And I let you—sometimes. But this time, when I thought I was making a choice, I really wasn't. It didn't matter where I went—it mattered that I went *when you told me.*"

"But we agreed it was the smartest thing to do."

"Yes, we did, and it *was* the right thing to do. But I'm talking about the way I felt about it later. The way I feel about it now.

"It's subtle and insidious, almost automatic, the way women allow themselves to give up a lot of responsibility to their men and at the same time pick up too much of the responsibility of trying to make sure that a relationship runs smoothly—become too accommodating, try to *make* it right— *do* it right, whatever *it* is. As a single person, an equation of one, I can stand on my own two feet, be accountable for my own feelings and actions. I don't know if I can do that in an equation of two—with forever-afters."

He laid a hand over hers on her knee and gave her a puzzled frown.

"But we share now. How would a diamond on your finger change that any more than diamonds on your ears?"

"It's hard to explain. Almost as if I would be agreeing to a contract that says everything we are now is okay and I accept it like it is. But there are still things we need to work out— things I need to work out. I'm always a little on guard against taking the easy way and letting you be responsible for me in ways that aren't fair to either of us."

"We wouldn't be carving anything in granite, Jess. We change all the time—learn new things about each other. I don't see that suddenly coming to some kind of halt if we formalize it."

For a second or two she was silent, considering, before shaking her head.

"I keep remembering a thing I learned a long time ago. If some part of a relationship doesn't quite work right, either I'm taking too much responsibility for someone else or I'm letting someone else take too much for me. I'd like to have a better moment-to-moment balance, not just hindsight. I'm not there yet."

He turned his head to look out at the waters of the cove, absent-mindedly rubbed Tank's ears, and puffed a cloud of fragrant smoke toward the nearest island. She watched his expressions shift as he thought over what she had said: puzzlement, disappointment, concern, mild amusement, and several that she couldn't identify. Eventually he nodded as if affirming something for himself, turned back to her, and smiled a little anxiously.

"But you're going to stick around and explore these ideas?"

"Of course. I love you, Alex, but I need unlimited time without pressure."

"Okay." He grinned. "Time we've got lots of . . . but the earring gets replaced."

Jessie laughed.

"I don't think you can buy just one earring."

"Watch me. Besides, I still owe you a birthday dinner."

"That's *right,* you do. And don't kid yourself—I intend to collect."

She stood up. "Come on. Let's go clean up Millie's kitchen."

He gave Tank a last pat and Jessie a mischievous grin.

"Naw. Later. Let's make the bed first."

"Hmmm."

Acknowledgments

As always, many thanks are due:

To my family and friends for their enthusiasm and support, without which being a writer would be a lonely occupation, indeed. Particularly to the Abbott clan for their trust and affection. To Pat and Ray Agen, and the mechanics at the Agen Automotive, for keeping my research vehicles running and for providing information on how to successfully damage a brake line. To Michael W. Eaton, M.D., magical orthopedic surgeon, for keeping this researcher running (well, at least moving) and able to sit at my computer without pain. To his office staff: Debra Ford, Linda Casey, and, especially, Barry McQuade for information on dislocations and their treatment.